Arresting Mason

by

Amber Daulton

Arresting Onyx Series

Arresting Mason

Cover Art by *Kristian Norris*

The Wild Rose Press, Inc.
PO Box 708
Adams Basin, NY 14410-0708
Visit us at www.thewildrosepress.com

Publishing History
First Crimson Rose Edition, 2018
Print ISBN 978-1-5092-2007-6
Digital ISBN 978-1-5092-2008-3

Arresting Onyx Series
Published in the United States of America

Desire trickled down her spine.

Mia nodded toward the passenger side of the car for him to hop in.

He confiscated her keys instead to unlock and open the driver's side door for her like a gentleman. Then he leaned closer and nuzzled her temple with his nose.

Not sure if he planned to seduce her in the parking lot or if he merely wanted to tease her, Mia pressed her hand to his chest and tried to think straight. "You're the first guy I've gone on a date with since my divorce. I haven't slept with anyone since Evan."

He tunneled his fingers through her wavy, chestnut-brown hair. "I haven't dated anyone in a long time either. We'll take it slow or fast, whatever you want, but I promise you one thing. After I'm done with you, you won't even remember that bastard's name."

Oh, God. She almost melted right then and there. "Fast. I want you, Mason."

"Take me to your place and you can have me."

Dedication

To Greg, my wonderful husband:
Thank you for all the late nights
when we would stay up and toss ideas around.
Because of you, I've found my way out of
embarrassing plot holes and dead ends.
You've read so many drafts of this story
that you know the characters almost as much as I do.
I love you so much!

Acknowledgments

I would like to thank The Wild Rose Press, Inc. staff, especially my editor, EL Felder, who never gave up on this submission and kept pushing me to make it better and better. I really appreciate your kindness, time, and hard work.

~*~

To the fans and readers: Thank you for giving this book and me as an author a chance. I absolutely adore Mason, and I hope you do, too.

Chapter One

"Oh, God. Are you okay? I swear I didn't see you."
Mia Eddison hurried from her car to the stranger on the
sidewalk. She'd almost hit him as she turned the corner
on the busy inner-city street.

The man swiped his hands over his dark, spiky hair
and smudged oil on his forehead.

Even in the midst of her horrible day, which now
featured a near accident, the gorgeous man with his oil-
stained clothes and skin nearly made her drool like a
starstruck fool.

"Are you hurt? Do you need an ambulance?" Her
throat constricted as she realized how screwed she
really was, and *not* in the way she wanted. "Damn, I
could've killed you. Are you gonna sue me? I'll have to
close my business. My brother will freak out."

"Calm down." The stranger's gruff voice tightened
her stomach into a bundle of knots. He wiped his hands
on his knee-length, cut-off jeans as though he'd just
noticed the oil, but he seemed determined to avoid her
gaze. "I'm fine, just a little shaken. You didn't hit me."

"Are you sure? I forgot to use the turn signal. I
think the speedometer read five miles or so an hour as I
gunned the engine. I'm so sorry. I don't mean to make
excuses, but I'm late for work and the idiot truck driver
behind me kept blowing his horn until I was ready to
scream or throw something at him. Let's go to the

emergency room and get you checked out." She would do *anything* to avoid a lawsuit. "My insurance should cover it. I just don't want to go to court." Mia glanced at the pedestrians on the one-way street, but no one appeared to pay her and the stranger any attention.

"I'm fine, really. Don't need a hospital. I won't sue you." He glanced at his wristwatch and stepped back. "I gotta go."

Mia frowned, grabbed his arm, and pulled him to a stop. His skin flared hot under her palm and his muscles twitched. Her chest shuddered as strength emanated from him like a cloak. A tribal-design tattoo circled his right wrist, partially hidden beneath his watch, and a second tattoo peeked out beneath his shirtsleeve, but she couldn't make out the design.

His eyebrow arched as he finally looked at her.

"I'm sorry, but you can't just leave like nothing happened. You could be dead. I nearly flattened you like a pancake." Heat crept up her neck and she dropped her hand. She should feel lucky he wanted to walk away—he could change his mind and claim injury, the longer they talked—and her panic ricocheted up another notch. "Why are you smiling? How are you so freakin' calm? I'm panicking here."

He shrugged. "It's not a big deal, sugar. My leg might've snapped if you'd hit me, but I wouldn't have met my maker."

His nonchalant words floored her. A chill filled her veins and surely blanched her skin. Her stomach cramped tighter.

He grimaced and struck his forehead with his open palm. "Fuck, I shouldn't have said that. I saw you just in time to throw my hands out. Everything's fine."

Air burned through her lungs as the world spun. The ground shifted and her knees weakened. The stranger caught her by the waist before she fell, strong and sturdy like a tree in the whirlwind of her bad memories. She leaned on him as he guided her toward a nearby bench. Several puppies yapped at them from a pet shop window. Mia bent and ducked her head between her knees to catch her breath.

He sat beside her. "You've been in a car accident before, haven't you?"

She forced air into her lungs and breathed through the pain that rushed through her like a tidal wave. Swallowing hard, she straightened and clenched her hands together in her lap. "Yeah, a few years ago. A truck hit my mom's minivan. My parents and the drunk driver of the truck died. Paramedics rushed my brother and me to the hospital. He's all I have left."

"That's terrible." He grasped her shaky hands. "But I'm fine. So are you."

Not sure why she'd shared her sob story, Mia stared up at the sun to fight back her tears. The warm May breeze lifted locks of brown hair from her nape. She tugged her hands free from the stranger and tightened her fallen ponytail. A side glance showed her his green eyes were at half-mast, his lips curved on one side of his chiseled face. Heat filled her cheeks. The hottie could easily grace the cover of one of those hunk-filled nudie magazines she and her friends would sometimes giggle over, but she didn't gawk or flirt with him as a normal woman would. Instead, she almost sent him to a hospital.

And I freaked out on him. Mia wanted to hide her face in a paper bag. *I'm so lame.*

Embarrassment squeezed her throat like a vise, but she pushed through it to find her voice. "I'm sorry about all this. I'm usually a good driver, and I've never had a panic attack until today. Thanks for calming me down. You aren't hurt and I've acted like a fool." With every ounce of strength she could muster, she slapped her hands on her knees and stood, and pushed all thoughts of her parents to the farthest corners of her mind.

He stood as well.

"You have someplace to be, right? I'll drive you and I'll be very safe. It's the least I can do."

"Nah, it's okay. I have to meet someone at the little diner on the next block, so I can just walk. I'll definitely watch out for traffic better the next time I cross a street."

"And I'll remember the turn signal." She tucked loose strands of hair behind her ears and offered him her hand. "I'm Mia Eddison."

"Mason Harding. Good to meet ya." He shook her hand and crowded closer to her. Two women nearly knocked him aside with their shopping bags as they walked by. He scowled at them and cast his gaze back toward Mia. "I moved back to the Denver area not long ago and people aren't as friendly as I remember."

"Yeah, not everyone has manners."

The women paused at the crosswalk and didn't seem to hear Mia and Mason's conversation.

Though her stomach still churned in hunger and nerves, her libido flipped back on like a light switch. She stood at five-feet-eight, and he was probably a little more than four inches taller. She couldn't help but wonder what it would be like to snuggle in his arms.

Be cool, Mia. Act confident. If you screw this up, you can't smash a rewind button and start over, you know. Not a fine pep talk, but it would have to do. She twirled a lock of hair between her fingers. "How long have you been in town, Mason?" Damn, his name sounded sexy on her tongue.

"Six months now. I'm originally from Aurora. I left about ten years ago but couldn't return until recently." Mason glanced at his watch again before he let his gaze travel down her body at a slow pace. "Are you busy Saturday? We could go for dinner."

Heat bloomed under her skin. She was grateful she wore a low-cut blouse, slinky black slacks, and peek-a-boo heels for a confidence booster, although she'd pulled her frizzy hair back in an unattractive ponytail that morning since her hairdryer had short-circuited. "I'm free." She dug through her purse, pulled a business card from her wallet, and handed it to him. "Call me and we'll set up plans."

His eyes widened as he read the card. "You own a store? That's awesome."

"Yep, Shadow Rose Boutique. Everything I sell is new or gently-used. I'm obsessed with books, clothes, and trinkets, so that makes up most of my merchandise. The store is in a renovated building downtown."

"Cool, I'll call you tonight."

"Tonight sounds great." A flirtatious grin spread across her face as Mason winked and turned away. The swagger in his step could knock a woman flat. Her gaze slid up from his ass to the tattoo on the back of his neck. Two black snakes crisscrossed each other like an X, their scales seeming to shimmer in the sunlight, and a woven black band encircled the wiggling serpents. He walked across the street and down the block as Mia gaped after him like an idiot, but she didn't feel like an idiot.

Nope, she'd just landed a date with a gorgeous mechanic. With a confident skip in her own step, she hurried back to her car and headed to work.

****

"You're four minutes late, Harding." Parole Officer Jeremiah "Jim" Borden leaned back in a plastic-vinyl booth and drank a cup of steaming coffee. "What happened?"

Mason sat across from him and glanced out the window in the direction where he'd left Mia. "A car nearly hit me on my way here. The driver hyperventilated and I talked with her until she calmed down. I came straight here afterward."

Borden tapped his fingers on the thick manila folder that rested on the table between them. "I've heard a lot of bullshit excuses over the years, including a few like that one, but I won't document your late arrival since you've never been late before."

"I want this to work out. You seem like a decent guy. I want you to think the same of me. I'm not lying about the woman." He could prove it by relinquishing Mia's business card, but the uptight officer would probably call her and verify, and ruin Mason's chances with her.

Their usual waitress arrived before Borden could respond. Mason ordered coffee, a cheeseburger with everything on it, and French fries—the same thing he always ordered during their mandatory monthly meetings—and Calista jotted everything down.

Borden's gaze locked onto her swaying ass as she

walked away.

Mason rolled his eyes. The beautiful blonde waitress didn't compare to Mia Eddison. The classy brunette fox deserved something better than slumming with an ex-con, and he had no idea why he asked her out other than the massive hard-on that strained his ragged-ass jeans.

Borden downed the rest of his coffee. "I meet most of my parolees at my office. I come to them if I think they're likely candidates for rehabilitation and if they're unable to make it to their meetings by the allotted timeframe. Like this with you." He held out his arms to encompass Demi's Diner. "If you're late again, we'll convene at my office across town from then on. You'll have one hell of a time getting there and back to work before your lunch break ends."

Mason bit his tongue. He *could* meet his babysitter at the office if the State had assigned him to a parole office closer to home.

"I deal with maybe a dozen or so decent parolees at any given time." The PO continued his lecture. "Most of them play by the rules for a few months until they sink back into their old lives."

"I don't wanna screw up, but you never know. I hate to say never. It always seems to bite me in the ass when I do."

Borden flipped open the manila folder, shuffled through several papers, and pulled out an evaluation form. He wrote the date on the document. "How are you, Mason? Any contact from old friends back home?"

Mason scratched at the old bullet wound on his right shoulder. "Not yet, but it's bound to happen since

Aurora borders Denver. As you know, Alan said a few of the guys I used to hang out with have cleaned up and moved on with their lives. Not all of them, of course. Even though I don't plan to visit or travel through Aurora, they could come to Denver." He worried about that every day. As far as he was concerned, his old life died when the judge at his hearing had sentenced him to fifteen years behind bars. "I want nothing to do with those people, even the ones who cleaned up. I don't want the memories. Besides, I work and live in clean areas. My old friends preferred slums and drug-infested strip clubs. I should be fine as long as I stay away from those places."

"How are your brother and his son? Are there any problems with that adjustment?"

"I feel comfortable living with them. I think they feel the same about me." Mason thanked Calista as she delivered his coffee.

She refilled Borden's cup, and the officer's attention shifted again as she walked away.

"Anyway"—Mason cleared his throat—"Alan gives me enough space but demands I adhere to the rules. He's taking the role of big brother seriously and my nephew is adorable. I don't want to set a bad example for Danny."

"How's your job at Ben's Auto Repair? You started"—the other man checked the file—"five months ago. Do you have any new altercations to report?"

"It's good and no altercations. I doubt I'd be employed anywhere if Alan hadn't secured the job for me." Legitimate employers in a struggling economy didn't usually opt for ex-cons. "The man who hit me a few weeks ago has left me alone since the boss threatened to fire him." Mason had backed down from the fight in order to not violate his parole, but that prick deserved a major kick in the ass.

"What was that argument about?" Borden searched through his files and found the right document. "Let's see... Right, I remember. You flirted with a coworker's girlfriend."

The muscle in Mason's right cheek lifted in an annoying tic. He rubbed his scruffy jaw to suppress it. "Yeah, but I didn't know that until he shoved me against her car and punched me. I didn't hit him back." He paused as the waitress arrived with their food.

The parole officer added a few notes in the current evaluation. "I see the anger management sessions have helped. A string of curse words usually follows the spasm in your face when I say something you don't like. Tell me about the meetings."

The tic beat again. Mason bit his tongue to silence his telltale cursing. "I haven't missed any weekly meetings. You'd know if I did." He popped a fry in his mouth and savored the greasy food he missed most while locked up. "I think half of what the therapist says is bull, but the other half makes sense. I have to control my temper. It's the main reason for my stupid mistakes."

"Why haven't you secured a means of transportation?"

"Alan demands I pay half the bills—rent, utilities, and groceries—since I live in his apartment. I wanna buy a car outright but haven't saved up enough money yet. I don't want to lease a vehicle because of the monthly bill."

"Are bills stressful for you?"

He rolled his eyes and swallowed a large bite of his cheeseburger. "You sound like the snobby therapist at my meetings. The prick charges me a hundred bucks an hour and tells me not to worry about money." He wiped a dab of ketchup from his mouth and licked his finger.

Borden dropped his pen and cut his chicken-fried-steak into several small pieces. "Stress is a trigger for anger." He chewed and swallowed a piece of gravy-coated steak. "And anger, as you just admitted, is the reason behind your mistakes. You may do something stupid to acquire more cash if you're stressed over money and bills."

"I'm not *that* stressed. I pay my bills every month and on time. My brother works a full-time job, as do I, but I have little money left over for niceties besides the money I'm saving for a car." He silently cursed. He would have to dip into those savings for his Saturday night date. A sophisticated woman like Mia probably wouldn't appreciate fast food for dinner. "Alan has extra money at the end of the month, but I refuse to ask him for a loan."

The officer scribbled on the document. "Any drug use?"

"No. Drugs were never my thing." He'd tried marijuana as a teenager, but it sickened him to the point of throwing up. He still couldn't believe the state of Colorado had finally legalized it. "I preferred alcohol back then, especially whiskey, and I assume I still would if I drank. That's a big no-no for my parole, though, so I haven't touched a drop of alcohol."

"Why not continue school? You could apply to one of the community colleges in the area. It would probably be easier to wait until fall, but you might make the deadline for the summer semester if you hurry. Did you look at those pamphlets I gave you?"

Mason pursed his lips. *Am I even college material?* He'd dropped out of high school at age sixteen but earned his GED in prison. "Benji, my boss from the garage, told me I needed an automotive certificate to qualify for a raise."

"That sounds doable. What's stopping you?"

"I'm on parole, Borden. That's a problem. I'd like to enroll and not just for a certificate or a damn raise." Mason wanted to prove he could do the academic work. He made damn near perfect grades in school before a few bad choices derailed his future. "Anyone can go to college, even people with records, but it wouldn't be easy. The admissions board would file a background check and call me in for a meeting, according to the pamphlets. I understand why, of course, but…" He couldn't finish the sentence as his cheeks heated.

"You're right, but wouldn't all that shit be worth it?"

Mason shrugged and stared out the window. "Don't know."

"All right. Are there any new relationships I should know about? Have you made friends at work yet?"

"Only Benji, but he's Alan's former brother-in-law, and I think Ben feels like he has to be nice to me. Most of the men there are okay to hang out with on the clock, but I wouldn't call any of them bosom buddies. Two of them are ex-cons, but their parole ended years ago. They don't offer support or anything, if that's what you mean."

"I know you associate with Benjamin Starwell outside of work, but what about anyone else?"

He fisted his hands under the table. "No. I just said I'm not friends with any of them."

Borden filled out the evaluation form while he ate. "What about other relationships? You have a girlfriend?"

"Nope." He unclenched one of his hands and smoothed his palm over Mia's business card in his jeans pocket.

"Have you visited any bars or clubs in the past month? Did you drink?" Borden tapped his pen against the table as Mason scowled. "Don't lie to me, Harding. Ten years in prison without female companionship or a damn drink of liquor would drive any man a little crazy. It's hard to believe you never indulged, especially since your crew smuggled alcohol in the prison. Anyway, it's time to enjoy a few vices since you're on parole. Am I right?"

"Dead wrong. I ended up behind bars because I lost control when I drank, so I quit. The wild, obnoxious person I turned into almost ruined my life. My prison shrink called me a *problem drinker*, not an alcoholic, and it's my choice to stay sober." But he sometimes had to remind himself of that. His mouth had often watered when inmates passed around a bottle and the heady scent filled his nostrils. Mason told himself a single sip wouldn't hurt, but could he stop afterward? Hell if he knew, so he always kept his paws off an open bottle. "You're right about the contraband and it's fully documented. I knew people who smuggled it in, but I never bought or sold it."

Mason straightened his back and met the officer square in the eyes. "I don't go to bars. I don't drink. I've admitted to flings before, even though my sex life isn't your business." The terms of his parole forbade him from entering establishments that distributed and sold alcohol as its primary focus, but he'd met several women over the past six months at various venues and stores across the city. After ten lonely years, he had a lot of time to make up. "I never committed a sexual offense, so your questions and insinuations are invalid."

"It *is* my business. You know that. Sex relieves stress and anger—that's common sense—and your temper is your biggest problem. I need to know all the ways you relieve that temper. So, no, the questions aren't invalid." Borden's eyes narrowed as Mason cursed under his breath. "Any flings this past month?"

"Of course."

"Have you paid for a woman's services?"

He hated the same old questions. With added sarcasm, Mason gave the same old answer. "My tats and scars draw the ladies like bees to honey. I'm too damn hot to pay for sex." He'd built his body to perfection in the prison yard and gym, and continued to work out in the morning before he headed to work and again before bed. "Most women find bad boys irresistible. My charisma, chivalry, and advanced vocabulary smoothes out the rough edges, so I have no shortage of available tail."

Mason flashed his sexiest smile as the waitress refilled their drinks, and he accepted his check from her as she tried to lay it on the table. He grazed her hand with the rough pads of his fingertips, his gaze flicking from her chest to her face.

A surprised but flirty grin lifted her lips. Calista sashayed away and her hips drew the attention of more than one male customer in the diner.

He turned back to Borden. "As you can tell, I don't need to pay for women."

Borden clutched his pen so hard his knuckles whitened. He slammed it down and shuffled through the documents inside the folder again.

Mason knew he shouldn't bait the asshole but couldn't help himself. "What a surprise. I'm not the only one with an anger problem. Would you like the number to my state-ordered therapist? I'm sure he can pencil you in on Friday after me."

Borden's forehead scrunched together in deep lines. "Shut the hell up and eat, Harding." He found a certain document, slammed it on top of the evaluation, and shoved a heaping pile of mashed potatoes into his mouth. He swallowed with barely a chew. "Be warned. I might stop by your apartment or work in a few weeks at any hour of the day or night. Your ass is mine for five long years. I'm the pit bull and you're the poodle. So play nice."

Mason bit back another sarcastic retort and gulped a long draft of his coffee as Borden tapped his fingers on the new sheet of paper, probably an at-home evaluation. Alan wanted Danny away at school, with a sitter, or at Benji's place while Borden inspected the apartment for violations. Mason couldn't predict or stop unannounced visits, however, but he didn't mind if the vengeful bastard visited the garage. His coworkers' opinion meant shit to him.

He refused to apologize. Parole Officer Jim Borden had just proven himself a first-rate dick, and Mason should've known better than to consider him a decent person. Authority figures only cared about two things: following the rules and screwing over anyone who didn't fall in line.

Mason picked up his burger and savored every ounce of cheese and beef. After so long without prime American fare, he doubted anything could ruin his appetite for a delicious burger and fries, not even the company of his angry PO.

Chapter Two

"What's so funny?" Mia lifted her eyebrow as Mason chuckled. They stopped on the sidewalk, and she lightly popped his arm as he shook his head. "C'mon, Mason. Tell me."

"It's nothing, really. I just didn't expect you to chug a wine cooler or choose a pizza parlor for a first date."

She glanced over her shoulder at the hole-in-the-wall eatery. They'd arrived before the dinner crowd and left just as several cars and a high school activity bus pulled into the parking lot. "You said over the phone you've never been there, so I knew we had to go. I think they serve the best damn pizza on the planet. Did you not like it?" Mia frowned, completely satisfied with half of an extra-large black olive-and-mushroom pizza in her tummy.

"No, I did. The pizza was great." Mason locked his hands behind his back. "I'm just surprised you didn't want something fancy and expensive."

"Ahhh, I get it. Don't worry. I'm a little high maintenance, but I'm not the type of woman to bleed a man's wallet dry." She laughed as blush pinked his cheeks.

They continued along the sidewalk. The quaint, inner city neighborhood thrummed with life, and Mia loved the way a busy city like Denver sometimes gave off a warm, inviting vibe. Adults chattered and children laughed all around them. Decorative lampposts dispelled the early evening darkness, and old-fashioned cobblestone buildings rose two and three stories high.

Mason glanced toward a few storefront windows as people shopped inside in the buildings. "Tell me about your business. I've never met anyone who owned a boutique."

"Well, it originally belonged to my parents. Mom wanted to own a clothing store, so they risked their savings and bought the building. Dad always supported her even though they had two little kids to raise, and I spent most of my childhood learning the trade." Cars honked and rushed by as she and Mason paused at an intersection. Three other people waited beside them at the curb for the *Walk* sign to flash. Mia swallowed the ball in her throat. "They left the building and business to me. That store is my life."

"I'll stop by sometime. I'd love to see it."

A breeze ruffled her hair as she stared into his eyes. "It's very girly. You'll love my store if you like beads, feathers, and the color pink."

Mason grinned. "Not really, but I'll still check it out." Traffic halted at the red light, and he grasped her elbow in a firm but gentle grip to lead her across the street. They reached the other side and he released her. "What did your dad do for a living?"

She arched her eyebrow. He stared at her as though interested in the conversation, not even aware of his chivalrous behavior. The idea of *protecting* seemed natural to him, and he definitely had the physique of a bodyguard.

Mia smiled, flattered. "He—um—he was a

policeman, a lieutenant when he died. My brother is a parole officer."

"Seriously?" He paused in his steady gait and glanced toward the street just as a police cruiser drove by. "Does your brother frequent this area?"

"Sometimes. He goes all over the city and county, plus neighboring counties, to visit with his parolees." Mia fought back a full-on grin as his face reddened. "He's protective, but he's not a psychotic brother who screens all my potential boyfriends. He treats me like a grown woman. Besides, I'm divorced. It's not like I haven't been around the block a few times."

"Divorced?" Mason stepped back and nearly bumped into a passing stranger.

She grimaced and rubbed the bridge between her eyes. "Damn it, I didn't mean to say that. You're just so easy to talk to."

He tunneled his hand through his hair. "It's no big deal. We all have skeletons in our closet. What happened, if you don't mind me asking?"

Mia glanced at her left hand as they resumed their walk. She didn't miss the wedding set that once circled her ring finger, but her skin sometimes itched with its absence. "Evan and I met in our senior year of college and married right after graduation. I thought we were happy, I thought he loved me, but I caught him in bed with a girl who worked at my store." She clenched her fists at her sides. "The marriage lasted about five years, and the bastard cheated on me for the last year of it."

"Damn, I'm sorry. When did you get a divorce?"

"About a year ago. We signed a prenup, but he still tried to claim half of everything I owned in the divorce hearing. *Unsuccessfully*, I might add." She fiddled with

18

the charm bracelet on her wrist. "Mom probably wouldn't have left me the boutique if I hadn't legally safeguarded my current and future assets with the prenuptial agreement. I didn't trust Evan with money, my parents didn't like or trust him, period, and none of us wanted him involved in the business. That mistrust should've been a red flag our marriage wouldn't last."

She'd lost her parents the year before and thought the world crashed down around her all over again when she caught Evan and his girlfriend naked together in *her* loft. She picked up the pieces of her shattered self-esteem over the following months, and though her friends tried to set her up on blind dates, her stomach churned every time she thought about trusting another man.

Mia never expected a barely avoided car accident to push her back into the dating scene.

"Oh, crap. I'm sorry I didn't ask earlier, but how are you? Are you in any pain?" She swished her hand dismissively in the air as he frowned. "I mean, from when I almost rammed your legs with my car."

"You're thinking of that now?" His lips stretched in a grin. A day's worth of scruffiness covered his cheeks and deepened his sensual appeal. His casual blazer hung loose around his muscled chest and his nipples pressed tight against his white dress shirt, and Mia couldn't help but stare. "You need to live in the moment, sugar. For me, that surprise attack happened ages ago."

Her mouth dropped open. Mia playfully pinched his arm as he laughed and held up his hands as though in surrender. "You're so mean, Mason, and it's condescending when you call me *sugar*. It's a good thing for you I know you're just kidding. You're lucky to be alive, you know."

"I am, really." He rubbed his shoulder.

"Is your shoulder hurt? Are you sure you're okay?"

"No, no. I'm fine."

Mia doubted that as she grasped his warm, rough hand. Their fingers twisted together. "What about you? Divorced? Kids?"

"Neither. I'm rooming with my brother and nephew for the moment. Alan and his wife divorced after Danny was born. The boy will turn eight in a few months."

"It must be tough to raise a child alone. I always wanted kids, but Evan didn't. I thought I could change his mind, but he always got so upset when I brought up the subject." A long sigh left her mouth. She'd confused infatuation and lust with love. Once divorced, she realized she never truly loved him and had wasted years of her life.

Mason glanced away. "I wanted to be there for Alan, but things got in the way. He offered to share his apartment in Westminster when I finally moved back."

"That's nice of him. Where were you?"

"Would you like to see a movie?" Mason nodded toward a busy theater down the block.

"Uh, sure." A little taken aback by the abrupt subject change, she grabbed her phone from her purse and checked the time. "But only if I pay."

"No. A gentleman pays for the lady."

Mia laughed behind her hand. "It's only fair. You paid for the pizza and drinks, though I don't understand why you ordered soda. Happy Hour cut all the beer and wine prices in half."

"What woman doesn't want things for free?"

"All right, let's make a deal." She pulled him to a stop and clicked her tongue. "You pay for everything tonight. Next time, I pay for everything. Sound good?"

"Next time?"

She flushed hot but refused to back down. "Yeah, I'd like to see you again."

Mason wrapped his arms around her waist and tugged her close. "Have I told you how amazing you look tonight?"

The blush surely deepened as heat consumed her face. He'd told her so twice already. Her slinky blue dress emphasized her breasts, hugged her curves, and reached above her knee with a high slit up one thigh. She'd overdressed for a pizza parlor but rarely wore her favorite outfit outside the loft. With a slick black jacket to downplay the sexy dress, the alluring armor bolstered her self-confidence.

Heat radiated from his broad chest as Mason embraced her. Strangers grumbled as they passed, but Mia hardly cared that she and Mason blocked foot traffic in the middle of the sidewalk. His scent teased her nostrils as she breathed, the bristles on his chin and cheeks a little rough under her palm, and she summoned every modicum of willpower she possessed to keep upright and not melt like a lovesick teenager.

Mason released her and stepped back. His sudden departure ripped the air from her lungs, but his eyes never left hers as he clasped her hand and kissed her knuckles. Mia assumed he sealed her deal with the kiss—she couldn't find her voice to ask—and she realized she'd forgotten what first dates were like.

No, scratch that. She'd never dated a man as

flattering or smooth as Mason Harding.

Mason rested his hand on the small of Mia's back as they walked toward the theater. The simple, protective gesture warmed her toes. She planned to see the newest chick flick with her girlfriends—her best friend, Belle, would slap her silly if Mia saw the movie without her—so she suggested an action-packed film that probably wouldn't bore Mason to sleep. After two hours of car chases, espionage, and hot sex between an even hotter couple, not to mention a kickass metal soundtrack, they returned to her sedan at the pizza parlor.

"Which one is your car?" She glanced around the crowded parking lot. A few streetlights pushed back the darkness and shadows. The restaurant served customers until midnight on the weekends, but no one loitered in the lot, at least from what Mia could see.

"Don't have one at the moment." Mason hooked his thumbs in the belt loops of his jeans. "I took the bus. It stopped a few blocks from here."

"Would you like a ride?" She pulled the car keys from her purse. "I feel a little ridiculous we met here tonight. I just wasn't sure if you were some kind of freak."

His eyebrow lifted, and he closed the distance between them as a tiger would zero in on its mate. A sexy, masculine smile curled his lips. "Have you made up your mind yet?"

"I'll let you know in the morning." Desire trickled down her spine. Mia nodded toward the passenger side of the car for him to hop in.

He confiscated her keys instead to unlock and open the driver's side door for her like a gentleman. Then he leaned closer and nuzzled her temple with his nose.

Not sure if he planned to seduce her in the parking lot or if he merely wanted to tease her, Mia pressed her hand to his chest and tried to think straight. "You're the first guy I've gone on a date with since my divorce. I haven't slept with anyone since Evan."

He tunneled his fingers through her wavy, chestnut-brown hair. "I haven't dated anyone in a long time either. We'll take it slow or fast, whatever you want, but I promise you one thing. After I'm done with you, you won't even remember that bastard's name."

Oh, God. She almost melted right then and there. "Fast. I want you, Mason."

"Take me to your place and you can have me."

Mia fought the impulse to shove him against the car and straddle him, and turned to enter the vehicle.

Mason yanked her back to him before she could climb in. Their mouths met in a frenzied rush of need. His tongue twisted with hers in an erotic dance as he circled his arms around her like two steel bands. The scent of aroused male hung thick in the air.

She moaned as Mason's mouth left hers and suckled the hollow of her neck. "Oh God, yes." Mia tilted her head to the side and gave him better access as he pinned her to the car. He palmed her waist and trailed his strong hands up to knead her breasts. Her back arched as she gripped his shoulders for leverage.

"Fucking hell, I could take you right now in this damn lot." Mason lifted his head and stared deep into her eyes. "We need someplace private."

She swallowed hard to toughen her raspy voice. "You drive. My legs are like jelly."

He helped Mia into the passenger side of the car

and settled himself in the driver's seat. "Tell me the shortest route, darlin', before I find a vacant alley and take you there."

****

Mason cut the engine to the sedan in front of a two-story building in LoDo, the lower downtown district of the city. Lampposts lit the street and a large, decorative sign titled *Shadow Rose Boutique* hung above double glass doors.

Mia snatched the keys from his hand and bolted from the car. She unlocked an old metal door several feet down from the storefront windows, ascended a flight of stone steps, and stumbled twice in her *fuck-me* heels.

A light bulb flickered above their heads as Mason followed her, and shadows danced on the brick stairwell walls. He grabbed her arm once they reached the landing, desperate to feel her, and pushed her against the main door. Her skin burned hot to the touch. He slid his hand past the slit in her dress and up her thigh.

She wrapped her smooth leg around his waist to grind against him.

Stars danced in his vision. "Get the door, Mia." Mason flipped her around and pressed her against the steel barrier. He buried one hand in her hair and yanked her dress up to her waist with the other.

She fumbled with the keys but finally unlocked it. A beep echoed as they tumbled inside.

Mason caught Mia by the waist and held them upright with a quick pivot of his feet before they fell. Her warm, tight body fit so right in his arms, but he let her go so he could slam the door shut and shove the lock into place. Shadows cloaked the loft. Light streamed in from street-facing windows, but Mason didn't bother to flip the light switch by the door.

The heat in Mia's eyes scorched him, but she held up her hands as he reached for her. Apprehension washed through him like an acid wave. He needed release, damn it. He needed her pliant body beneath his and her soft cries in his ears.

Mia circled around him and headed back to the door.

He thought for sure she'd tell him to hit the road. If she did, he'd call her a prick-tease and tell her for future reference a smart woman should never invite a man home and dump him before putting out, just for her own safety.

She pressed a few buttons on a wall-mounted security panel, and the alarm ceased. A flirty smile teased her lips. Her gaze swept down his body as if she was mentally undressing him.

Mason chastised himself for those stupid negative thoughts.

"Now, where were we?" She braced her hands on her hips and flipped her dark hair over her shoulder like a wild mane. Little flames of fire lit her eyes, the darkest brown eyes he'd ever seen.

Her come-get-me look drove the last shred of his self-control out the window. He backed her against the wall and jerked her jacket down her arms. A growl rumbled in his throat. Creamy cleavage pushed against the low neckline of her dress. Mason could barely think or see as the red haze of desire clouded his mind. She twisted her arms around him, gripped the back of his blazer, and he jammed his knee between her legs to part them.

Her heels clanked on the floor as Mia stood on her tiptoes and straddled his knee to keep upright. A moan escaped her mouth.

"You're so damn beautiful." He pressed hard little kisses along the curve of her neck. "You smell like flowers."

"My perfume." She trailed her fingers up his nape and through his hair to cradle his head to her neck.

Her silk-covered ass fit perfectly in his palms as he lifted her into a better position between the art-deco brick wall and his body. Air sawed in and out from his lungs. His ears rang and his muscles twitched in anticipation.

Mia wrapped her legs around his waist, and her panties offered little resistance as he slid his fingers beneath them to stroke her clit. She squirmed and gasped.

The pleasure on her face heightened his lust, and he pushed two fingers into her moist center.

Her sharp cry filled the room.

"Damn, you're tight." His penis throbbed painfully hard in his jeans, and he thrust his hips into the circle of her body to ease the pressure. Her pulsating, hot sheath stretched as Mason wiggled his fingers in and out, back and forth, and he drove in a third digit to push on her G-spot.

"Oh God, Mason. That's so amazing."

He blew warm air in her ear. "Just wait until we're naked. I'll rock inside you so hard you'll scream for more."

"I can't wait. Take me to the bedroom. Now."

Her heat slicked his fingers as she bucked against

him. He wiggled his fingers harder, faster, and pushed on her little button with his thumb.

She slapped at his chest, whined for more, and clung to him as though she needed a lifeline in a storm. Fine creases spread at the corners of her eyes as tension surely built in her womb.

Her feminine muscles contracted around his probing fingers, and Mason captured her shout of pleasure with his mouth.

Mia stopped thrusting after her quick release, and she lay limp on his chest.

"That's a good girl." He brushed a kiss on her head and withdrew his hand. Her legs slid from his waist and he steadied her against the wall. He licked his fingers clean. "Now, I'll take you to the bedroom."

"I—I don't know if I can take anymore. That hand job was top notch."

Mason gripped her chin and forced her to meet his gaze. "I want you, Mia. I haven't felt so ravenous for a woman in a long damn time." He'd slept with several women over the past few months but didn't crave any of them as he craved Mia, not even the first woman he screwed after a decade of incarceration.

His heart stuttered in his ribcage. He'd never mentioned his prison term to any of those women and even though Mia matched their sexual prowess, he didn't consider her a slut or just a way to pass the time. She respected herself and probably saw this encounter as a spontaneous, carefree night of passion. In fact, she admitted she hadn't dated or slept with a man since her divorce last year. She deserved the truth.

He cursed and released her. Pressure pounded in his cock so much it ached, and he rubbed himself for relief. Mia's curvy, lithe body promised heaven, but now he couldn't touch her. He rarely acknowledged the gentler side of his personality unless he was around his nephew, but he wanted to with her. Mia deserved better than a rough romp with an ex-con—unless she wanted the romp and nothing more.

Mason clenched his fists and sighed. He stepped away from her.

"What's wrong?" Mia rested her hand on his arm before he got away. Her eyebrows scrunched together, worry clear on her face. She brushed at his sleeve as though to clean off stray hairs. "Why are you mad?"

"I'm not mad. I just need to tell you something."

"Oh crap, you're married? You said you weren't." She grabbed his left hand and frowned. "Is the ring in your wallet? Do you have a disease?"

"No, it's nothing like that." He locked his hands behind his back to keep from jerking her into his arms. "You're heat and innocence, wrapped in one delicious package. I don't want to hurt you, Mia." The male, possessive part of him demanded he ravage her body until sunrise, yet he wanted to shelter her with equal fervor. She needed him as much as he needed her—the proof blazed in her eyes and in the blush of her cheeks—but she'd probably kick him from her home in disgust after he told her the truth.

So be it. I have to tell her.

Mason glanced around the spacious loft, desperate for a distraction. The living room, along with the adjoining kitchen and dining room, equaled about the size of Alan's small but comfortable apartment. A padlocked steel door in the dining room likely led downstairs to the store. Painted dark gray for an artsy feel, mechanicals systems and piping lined the stucco ceiling and exposed brick walls. A plaster ceiling and a row of drywall sectioned off about a third of the loft at the far end, and three closed doors faced the large living area. Valances and mini-blinds hung suspended from the top of two windowsills in the main room, and the urge to release the bundled blinds to darken the loft tightened his gut.

He met his date's gaze. "You have no idea how much I want you, how much I'd like to get to know you better, but you need to know some important stuff about me. I did things in my past that might offend you. You probably won't want to see me again. In fact, I'm sure of it, but I have to take that risk or I'll hate myself later."

She chewed on her bottom lip. "Okay. I'm surprised you decided to tell me this *before* we have sex. Most men would wait until after or never say it at all."

"I don't want to use you like that. I already feel guilty for this." Mason nodded toward the wall where he'd made her scream. "I took you like an animal."

"I'm not complaining."

"Not yet." He clutched his fingers in his hair and tugged until his scalp burned. "Fuck, I just need to say it. I spent the past ten years in prison, Mia. I'm on parole."

"Prison?" She stepped away from him. "For what?"

"Attempted murder."

Chapter Three

"Murder? You're joking?"

"No, *attempted*—there's a big difference—and I would never joke about something like that. Two men almost died and I'm responsible." Mason pressed his fingers to his temples as images of blood ran through his mind. "God, I fucked up so bad back then. I'll go. I don't mean to scare you."

"I'm not scared. I'm just—just a little shocked." Mia straightened her dress around her knees and grabbed her jacket from the floor. "What happened?"

Mason frowned as she shook out the wrinkles in the jacket and draped it over the back of a plush chair. He glanced unsteadily at the door. "Don't you want me to leave?"

"I'm not sure yet. I don't know what you did or why. I don't know if I should be afraid of you."

"I'm not dangerous. I made a huge mistake and I paid for it."

"An accident?"

Mason dropped his gaze. Exhaustion weighed on his chest like a pallet of bricks. Drained from his stupid choices and the self-loathing that ate away at him, he craved a moment of peace and a way to forget everything he'd done. Alcohol offered a way out for some people. For him, it pushed him on a downward tailspin of mistakes, and he'd vowed to never lose control again.

"I thought you would yell at me to leave, not want an explanation."

"Leave if you want, Mason. I won't keep you here against your will."

"I'd rather stay." He'd *rather* wrap her in his arms and promise her he would never hurt her, but he maintained his distance.

"All right. Have a seat on the sofa if you like. I need to grab a towel so my messy clothes won't stain the cushions." Mia hurried across the living area without waiting to see if he sat.

Anxiety warred in his stomach. She opened the middle door on the far wall and likely headed inside the bathroom. A small part of him wished he'd kept his big mouth shut and pleasured himself with her body, but then he would feel even more like shit. Mason scrubbed his hand down his face and mulled over his next words as she returned with a towel clutched in her hand. She nodded toward the sofa and Mason finally obliged.

He couldn't fathom how much she spent on the overstuffed piece of suede furniture and two matching chairs. The soft fabric and cushions were comfortable, but tension knotted his back so tight he couldn't enjoy the luxury. A telephone, a lamp, and a few picture frames occupied the end table beside the sofa, but from his angle, he couldn't see the faces of the people in the photographs.

Sculpture-style art decorated the walls. The scent of cinnamon wafted from the bowl of potpourri on the low-rise coffee table. Then there was the huge television armoire that stood between the two large windows and faced the sitting area. A plush Oriental rug connected the furniture. Everything about her home, even the *type* of home Mia lived in, screamed class and money.

She unfolded the large towel and laid it flat on the far end of the sofa. Her gaze averted, she sat and clasped her hands on her lap. A strained smile lifted her lips as she finally looked at him. "I had a lot of fun tonight. More than I expected. Why are you possibly throwing all that away to tell me this?"

"Because I like you, Mia. I don't want you to accuse me of lying if I keep quiet and you find out later."

"You've got a point." She swiped locks of her tousled hair behind her ears. "Start from the beginning. Get everything off your chest."

"The beginning? Okay." Air whizzed through his teeth. "My parents divorced when I was fifteen years old. It sounds like an excuse, but it messed me up bad. We used to be so happy. I used to respect them, especially my dad. He taught me everything I know about cars. Once he cheated on my mom and they started to argue, well, I just lost it. I couldn't understand how two people could hate each other after twenty years of marriage."

He still didn't get it, even though he understood *hate* well.

"Mom won custody of me, and Dad left the state with his girlfriend after the divorce finalized. Alan was attending college at the time and lived in a dorm, so he didn't deal with their shit often. I don't think he ever understood how much they fought or why I acted out."

His memories of his parents' nasty screamfests sometimes weighed harder on him than when he dreamed about roll call and clanking bars. Sometimes he feared he'd imagined his past few months of freedom and he refused to fall asleep at night, too afraid he would wake back up inside the slammer.

Mia reached halfway across the sofa as though to hold his hand, but she drew back and rubbed her cheek. She tapped her feet in a nervous rhythm on the floor.

"Anyway, I befriended some local losers after the divorce and dropped out of school as soon as I turned sixteen. I ran away from home countless times, but the police always dragged me back." Mason pounded his fist against his tattooed wrist. "Mom grew tired of my bullshit, and Dad didn't give a damn. Alan never gave up on me, though, and I hated him for it." He'd just wanted his friends and thought they were the only ones who understood him. He hurt Alan so much back then and would never forgive himself for it.

"What about drugs?"

Her abrupt question took him aback. "I rarely used any. Pot made me sick and I never tried anything harder, but I handled alcohol like a man twice my age and body weight. *That* was my drug."

Tension radiated around Mia like an impenetrable bubble.

The scent of her womanly musk doubled the saliva in his mouth. He stood to pace behind the sofa, too antsy to sit still. His skin hot and a little clammy, he shrugged off his blazer and dropped it on the sofa. His back stiffened as Mia shifted sideways to watch him, but he wouldn't meet her gaze.

I could really use a drink.

Not a damn thing tasted better than whiskey as it burned a red-hot track down his throat. He brought his right hand up to his nose, sniffed Mia's scent, and imagined what his drug of choice would taste like if poured over her hot little vagina. His cock strained in his jeans again.

Keep going. Can't stop now, not when I'm the white-trash idiot who brought this up.

"I hit bottom a few months after my eighteenth birthday." He folded his arms across his chest to hide his shaky hands. "The drugs and alcohol ran dry at a party, a three-night bender, and my friends and I decided to rob a little liquor store. Jeston's Liquor. I refused at first, I knew it was wrong, but I wanted more whiskey and the guys nagged until I agreed. Four of us went. My friend, Joe, gave me a gun—for intimidation, he said—but I never used it."

Memories rushed through his mind, wave after wave of mistake. "It all happened so fast. Joe screamed at the cashier and demanded money. He waved his gun around like a fucking cowboy. The other guys and I rushed down the aisles and stuffed hundreds of dollars worth of high-end bottles into our bags. Lenny and Tom threw bottles of the cheap stuff at the walls and knocked over shelves. I watched them do it but didn't help them trash the store." Disgust had gnawed in his gut and a pounding headache dogged him throughout the robbery.

Just thinking back on it churned his stomach.

"Joe freaked out when he heard police sirens, and he grabbed the register to smash on the floor. The cashier, Walter Jeston, grabbed a handgun from beneath the counter, and Joe shot him in the chest just as the old man fired. The slug hit me, not Joe." He rubbed his shoulder and grimaced. "A clerk emerged from the back room and blasted a damn shotgun. Joe went down. His blood sprayed all over me, so slick and wet. I shook so bad you would have thought I had palsy or something. Before I knew it, Lenny shot the clerk."

Mason pinched the bridge of his nose. "Joe died. Lenny and Tom grabbed the bags and hightailed it out of there. I wanted to run, too, but my feet wouldn't move. I thought Joe killed the cashier, and I knew the clerk would die if I didn't do something. Blood bubbled out of his stomach, so thick and red like you'd see in a horror movie, and I pressed against the wound with my jacket. The police and paramedics arrived minutes later."

Guilt swelled in his throat. Mason swallowed hard to breathe and stalked to the nearest window. Dull light streamed in and bathed the living room in a dark glow. Cold air blew from an overhead vent, and he leaned his forehead against the cool glass windowpane to stare down at the deserted street. A few cars occupied parallel parking spots, and even fewer lights glowed from upper level windows of nearby buildings. The beauty and the vast openness of the night unnerved him. He'd spent so many years in a small cell that he needed walls to feel safe.

"What were the charges?"

He turned to face Mia.

The beautiful woman sat with her legs crossed and her shoulders straight. Her voice sounded even and smooth, perhaps a little cool, but he couldn't gauge her mood. He should have made love to her when he had the chance.

"The State slapped me with one count of attempted murder in the second degree as an accomplice, a class four felony, and one count of attempted aggravated robbery, a class three felony. The initial charges were much worse before I accepted a plea bargain."

"Right." Mia drummed her hands on her knees and stood. "The state of Colorado holds all accomplices accountable for the same actions as the main perpetrators, which sounds like Joe and Lenny, so I assume the DA originally charged you with two counts of attempted murder."

Mason scratched his scalp, surprised she knew the law. *Of course she does. Her dad was a fucking cop.* He pushed away the reminder.

"You're right. The plea bargain canceled out the attempted murder charge of the clerk, Ronnie Jeston, and reduced the armed robbery charge since I didn't leave with any stolen goods. I didn't bother to aid Walter Jeston, so that charge remained." Mason clenched his hands behind his back as she avoided his gaze. "I spent two months in the county jail and the judge sentenced me to fifteen years in a correctional facility, up for parole in ten. I'd still be in prison if either of the Jeston men had died."

Mia hummed as though in agreement. "What about your friends?"

"The district attorney sentenced Lenny with two counts of attempted second-degree murder, one as an accomplice and the other as the main perp, and Tom as an accomplice to both charges. Since they left with alcohol, he also sentenced them for armed robbery." Mason stroked his bristled chin. "Unlike me, they didn't remain at the scene or cooperate with the police. They eventually accepted plea bargains, but the judge showed little leniency when he sentenced them."

His cheek twitched as Mia walked behind the sofa as though it could protect her.

Do I not look capable of jumping over a coffee table and a sofa?

Unlike most of the macho jerks on his block, Mason had divided his free time between the gym and the prison library to read anything he could find, though he preferred literary classics. Closer to his parole, he'd joined the automotive repair work/study program to relearn the trade. A few pieces of wood, upholstery, and springs couldn't stop him if he wanted to reach Mia.

He rubbed the damn tic away, grateful it never caused him pain, just an uncomfortable twinge now and then, and hoped she didn't ask about it. Though he needed to get the conversation about his prison sentence out in the open, he'd trash his ability to get a stiffy for the night if he told her the reason for the facial tic right now.

Mason bit his nails into his palms to soothe the irritation in his veins. "The DA focused more on the robbery than the two attempted murders in my case since neither victim died or sustained lifelong injuries. The store surveillance cameras caught everything on tape, so he had a lot to work with. The judge later ruled my gunshot wound and Joe's death as self-defense for the Jestons." A ruling he hated at the time but now understood.

"Do you have a scar from the gunshot?"

He nodded and slid free the first three buttons of his dress shirt. "An ambulance took me to the hospital with a police escort. Two pissed-off cops arrested me after a doctor removed the slug and sewed up the hole." He pulled back the fabric to reveal his scar as Mia neared. Her flowery scent enveloped him, and his heart thumped an unsteady beat.

She peered at the circular, rigid blemish with a little frown on her face and stepped back with her lips puckered. Compassion, not condemnation, flooded her eyes as she blinked up at him.

A deep breath thundered through his lungs. His nostrils flared at her feminine aroma. Tension bubbled around her and thickened the air, and he stepped back for space. "I'm relieved I went to prison. I finished school and got my life together there. If I'd stayed out, I probably would've died in a fight or from alcohol poisoning."

"That's quite a story."

"Do you want me to leave? I won't take offense."

"I'm not a heartless bitch, Mason. You just bared your soul to me, trusted me with secrets I doubt many people know, and I won't throw you out as if you or your confession meant nothing. I'm grateful you told me this *before* we slept together—that's a major plus for you in my book—and I'm sure you have a ton of baggage, but I'm not scared of you."

"Why? How can you be—I don't understand."

"People do things when they know they shouldn't, but that doesn't make them bad people, especially if they feel guilty about it and turn their lives around. You've paid for your mistakes." Mia pulled back his shirt and traced her fingertip over the scar. "That clerk might have died if you had run off that night. You stayed because it was the right thing to do."

"Ronnie would've died, but I saved his life, according to the doctors. The DA and my public defender offered a damn good plea bargain because of it." His chest heaved as her soft touch set fire to his skin. "I refused it. They wanted me to rat out a few other friends who they suspected of auto theft in exchange for probation, if not just a year or two in prison, since the Jestons survived. In hindsight, I should've accepted it, but at the time I didn't want to get the guys in trouble."

"What about this one?" Mia trailed her fingers from the bullet wound to a rigid white scar that reached from his collarbone to just above his right nipple.

"A few weeks after I arrived at the facility, a neo-Nazi skinhead attacked me with a shard of glass. I fought back, broke his nose, and the guards tossed us both in solitary for a week. The warden later transferred the asshole to the state pen." He grasped her arms to push her away. "Mia, you shouldn't—"

She kissed the old bullet wound.

Everything inside him stilled. Her sweet lips trailed a brush of heat to the rigid slash, and he closed his eyes to savor the gentle swipe of her tongue. Desire surged through him. He stepped back and knocked into the armoire.

She trapped him between the sturdy piece of furniture, the window, and her body. Her thickly fringed eyelids batted up and down as she stared at him. Curiosity arched her eyebrows.

He fidgeted in the makeshift corner. Goose bumps mauled his skin, and his pulse raced too damn fast. He couldn't find his voice.

Mia backed up. "Now I understand why you acted so nervous tonight. I mentioned my brother works for the State, and you looked ready to run."

He maneuvered around the armoire and used the

coffee table as a blocker. How the tide had turned, Mason didn't know, but only a coward relied on furniture for distance and protection from a beguiling female. *Fine, I'm a fucking coward.*

"I shouldn't run at the mention of cops or even parole officers. I want to, it's instinctual, but I served my time. If I want to date a PO's sister, there's no law to stop me."

She grinned, opened her mouth to speak, but quickly closed it.

"What is it, Mia?"

"I'm not sure you know what you just said."

He repeated the words under his breath. "Date?" Mason rubbed his temples and cursed. "I wouldn't have said all this if you were just a fling or a one-night stand to me. If that's all you want, I accept it. If you want nothing else, all right, but I'd like to see you again."

"Don't retreat from me. I'm not angry or afraid of you." She followed him around the coffee table and stroked his rough cheek with her soft palm. "I'm shocked, but I won't hold your past against you. I do have one more question, if you don't mind."

He nodded, not sure what to say.

"I drank a wine cooler at dinner. Did that bother you? I mean, are you okay if people drink around you?"

"Oh? Yeah—um—I'm usually fine with it. The temptation is harder to ignore if I'm angry or stressed and a bottle is right there in front of me, but I've been sober for over ten years. I don't plan to fall back down."

"That's good to hear. We should definitely go out again, but I want to continue *this* date first. C'mon, I'll show you to the bedroom."

His jaw dropped. Mia twisted her fingers with his and tugged his arm so he'd follow her, but Mason's feet felt like solid granite. She pouted her bottom lip and he snapped back into gear. He grasped her narrow waist, hauled her over his shoulder, and carried her through the living room and past the dining room. Her girlish gasp of delight played like music to his ears. He kept a tight hold on her ass to keep her pinned and safe, but she dug her nails into his back as though to hold on anyway. Not that he minded. He liked it rough.

"Which door, darlin'?"

"The left. The one left of the bathroom."

He entered the room and dropped Mia gently on a large bed in the corner.

She kicked off her heels and scurried back to the massive headboard.

Mason crawled up after her, grabbed her ankle, and jerked her back down beneath him. He blanketed her body with his and kissed her. He should slow down, but he couldn't think. He needed to feel her body beneath his. He needed to pleasure her and savor her cries for more. After everything he confessed, her acceptance surprised him. He didn't know what to do with that precious gift except to kiss her body in gratitude.

Grabbing her arms, he pinned them above her head and leaned up to stare at her. Her dark eyes reminded him of sweet chocolate morsels, and the trust that beamed through them silenced his shock and reservations. Mia Eddison deserved the best he could give her.

Lucky for her, he always craved a challenge.

Chapter Four

Mia gripped the pillow above her head as Mason straddled her waist. The raw, animalistic sheen in his eyes quickened her pulse, and desire coursed through her veins like lava.

She wanted, *needed*, his strong hands on her body. He jerked off his dress shirt and tossed it over his head. A gasp lodged in her throat. Tattoos decorated his torso and arms. A black-striped snake slithered across his waist and curled around his stomach with its jaw opened wide as though to consume his belly button. A large, snarling skull with dark flames spiraled around it bulged on his right biceps. A tribal-design black phoenix took flight on his left.

"Are you all right?" His forehead creased as Mason glanced down at his body. "Fuck, the tats. I should've warned you."

Mia swiped her tongue across her upper lip. "It's okay. You're just full of surprises. How many do you have?"

"Five."

"I only see four." Her gaze drifted to the tat partially hidden beneath his watch, but she couldn't spot the elusive fifth tattoo. "On your legs? No, wait. On your neck. I saw it the day we met."

"Yep, right here." He patted the mini snakes inside the circle. "All of them are prison tats except for the one on my wrist. I'd just turned sixteen when I got that inked."

She reached up and traced the snake on his torso with her fingers. "I want a butterfly on my back, but I never had the guts to step foot in a tattoo parlor. That's pretty lame, huh?"

"Nah, I don't think so. Some shops are shady and you never know what might happen, but others are reputable. I could take you to a parlor sometime, my treat." He flashed a crooked smile and wiggled his eyebrows. "I'd lick your tat, wing from delicious wing."

Slow, sensual warmth filled her like a chocolaty, nutty candy bar after a long day. She nodded, and though she really did want a tattoo, she'd probably agree to anything he desired as long as he stared at her with that ravenous look on his face.

Several little scars marred his arms and chest, even a few beneath the prison ink. A few looked rigid and rough, but most were long and faint as though knives had grazed him. Only one resembled a gunshot wound.

Mia trailed her fingers across his pecs and flicked his hard nipples. His tanned chest, broader than she imagined, heaved under her exploration. Dim light streamed in from the bedroom window and sharpened his sculptured muscles in stark relief. She considered flipping on the bedside lamp to better see and memorize every sharp, yummy inch of the bad boy who pinned her down, but she didn't want to move out from underneath him.

Mason cupped her breast and thumbed an achy nipple. Then he shifted his bent knees and reached between their bodies to jerk up her dress.

Mia lifted her back so he could yank it off her, but she crossed her arms over her chest as his gaze dropped to her silky black bra and panties.

"Don't hide them, Mia. They're beautiful."

Her lover pried her arms away. Her puckered nipple blossomed to life as he lapped it with his tongue, the silk a thin barrier between them. Ripples of fire coursed through her with his strong but gentle bite, and he licked away the sting before he switched to her other breast. Mia bucked her hips, rubbed her silk-sheathed vagina along the thick fabric of his jeans, and nearly cried out at the brief sense of relief.

"You ache, don't you? Tell me you ache."

Her eyelids fluttered closed. She moaned, unable to form coherent words.

His hands roamed over her chest and stomach, cupped every curve and teased every valley, and swept her up in a fierce storm of need.

As the weight of his body lifted from hers, her eyes snapped open and a whimper crawled up her throat. Mia fisted her hands in his hair and shuddered as he brushed his lips across her forehead and down her nose.

A seductive smile spread across Mason's cheeks. Time seemed to stand still. With a slow, lazy twist of his hands, he grasped her wrists and pressed just hard enough that her fingers weakened and slid free from his hair.

Mia licked her lips. Her heart hammered and echoed in the room—or maybe just in her own ears, she couldn't be sure—and her heavy panting matched the rhythm of his.

He kissed her and moved to the side of the bed. The muscles in his back gleamed and rolled as he bent over to unlace his boots and kick them off along with his socks.

She reached out to stroke her nails down those taut muscles, but he stood and shook his head at her with a *no-no* look in his eyes. The reprimand coiled a wave of lust in her stomach. Tempted to pounce on top of him, Mia clutched the blanket to keep her body firmly on the mattress and her hands to herself.

He grabbed a condom from his wallet and stripped off his jeans, wickedly commando beneath. The head of his thick cock glistened as he pumped the shaft with his hand. Mason returned to the bed, licked a trail of decadent heat up her calf and over her thigh, and hooked his finger under the hem of her panties to pull them down.

Mia hardly breathed. Her vagina still moist from the earlier hand job, the cool air in the room tightened her sensitive clit into an aching, throbbing bundle of nerves.

Mason lifted her legs over his shoulders and speared her labia with his tongue.

Mia tossed her head back and cried out. His slow ministration teased and tantalized her, heightened her pleasure, and drove her insatiable need to nearly insane levels. She begged for release and told him to go faster, but he continued the languid caresses on her folds.

Mason gripped her thighs with his strong fingers and squeezed just hard enough that she arched her back to thrust her lower body closer to his mouth. His tongue jutted deep inside her, retracted and plunged in again, and picked up speed with each thrust.

Mia bit her lip and cursed as her climax rolled through her.

He drew back and licked his lips. As he rubbed his hand over his forehead, he streaked some of her release into his hair. He winked at her. "A woman's release makes excellent hair gel, you know. I could bottle yours and make a fortune. It smells amazing and tastes even better."

Mia burst into giggles. "That'll be a joint venture. We'll cut the profits down the middle."

"Deal." Mischief twinkled in his eyes. He lapped at her labia again and blew warm air over her center.

A sharp hiss tore through her throat.

He rose up above her, her legs still braced on his shoulders, and poised his stiff cock at her entrance. Mason slid on the condom and plunged in, almost to the hilt. His balls slapped her ass as he groaned.

Her vision blurred. Her feminine muscles clamped around him so tight she burned.

"You wanted fast. Right, Mia?" He pulled out and teased her clitoris with his head. "You got it."

The all-male smirk on his lips lit her blood aflame. Mia cried out as he shoved back in.

Mason bucked his hips, his relentless momentum a godsend, and he lifted her bottom off the bed to deepen his invasion. His length and girth fit snug inside her. His strong, possessive strokes seared her.

She braced her shoulders on the bed for better leverage and pushed up against him.

"You're so damn tight, Mia."

She dug her fingers into his biceps. "Not my fault. You're too big."

"Sit up for me, darlin'." Mason untwisted her legs from around his shoulders and wrapped his arms under her back to help her up. Still buried to the hilt, he leaned back on his knees and drew her onto his lap. "You have far too many clothes on." He snapped the hooks of her bra free and tossed away the scrap of silk. Her breasts bounced and he licked each rosy nipple.

Mia tried to wrap her sore legs around his waist, but he popped her hip with his palm. He gave her another *no-no* look, a determined gleam in his eyes, and her nerve endings hummed. She dug her toes into the rumpled blanket to keep her legs sprawled and away from his body as he gently thrust into her. Tension tightened in her thighs. Her muscles strained. Her orgasm grew like an inferno, but his easy strokes kept her on the edge of the cliff. He lightly popped her hip again, and she wrapped her legs around his waist without wasting another second.

"Good girl. You learn fast."

Butterflies fluttered in her stomach.

He clamped his mouth on her neck, his bite a little too sharp, but his tongue soothed the sting.

"Kiss me, Mason. I need to taste you." He relinquished his hold on her neck as though she snapped her fingers. Mia palmed his bristled cheeks and nearly melted. His sultry bedroom eyes turned her on almost as much as his rock-solid body. Her tongue delved into his mouth and her taste buds tingled. His pouty bottom lip swelled as she suckled it between her teeth, and she pulled it hard.

"Damn, girl." Mason groaned and wrenched his face away.

The scowl he leveled on her would probably scare most people, but the lust in Mia's veins burned hotter.

As though he knew his scowl didn't work, he slowed the rhythm of his thrusts until he gently pulsated inside her. "I thought you were a good girl. Which is it, Mia? Are you naughty or nice?"

Her heart skipped a beat. Mia bit her lip to keep from apologizing and begging him to pick up the pace. A wave of excitement and naughtiness washed through her—what kind of woman invited a virtual stranger to her home?—but she considered herself a good girl when it counted. She breathed deep to steady her voice. "I'm both, but I'll only let you boss me around in the bedroom. Sometimes I might want to boss *you* around. Off the mattress, though, I expect you to treat me like a lady." She clutched his shoulders and undulated her hips against his for friction.

His eyebrow cocked up. He thrust a little faster inside her, and she gasped. "All right, darlin', I accept those terms. I'm definitely a lucky man." He teased his fingers down her spine, sensitized a normally dull part of her body, and plowed deeper inside her.

Sheer bliss consumed her. Caged between his chest and his arms, her breasts smashed against him, and her diamond-hard nipples could probably carve holes into his body. He didn't seem to care. They thrust in unison, met each other's tempo like a musical number, and the pressure in Mia's womb threatened to overtake her.

Sweat gleamed on his scrumptious skin, and she licked the beads that slid like raindrops down his thick neck. "Yes. Hurry, Mason." She tilted back her head as he dug his fingers into her waist and thrust with the intense rhythm she craved. "Please."

The gorgeous man gripped her long hair. "Are you done already?" His deep voice teased her senses.

Mia tried to shake her head, but his grip tightened. She quivered all over. "It's too good."

"Relax. Just take it." He released her hair and eased her down on the mattress.

The cool blanket offered little relief to her hot skin.

Mason braced his hands on the sides of her head and no matter how hard he thrust into her, he seemed intent on not crushing her body with his.

The emotion in the depths of his eyes took her breath away. Not lust or excitement, but a sensitivity she didn't expect. His surprise and gratitude when she'd accepted his troubled past and in essence, *him*, accumulated in his eyes like a beacon of hope. His admission shocked her more than she let on, but she knew deep in her heart he wouldn't physically hurt her. No matter his sins or the crimes from his past, she believed everyone could change.

The man who made love to her now just wanted to move on with his life. He said as much earlier, and she believed him. After what she went through with Evan, she didn't know if she could ever fully trust a man with her heart again. Mason may want a better life, but that didn't mean he wouldn't trample on her emotions and run down her heart in his pursuit of it.

She pressed a kiss on his lips and smiled. Tenderness lit his face, but he took her so damn hard that each thrust pushed her closer to release. Every time she clamped around him and pinned him inside her, he undermined her authority and pulled out to toy with her sensitive folds. Like a fool, she believed he would slam home each time he pushed his mushroomed head back into her moist heat, but he would pull out to tease her button all over again.

His skill impressed her. He certainly knew how to draw out her pleasure and keep her climax suspended on a precarious ledge. Mia couldn't imagine how he honed his technique with his lengthy prison stint, unless he'd practiced like crazy once he got out. *Nothing else explains it.* Mason treated her body as her past lovers failed to. He put her satisfaction before his own and pleasured her so thoroughly, so hotly, that she begged for more.

Begged! She couldn't help herself. Mia pleaded with him to finish, ordered him to take her over the edge, and she even struck his chest a few times with her hands.

He just grinned at her, his ego surely soaring to the clouds, and he licked the tears that slid down her cheeks.

The knot of need that wound her body so tight finally spiraled out of control and exploded inside her like fireworks. Her scream of bliss and relief echoed in her ears. A myriad of colors danced in her vision. Her liquid heat flooded his manhood and his body stiffened as he orgasmed. She wrapped her arms around his shoulders to hold him close as he shouted at the top of his lungs.

Mia untangled her legs from around his waist. Sweat slicked her skin and cold chills racked her body. She stroked his jaw, the strain in her muscles and the weakness in her arm a surprise to her, and her heart fluttered as he kissed her fingers that trailed over his mouth.

Mason's arms shook as though he struggled to keep upright and not collapse on top of her. After he kissed her nose, he flopped down beside her and drew off the condom to dispose of it in the little wastebasket beside the bed.

Exhaustion bore down on her limbs, but Mia managed to yank the twisted blanket out from under their legs to drape it over them.

Her throat clogged as she tried to tell him what this night meant to her, but Mason brushed his lips over hers as though he already knew. The warmth of his embrace soothed her chills, and Mia cuddled into the crook of his arm to fall asleep.

She stretched in bed early the next morning.

Mason slept peacefully beside her with one arm tossed over his face. Purple hickeys dotted his neck, chest, and stomach.

She traced her fingers over the large snake tattoo, her favorite one, and pressed a kiss to his bullet scar. As sunlight dispelled the shadows in the room, she slid off the bed and pulled the blinds over the large window—something she should've done hours ago. She and Mason probably gave the nosy old neighbor across the back alley a private show.

After a quick shower, Mia stared at herself in the bathroom mirror to admire the hickeys on her neck and breasts. Little bruises marred her waist, stomach, and hips in the shape of fingerprints. Tempted to walk around naked to show off the sexy marks—she flushed red from the thought—Mia donned her silk bathrobe and tied the sash around her waist. Though she longed to use her new hairdryer, it would be a waste since she hoped to shower again in a few hours with Mason and his talented fingers at work. First, she planned to surprise him with breakfast in bed and another romp.

Mia headed to the kitchen and pulled out a carton of eggs, pancake mix, and milk from the fridge. Though she should ask Mason what kind of eggs he preferred, she decided on the simplest kind—scrambled eggs—in the hope she couldn't go wrong.

A buzzer echoed through the loft in quick bursts of sound, and she hurried to the living room to answer the intercom mounted by the door. A red light flashed on the panel, and she cursed. Mia entrusted her spare door key to just one person, and he likely used the buzzer as an impromptu doorbell before he unlocked the door himself. She switched off the security alarm, pulled back the heavy latch, and opened the door. Mia scowled at her brother as he headed up the stairwell, and she used her body to block his entrance into her home.

Jim Borden didn't seem to notice her tense body language and pushed her aside to enter. "Good morning." He hugged her with one arm and frowned at the hardwoods. "There's something sticky on the floor." He scraped his shoes over it a few times and headed toward the kitchen. "What's for breakfast?"

"Why are you here?" Mia shut the door, grabbed the towel she'd left on the sofa, and used it to cover the evidence of her desire on the floor. The last thing she needed was for her brother to realize what that *sticky* substance was. Her gaze darted toward the telephone and answering machine combo in the living room and back to Jim as he picked up the pancake mix. The U-shaped kitchen occupied one half of the loft's airy floor plan, and she could see into the kitchen through a gap between the upper and lower cabinets. "You know to call first. I don't have any messages on the machine, and I doubt you called my cell phone."

"I'm in the neighborhood to see a parolee for an unexpected visit—well, unexpected for him—but I thought I'd stop by to see you first." Jim sat the box aside and opened the fridge door. "You have any more blueberry muffins?"

"No, you cleaned me out the last time you showed up unannounced." She crossed her arms and glanced at the closed bedroom door. "Jim, you need to leave." She'd rather shave her legs without aloe-infused shaving cream or live a whole month without a hairdryer than introduce her parole officer brother to her parolee—boyfriend, perhaps?—the day after the best sex of her life. Talk about awkward.

"What's the rush? I haven't seen you in a few days." He grabbed an apple from the bowl on the counter and rubbed it on his polo shirt to shine the fruit before he sank his teeth in. "Why are you so uppity?"

"I'm in a bathrobe, Jim, and you're irritating the crap out of me. I have plans today and need to get going."

"I bought you that robe for Christmas last year. It's nice to know you use it." He glanced at the food on the marble countertop. "Looks to me like you were about to fix breakfast. Pancakes are fine since you're out of muffins."

Her blood pressure rose. She wrapped her hand around Jim's arm and dragged him out of the kitchen as a noise resonated from the bedroom.

"Wait a minute. What was that?"

"Just rats. Come on." Mia jerked on his arm again, but he refused to budge.

Jim shook off her hand, took a step toward the bedroom, and stilled. "Oh God, there's a man in there. No wonder you want me to leave." He scowled at the splotches on her neck as though he just noticed them. "That's very professional. What will all those snooty ladies say tomorrow after you open the store?"

She clasped her neck. "Leave, Jim. I don't want you to ruin this."

"Fine, I'll go." He patted the gun he always wore beneath his loose blazer. "Don't worry. I won't have a problem with him as long as he's not Evan."

She doubted that. Evan was blond, gorgeous, and an up-and-coming photographer with a great body. Jim hated him on sight. Mason, a tattooed ex-con who worked at a garage, wouldn't stand a chance unless Mia buttered Jim up first.

"Just to be sure." Mia grabbed her brother's arm again. "We can meet for lunch tomorrow and I'll tell you about him." A door creaked open behind her, and she whipped her gaze toward the bedroom just as Jim did.

Mason paused in the doorway, dressed in his jeans and wrinkled dress shirt. The shirt hung open and revealed his sexy snake tattoo. His eyes widened like saucers.

"What the hell?" Jim dropped the apple on the floor and jerked free from Mia's hold. A dark glower morphed his face into a mask of anger, and he leveled that hate-ridden stare on her new lover. "Mason Harding. What the fuck are you doing here?"

Mason folded his arms across his chest and leaned against the doorframe. His lips sealed together in a thin line as his right cheek twitched. Tension palpitated so strong between the men she feared the windows and light bulbs would shatter at any moment.

"How do you know him, Jim?" Mia swiped damp strands of hair behind her ears, a little afraid to know the answer.

Her brother spun toward her and fisted his hands. "He's one of my parolees."

Oh God, no. She covered her mouth with her hands. *I'm gonna throw up.*

"Did you know he's an ex-con?" His scowl deepened as she nodded. "What's going on with you? Damn it, Mia. I knew you were upset over that cheating piece-of-shit Evan, but I never thought you'd go slumming with someone worse."

"Shut up, Jim. He's ten times better than Evan."

"How did you even meet him?"

Mia sheepishly glanced away. "I nearly hit him with my car."

A shudder rolled through her brother. He snatched the apple off the floor and slammed it hard on the countertop before he faced Mason. "You're one stupid son of a bitch to screw your parole officer's sister, Harding. I know parolees do some god-awful, reckless things, but this blows it. I could revoke your release like that." He snapped his fingers.

Mason fisted his hands but remained silent.

"Damn it, Jim. Don't act like an asshole. You have no right to speak to him like that." Mia itched to hit her idiot brother and jerked him back around toward her. "It's not a parole violation to sleep with me. If you go before the parole board about this, those stuffy superiors of yours will laugh you out of the meeting. You can't do anything to him."

"What do you think Dad would say? Do you know how ashamed he would be of you?"

Jim caught her arm as she tried to slap him, and he squeezed hard. "You screwed a convicted felon. Just look at him, Mia. What kind of man tattoos his body like that? I won't stand for this."

"You don't have a choice."

"Fuck that. You're my responsibility. After Dad died and once you left Evan, you became my responsibility."

"Oh, really? Stupid me, I thought we were friends and equals." Tears burned in her eyes, but she kept a tight leash on the waterworks. Jim crossed the line when he brought up their father, but Dad probably *would* be disappointed in her. Still, no matter their shock, she hoped her parents would've eventually accepted Mason if she chose to keep him in her life. Not that she would ever know.

Mia tried to jerk her arm from his rough grasp, but he latched on tighter.

"Let her go."

Her gaze connected with Mason's. His hard eyes and set jaw quickened her pulse.

He looked savage and ready to punch the hell out of Jim. Even his snake tattoo seemed ready strike with razor-sharp, poisoned fangs. Her brother may deserve it, but any strike Mason threw in her defense *would* definitely land him back in prison.

As Mason stepped away from the doorway, she held out her free hand to stop him. Jim finally released her, and she quickly intercepted Mason's course to her brother. "I'm fine. He didn't hurt me." Mia resisted the urge to rub her sore forearm as she lied. She pressed her hands against Mason's barrel chest and blocked his path, determined to keep him safe from her livid brother *and* to protect Jim from Mason.

Jim tapped his foot. "Don't pamper him, Mia. He's a criminal on parole because of good behavior. You don't know him. You don't know what he's done."

She flipped around to face him. "I do. He told me. Just go. Okay? We'll talk later." When Jim's temper flared like this, nothing and no one could get through to him.

"I won't leave you alone with an attempted murderer."

"He's not dangerous. If he wanted to hurt me, he could've last night. I trust him." A headache throbbed in her temples and her stomach churned. She gripped her hands to hide her sudden shakes as Mason settled his hands on her waist and braced his body up against hers from behind. His possessive touch burned right through the silk barrier of the robe, her skin flared hot, and the thick denim of his jeans teased the crease of her buttocks.

Jim snarled like a rabid animal.

Oh my God. Mason's crazy. Why is he baiting Jim?

She knew big balls hung between Mason's legs—everything about him rated *bigger* than average—but she didn't think his balls weighed like anvils. If she pushed his hands away, and in essence, his claim on her, Mason would likely ditch her without another word.

She wrapped her arms around her waist and clasped her hands over Mason's to claim him back. "I like him, Jim. Don't ruin this."

"I have to, Mia. I love you. I know you're an adult, but this is a huge mistake. I refuse to stand by like last time and let you toss away years of your life on a man who won't respect you." Jim rubbed the bridge of his nose and shifted his gaze to Mason. "Meet me at Demi's Diner at noon. We need to have a long talk."

With that, he stormed out of the loft.

Mia shuddered as the steel door slammed shut. Mason's strong arms wrapped around her, offered the comfort she needed, and she turned in his embrace to meet his angry gaze. "I'm so sorry. I—"

"Don't." He pressed his finger to her lips. "I like you, too, but I won't go back to prison over this. I'll meet with Borden today and find out what his demands are."

"You did nothing wrong. I understand you're worried—you have a right to be—but don't throw away what we could have because of fear. He's just threatening you. He can't really do anything." She laid her head on his chest and breathed in his masculine scent. "Jim is a good person. He won't falsify paperwork or get you blamed for something. As long as you abide by the terms of your release, he can't touch you."

"I should go." Mason grasped her arms and set her away from him.

Apology after apology clogged her throat. Mia followed him to the bedroom and waited by the door as he shoved on his socks and boots. The rift between them stung like a thousand bees. The air conditioner blew cold air, but his reserved, icy attitude chilled her to the bone. He hastily buttoned his shirt, lining it up wrong, and stepped toward the doorway as though he meant to leave without acknowledging her.

She blocked his path. "At least let me fix your shirt."

"Don't worry about it. I'll call you, Mia." Mason brushed a kiss on her cheek, snatched his blazer from the sofa, and left.

Chapter Five

A cool breeze hit Mia as she slammed her car door. Several puffy gray clouds filled the sky. Though the weather report she'd heard this morning called for scattered rainstorms in the early afternoon, the sky didn't appear dark enough to rain yet. Dark clouds churned in the far distance and matched her ill mood far better than the puffs above her.

Mason had ignored her phone calls for the past several days. She assumed his home phone number belonged to his brother, Alan, so she'd kept her messages brief. Jim ignored her calls and texts as well, probably because she'd cussed him out every time she left a message on his cell and his home phone answering machine. Jim couldn't hide from her forever, but she deserved some sort of explanation from Mason if he intended to never see her again.

Mia took Friday off from work, and like a stalker, drove by Ben's Auto Repair twice before she pulled in. Located on the outskirts of LoDo, the establishment always looked rundown and seedy to her. Perhaps she was a snob or just a careful woman, but she preferred the overpriced chain garage a few blocks away.

When it came to Mason, though, she threw all caution to the wind and dove in headfirst.

Casting a quick glance around the parking lot, she wished Mason owned a vehicle so she'd at least know if he was currently working.

Several mechanics slaved away inside four attached garages, but she didn't spot her target. Someone had painted the name of the business in big blue letters on the front wall of the lobby, but time and weather had faded the colors.

She headed across the uneven asphalt, and cold air rushed around her once she opened the door and stepped inside the lobby. Dim overhead lights soothed her eyes. A sizeable selection of tires occupied the left half of the small building and exuded a strong rubber smell. Vending machines and half a dozen chairs surrounded an old TV on the right side. She walked up to the counter that blocked access to the manager's office and the bathrooms on the far wall.

The thin, lanky man at the register set his car magazine aside and looked her up and down. A flirty grin spread across his face.

Dressed in a pink tank top, a floral knee-length skirt, and heels, she lifted her chin at a lofty angle, even though she wanted to bury herself in an oversized coat.

A heavyset patron sat on a barstool at the counter and tipped his hat at her in greeting. An elderly couple watched a TV sitcom in the mini waiting room and didn't bother to glance in her direction.

Mia swallowed hard to find her voice just as a tall, broad man, probably in his mid-thirties, left the office. "Excuse me, I need an oil change." She caught the man's gaze and refused to drop it as he nodded toward the other employee.

The manager sighed. He approached the counter and grabbed a clipboard with a form already attached to it.

She swiped several strands of hair behind her ears in a nervous jitter and refused to acknowledge the other men except for the one who appeared to be in charge. Although he didn't wear a nametag on his T-shirt or even an official uniform, she assumed the handsome redheaded man was Benji, Mason's former brother-in-law by Alan's marriage.

"All right. Which car is it?" He held out his oil-smudged hand for the key while he peered out the large bank of windows that overlooked the parking lot.

"Is Mason working today?"

The man arched a bushy eyebrow at her. "Yeah, he is. Why?"

"I want him to do it. I'll give him the key."

"Ma'am, he's been in an awful mood lately. He snaps at anyone who speaks to him."

She smiled. *Good. Maybe this crappy situation doesn't sit well with him, either?* "Thanks for the warning, but I'll take my chances."

The manager nodded and left the lobby through a glass door that led into the series of garages. A *ding-dong* noise hummed in the air.

Mia released a long breath and stared around the room. A pin-up calendar with a bikini-clad model hung next to the men's bathroom. Several car posters and automotive awards decorated the paneled walls. The pungent smell of grease, rubber, and sweat, oddly mixed with fragrant flowers, nearly suffocated her. The employee retrieved his magazine but glanced up every now and then to stare at her long legs. She refused to make eye contact with anyone and stayed at the counter to wait for Mason.

A few minutes crawled by before the low *ding-*

dong echoed again. She turned to face whoever had opened the door.

"How may I help—" Mason paused in mid-sentence once his gaze locked with hers. A scowl darkened his face as the door swung shut behind him. "Why are you here?"

Mia folded her arms across her chest.

Black smudges marred his skin and clothes. Sweat glistened in his hair and spiked the jagged strands.

Her libido kicked in and weakened her knees, but she refused to salivate like a teenager. Instead, she tilted her head in challenge. "My car needs an oil change. I want you to do it." She held out the key.

"Don't do this, Mia. I want you to go."

"Do what? My car needs maintenance. That *is* your job, right?"

Mason turned his scowl on their audience—his coworker and the heavyset customer—but neither man looked away. "Fine. It'll be about thirty minutes." He snatched the dangling key from her hand and stalked back through the garage-entry door.

Her mouth dropped open. She watched Mason through the windows as he headed toward her silver sedan. Ready to strike like the snake on his torso, a tattoo she missed licking and petting, she stomped to the door and flung it open. The telltale noise spurred her on. Dry heat assailed her. Machines whirled and engines revved. She ignored the stares of several mechanics, stomped through the first garage, and entered the second just as Mason drove into the slot.

The dark look in his eyes scorched her as he exited the car. "You're not allowed back here." Mason slammed the door shut with a deafening thud as she stomped toward him.

"What's your problem, Mason? Are you so afraid of my brother you'd rather throw me away than stand up for yourself? For *us*? It may sound pathetic—hell, I know it will—but I thought the time we spent together meant something to you. I don't believe for an instant you only wanted a one-night stand." Why else tell her about his prison time, if so? Did he tell the story to all his dates? Did it get him laid more often than not?

The questions sickened her.

"I thought you were different. You told me you grew up. I didn't judge you over the crap you did back in the day. I accepted it. I accepted *you*. I know prison hardens people, but are you really so heartless to not care about my feelings?" She jabbed her finger against his chest. Hard. "Goddamn you! I wouldn't have agreed to a date, let alone invited you to my home, if I'd known you would just take advantage of me and squash me like a damn bug. But hey, maybe it's no big deal. Maybe I shouldn't bother with relationships. Meaningless flings are obviously the way to go."

Mia didn't want that. Though the past week didn't compare to her failed marriage and the nasty breakup, the same self-doubt that ate away at her the months following her divorce rushed back in. At twenty-eight years old and childless, her biological clock ticked like a bongo drum. More than her desire to have a child, she wanted to grow old with the man she loved.

She just needed to find the man first.

"At this point, I don't care if you want me or not. Just do me the fucking courtesy and tell me the truth. Don't ignore my calls. Be a man and break off whatever we had between us to my face. You owe me that much." Mia braced her hands on her hips. "Why the hell are you grinning?"

Chuckles caught her attention. Her pounding heart stilled. Her narrowed gaze branched out and encompassed the garage.

Several men watched her from across the connected slots and a few others stood by various shelving units a few yards away. Every one of them grinned at her.

Her cheeks flamed hot like two fiery coals. She stepped back from Mason, unaware she'd pinned him against her sedan, and swallowed the lump in her throat. The arrogant grin plastered on Mason's whiskered face lengthened, and she wanted to slap it off.

"You finally realized we're not alone, huh?"

"My words stay the same." She softened her tone, but his smug comment set her teeth on edge. "Do you have anything to say?"

Mason glanced away. The muscles in his arms and neck bulged as he tensed.

"Fine. Goodbye, Mason Harding." Mia snatched the key from his hand and pushed him away from the driver's side door to leave.

A hard hand grabbed her arm.

She whipped her gaze to Mason as he trapped her in the cage of his arms and backed her up against the car.

His demanding lips descended on hers.

Fight this. Push him away.

Mia wrapped her arms around his neck instead. Her ears buzzed. A hint of mint teased her senses as his tongue swiped over her teeth, and the smell of sweaty, untamed man mixed like an aphrodisiac with the stench of oil. After several seconds, or maybe minutes—she couldn't be sure—she pulled from his delirious kiss with all her strength to suck a mouthful of air into her lungs.

His emerald-green eyes sparked with longing and burned her all the way to her soul.

The ringing in her ears faded. Hooting took its place as their audience laughed.

A few of the men even made crude sexual gestures with their hands while others shouted Mason's the man and shook their fists in the air.

Mia didn't care. She waited for Mason to speak. She needed to hear his voice, even if he meant the kiss as a goodbye. *I just need to know where this relationship stands.*

Mason brushed his rough knuckles across her flushed cheek. Black smudges marred his skin, T-shirt, and cargo pants, but he didn't seem to care.

Neither did Mia.

"I'm sorry, darlin'. I'm game if you wanna work this out, but we have a lot to discuss." He clasped her hand and brought it to his lips to kiss.

A shiver coursed up her arm. Mia clasped his face with her palms and pushed up on her tiptoes to kiss him. The floor beneath her feet disappeared as he circled his arms around her waist and lifted her up to spin her around. The laughter and cheers of the other mechanics escalated, but she drowned out the sound. She wouldn't forgive Mason for hurting her just yet, but his arms offered the warmth and hope she craved.

The fine hairs on the back of her neck rose as Mason set her on her feet.

The man she spoke with earlier stood a few feet away. A smug smile curved his lips.

Mia twisted free from Mason's embrace and sidestepped him to meet the manager's gaze. "I'm sorry. I-I know I shouldn't be in an employees-only section." The apology squeaked from her mouth. She turned back to Mason and grasped his hand. "I hope I don't get you fired."

Mason laughed as the other man shook his head.

"Well, I'm liable if a pretty lady in heels like those falls down." The manager nodded toward her pink two-inch heels with the bow on each toe. "It's a lawsuit just waitin' to happen, but I'll give you a pass this time. You got this grump to grin, so any woman who can do that is okay in my book." He looked at Mason. "Are you gonna introduce us or keep staring at her like a puppy dog?"

Mason settled his hand on her waist. "Mia Eddison, meet Benjamin Starwell. Benji, my parole officer's sister."

Benji's blue eyes widened like the tires on a huge pickup truck. "No kidding? Well, that explains your bad mood and her tirade. Glad to meet ya, ma'am." He offered Mia his hand.

"Likewise." She shook it. "I really am sorry for the interruption with you and your crew. I just lost my head for a moment."

He laughed. "Mason will do that to you. I swear his brother is just the same. Pigheaded and stubborn. Have you met Alan yet?"

"No, but I'd love to. I can't wait to meet Danny too."

"You'll love the kid."

"Mia? I need your car key." Mason released her and held out his hand for the little piece of metal. "I should get to the oil change."

"Oh, that?" She toed a stain on the concrete. "I went to another garage about a month ago for an oil change and to have all the liquids topped off, but you can go ahead if you want."

Benji chuckled as Mason's brow arched to his hairline. "You know, Mase, it's almost time for your lunch break anyway. Head out early, talk with this little firecracker, and I'll see you back here at one o'clock. Sound good?"

"Yeah. Thanks, Ben."

Mason backed the car off the metal risers and into the parking lot before Mia settled down behind the wheel. A few mechanics still hollered, shit-eating grins splitting their faces, and Mason jogged around the car to open the passenger side door. He flipped them his middle finger, which garnered a round of applause, and he entered the car.

Butterflies took flight in her stomach as Mason grasped her leg. Though she wanted to head to her loft and soap Mason down in the shower, she wouldn't sleep with him until they worked through their problems and decided what to do about her brother. Relieved part one of her plan worked, Mia shifted gears and left the garage.

****

"I'm gonna kick his ass. I can't believe Jim implemented an eight o'clock curfew."

"Calm down, Mia," Mason whispered as he stirred several pieces of Mandarin chicken with pork-fried-rice. Soft Oriental music filled the semi-crowded

Chinese restaurant, and the cool blue walls soothed his nerves. "Borden issued an ultimatum because he couldn't revoke my parole. I either stop seeing you or deal with a curfew, weekly mandatory visits instead of monthly ones, more random drug-and-alcohol tests, and more unannounced inspections of my home and work. I'm not surprised he followed through with it."

After Mia bombarded him at work the previous week, he'd spent Friday night and all of Saturday at her loft and enjoyed his woman's body as much as he did the first time. His dickhead parole officer left a message on Mia's answering machine early Sunday morning and told them the new restrictions would go into effect on Monday. Mason figured Borden stopped by Mia's loft sometime on Saturday and saw Mason through an open window.

Mia called her brother after she'd played the message, but he didn't answer or return her calls.

"I'm happy you wanted to meet tonight." Mason ducked his head to catch her gaze, but she didn't seem to notice him as she stared daggers at her plate. "We should spend as much time together as possible on the weekends since the curfew and other stipulations take away time during the week."

"I don't know how you're so calm." Mia jabbed at her beef chow mein with a pair of chopsticks. "I'd love to shove these in Jim's neck. Hell, I might do it if he stood in front of me right now."

Mason shrugged with a nonchalant air, but the venom in her words and tone were a surprise to him. Though he acted calm, he wanted to plow his fist through Borden's teeth. He doubted Mia would ever attack her brother, with or without chopsticks, but she could probably benefit from a session with his shrink. Still, her temper turned him on and heated his blood to boiling as few things could.

"Mia, please." He grasped her hand from across the table. "Let's enjoy dinner."

"An *early* dinner. It's six o'clock on a Saturday night. You can't even come back to my place tonight. How are we ever going to have sex again?"

The elderly couple at the next table scowled at them, but Mia seemed to ignore them.

Mason blushed. "We can be together during the day and have phone sex at night. We'll manage." He wiggled his eyebrows at her, but she didn't take the bait.

"I know there are ways around it, but I'm a grown woman." She pulled from his grip and rubbed her temples. "My brother shouldn't restrict who I can or cannot date, and he especially shouldn't punish you for having a girlfriend."

"True, but what can we do about it?" Aggravation rolled through him. He grabbed the glass bottle of soy sauce and poured a small amount of the dark liquid on his rice. "Go to his supervisor or the parole board to appeal it? Sure, but I doubt it would do any good. The law states a PO can designate any terms, or special sanctions, he deems necessary. He doesn't need a good reason behind it."

Fucking bullshit.

Thanks to a series of mind-numbing law books in the prison library, Mason had studied up on Colorado-state parole laws a few months before the board decided to free him from hell. From what he'd read, the board should've denied his parole request. He'd misbehaved more often than not, and though he cleaned up over the last few years, the bad things he did outweighed the good. He considered it pure luck the board released him anyway, and he wouldn't take a single day of freedom for granted.

He assumed Mia understood Colorado laws better than most civilians since she grew up with a policeman father. Even though Borden won this battle, she seemed determined not to let him win the whole enchilada. Mason respected her for it. If they could only see each other on limited terms, so be it.

"The weekly visits start this Monday, right?" She twirled several noodles around her chopsticks as he nodded. "Jim doesn't have time for this. He's probably putting off other cases to harass you. I'll stop by his office next week and try to knock some sense into him. I should've done so already, but it's a hassle to go through the security checks for a visitor pass. Unless Jim plans to jump from a two-story window, he won't be able to avoid me."

If only the prick would try, and break his neck. Mason shook his head to dislodge the cruel thought.

After she swallowed the noodles and dropped the chopsticks on her plate, she tapped her fingers on the tabletop. "Is Benji okay with all this? I mean, you said he lets you take an hour-and-a-half break for your monthly meetings instead of the normal hour for lunch."

"Ben thinks Borden's an ass, but he accepted the new terms, otherwise he'd have to fire me. At least Borden still wants to meet at the diner, not at the parole office. As you know, it's clear across town and I couldn't swing it without a car." He retrieved her hand.

"Listen, Mia. I'd missed you so damn much over the week I ignored your calls. I wanted to call you back—I wanted to see you and kiss you all over—but none of these new rules seemed worth it. When you blindsided me at the garage, dressed so feminine and with that righteous fury in your eyes, I knew I couldn't say no to you. You're very special to me."

Her cheeks pinked. "You're right. I shouldn't complain. I'm grateful you didn't tell me to hit the road after I embarrassed you in front of your coworkers."

"Embarrassed me? Didn't you hear those fools shouting? I'm like a god to them now." He laughed as she rolled her eyes. "You know—"

"Mason Harding?" A deep voice resonated across the restaurant. "Is that you?"

Mason looked up as the attractive Asian hostess escorted two men to a corner booth. She laid down their menus as the men veered away from their assigned table and headed toward him.

Fuck, no. This can't be happening. Not now.

"Who are they?" Mia wove her fingers through his. "You look pale."

"Don't speak to them, Mia. Don't make eye contact."

Her eyebrows rose into sharp arches.

With a quick squeeze of her hand, he released it and stood to greet two old friends he once thought of as brothers.

No older than their mid-thirties now, Trent wore biker boots, faded denim jeans, and a dark T-shirt while Pedro sported moccasins, dark jeans, and a leather vest with nothing underneath the cowhide except tattooed skin.

He shook Trent's hand and hugged him, and acknowledged Pedro the same way.

"When did you get out?" Trent clapped Mason on the back as the elderly couple gathered their belongings and rushed from the restaurant. A few other customers glanced over but continued to eat their meal.

"About six months ago." Mason swiped a hand through his hair, his voice pitched low.

"Six?" Trent laughed. "Damn, man. We need to catch up. Why didn't you tell anyone?"

"It never crossed my mind."

"Well, you should swing by my place for a party tonight. It's the same apartment from years ago. We have some badass associates who will be there. Trust me, man. These people have connections that will blow your mind." His eyebrows wagged. "You in?"

"Tempting, but no can do. I have plans."

"No prob. We have parties all the time. Any of them can be your *welcome back* shindig."

Pedro cocked his head to the side. "You're bigger now, *amigo*. You look sober too. That's rare," he stated with a smooth Latino accent.

Mason smirked. "I grew up, Pedro."

"Who's this?" Trent leaned against the booth with his arms crossed over his chest, and he blocked Mia inside with his muscular body.

The grin he flashed at her surely knocked most women to their knees, but not Mia. She sipped her tea as though not bothered by the interruption, but Mason knew her better than that. She'd swiped her hair behind her ears twice already, a nervous gesture he found adorable, and she sat far too straight in the booth to be at ease. Trent gawked at her breasts, pressed tight in her

V-neck cotton blouse, and Mia lifted her gaze from her glass to peruse Trent with a hard stare.

The blond idiot winked at her.

"My girlfriend." Mason fisted his hands. "So don't stare at her chest."

"You haven't wasted any time. She's fucking hot."

The muscle in Mason's cheek twitched. "Listen, guys, we're in the middle of dinner."

"Dinner?" Trent turned away from Mia. "It's been a damn decade. Can't you spare a few minutes for some old friends?"

"My asshole PO follows me around, so, no, I can't." Though he used the lie as an excuse, Mason hoped Borden would never stoop that low. If the man did, Mia would surely give her brother hell and send him packing.

"Ah. Gotcha." Trent glanced toward the large window by their table. Pedestrians littered the sidewalk as several cars sped by on the busy road that connected Denver to Aurora. "I did a two-year stint for larceny a few years back. PO's are bastards."

"Catch you later, *amigo*." Pedro fisted Mason's hand in another grip.

"Keep cool." Trent hugged him again. "Don't be a stranger."

Once they settled down at their table across the room and grabbed the menus, Mason returned to his side of the booth. He gripped his hair in his fists. Nausea rolled through his stomach and soured his dinner.

"Mason, are you okay?" Mia grasped his clenched fists and tried to gently pull them from his hair. "C'mon. Ripping hair from your scalp won't help."

"This fucking sucks, Mia. I'm so screwed." He released his grip and dropped his hands hard on the table.

"We'll just avoid this restaurant from now on."

"And every other restaurant in this area, not to mention stores, parks, everything. We're too damned close to my hometown."

"I'm sorry." She plucked at her napkin. "I wanted to come here, but I didn't realize it might be a problem if you ran into someone you once knew."

"Don't apologize. I should've told you." He rubbed his stiff neck. "I have to tell your brother about this. As a stipulation of my parole, I must notify Borden if I make contact with former friends. If I don't tell him and he finds out later, he'll revoke my parole. The bastard will probably grin from ear to ear as he writes up the paperwork and shoves it in my face." He leaned back in the booth. "Damn it, Alan will never forgive me if I go back to lockup."

"Jim will help."

"He wants me away from you. He *needs* me to violate parole. Borden just added restrictions to my parole *because* of you." Regret tightened around his heart like barbed wire. *No, not because of Mia, but because I decided not to throw away the best thing in my life.*

She flinched, but Mason didn't retract his statement, at least not verbally. Determination narrowed her eyes. "Jim will do his job, especially since I refuse to leave you."

"You should, Mia. We shouldn't see each other for a while." He held up his hands as her mouth fell open. "I know we just made up, but I'm not acting selfish and stupid now. You don't know these guys. I'd never forgive myself if something happened to you."

"I'm crazy about you, Mason. Doesn't that mean anything to you?"

"Of course it does, but I don't want you hurt. Trent and Pedro won't take no for an answer. When they find me either at Alan's apartment or at work—and they will, it's just a matter of time—I'll tell them to fuck off but it won't go down well." He pushed back his watch to fully reveal the tribal tattoo wrapped around his wrist. "A group of us stupid kids got the same tattoo. It meant brotherhood and unity. I took the idea seriously back then, but now this symbol disgusts me. My petty little hoodlum days are long gone, but the tat reminds me that I once belonged to them."

Mia reached out, grasped his wrist, and traced the sharp curves and points of the design with her fingertips. As she pressed a small kiss on top of the pulsating vein beneath the ink, time seemed to stand still.

Her touch stirred the monster inside him, not the decent man he tried to be around her, and he wished to the Devil himself she would leave him over the things he told her.

At least she would be safe that way.

"Some of those guys left town for a fresh start. The ones who stayed in Aurora continued with that wild lifestyle and probably joined real gangs. Trent and Pedro won't kill me—I never ratted on them about the auto theft to the police, so they owe me—but I'll still piss them off. Maybe I'm naïve to think that way, but they used to follow a code. Perhaps they still do."

He thumbed her knuckles. "At best, I'll kick their

asses. At worst, I'll spend some time in the hospital and go back to prison. I'll be fine, but I don't care what happens to me. Not really. I'm worried about you." Mason gritted his teeth as she rolled her eyes again. "Think about it, Mia. You're a woman, and a beautiful one at that. Those assholes know who you are. Not by name, not yet, but they know you're mine. They'll find you if they want to, especially if these *connections* are legit."

He brought her hands to his mouth and inhaled deep to take the scent of her skin into his nostrils. He shuddered, and his shirt pulled taut over his biceps and tense shoulders. "Don't you know what violent men do to pretty women? To any woman who stands in their way? They rape them. Beat them. I swear I will butcher anyone who touches you."

Her throat convulsed as though she swallowed hard. "Say whatever you want, Mason, but I won't budge on this issue. You just claimed me as your girlfriend, so that makes you *my* boyfriend. It's your job to protect me, if needed, and my job is to protect you." She tilted up her chin and maneuvered her hands free. "When I decide to enter a relationship, I go all the way. I don't half-ass it. That gives Jim every reason to help. He'll do whatever it takes to fix this."

"Goddamn it, I don't need his help." Mason slammed his fists on the table. Dishes rattled. His glass fell over and water spilled everywhere. His old friends laughed across the restaurant, and several strangers stared at him as if he'd sprouted horns on his head.

Mia's face reddened. She grabbed a stack of napkins to sop up the water.

Real smooth, Harding. You're a fucking jackass.

Mason fished his wallet from his jeans pocket and threw several bills on the table for the check and a hefty tip. He grabbed Mia's hand in her mid-cleanup job and they left the restaurant. His skin clung too tight to his strained muscles, the world around him seemed to double in size, and he longed for a private, enclosed space to hide in. Shit, he actually missed his prison cell.

"Take me to Alan's." He flattened his palms on the roof of Mia's car so he wouldn't scratch his arms until they bled. Car exhaust tainted the air. A myriad of warm hues streaked across the sky as the sun slowly descended. "This date is over."

"It's just past six o'clock."

"I don't give a shit."

"We might as well part now if you plan to run every time crap happens, but I refuse to believe you're a coward. You need help, and you've got me in your corner. So, yeah, I'll take you to your brother's place, but I'm coming in to meet him." Mia unlocked the driver's side door, and the anger in her eyes seared him. "You're a stubborn ass, Mason, but I'm worse. It's time you realized that." She jerked open the door, hit a button to unlock the passenger side door, and climbed inside the vehicle.

Angrier than he cared to admit, Mason breathed deeply to calm down and joined Mia in the car. He would do anything to keep her from the line of fire, but none of his hopes and wishes mattered if he couldn't protect her from himself.

Chapter Six

"Alan? You here?" Mason flipped on a light switch in the living room and stuffed his apartment key back inside his pocket. Silence greeted his call. He stalked to the adjoining dining room and kitchen to flip on another light as Mia closed the front door. "Damn, I forgot. Alan's on a date. Benji is babysitting Danny."

"When will he return?"

"Tomorrow, if the date goes well. If not, probably soon."

Mia hung her purse on the coat rack. "It's good he's not here. We should talk in private."

"You could've talked on the half-hour drive up here." He thought she'd changed her mind and decided to leave him as a smart woman should since she sealed her lips in the car. "I need you far away from me when everything blows up."

"*If* it blows up."

Frustration rubbed his nerves raw. Torn between dragging her to his bedroom and tossing her ass out the door, Mason flopped down on the sofa to escape the look of concern on her face. The past six months of freedom had softened the hothead he used to be, and he knew he would never meet another woman like Mia. Though they'd only known each other for a few short weeks, he'd already fallen hard and fast for her, but he didn't want to slow down. He *needed* to, though, if only to protect her from the trouble bound to mess up his life sooner or later.

If only Mia listened.

He loved her strength, her stubbornness, and her unwillingness to give up. She treated him as someone special and honorable, but trash like him only deserved trash.

Bands of red-hot heat ignited under his skin as Mia sat beside him. The hair on his arms stood erect. Ready to say whatever he needed to convince her to leave him—just temporarily—she grasped his hands and the words clogged in his throat.

"You're a good person, Mason. Besides, you didn't shoot anyone. You—"

"I still participated. I deal with the guilt every day."

"You've changed for the better."

"Maybe, but I won't let you suffer for my past mistakes." He feathered her knuckles with his thumb. "I'll blame myself if someone hurts you."

"Then don't push me away or make me worry about you. *That* will hurt me. Let me help. You need a friend, a real one. Not someone who will use you and later throw you aside."

"Every girl I've ever cared for betrayed me on some level, whether she lied, cheated, or left." Heat filled his cheeks but he needed her to know. "It's not like I deserved better. I've cheated on my fair share of girls before my incarceration and treated the women I met afterward as nothing but toys. I don't deserve your trust, Mia."

He clenched his jaw to silence his next admission. He once believed the opposite sex couldn't be trusted, and he learned the hard way to lie and cheat first before the girl he cared for stabbed him in the back. Then a spitfire like Mia with her kind soul and zest for life revived his faith in women. Everything he knew and wanted from a female changed. For her, Mason would remain loyal, but he couldn't admit any of it and keep his pride. If he gave her that kind of power over him, he'd probably find his heart ripped from his chest and stomped on the ground.

"We both have baggage but we can work through it. I'll never forget what Evan did—I won't tolerate that kind of betrayal—but I'm not angry with him anymore. We weren't right together. We didn't mesh." She scooted closer to Mason until their knees touched. "Mistakes are a fact of life. It's how you respond to those mistakes, or how you cope, that defines you as a person. So don't use your past as an excuse, Mason. I care for the person you are now. That's the man I laugh with and the one I make love to."

"How can you be so supportive?"

This is too much. Everything's happening too fast. He released her hands and rubbed his palms on his jeans. *Dear God, I don't want to lose her.*

Her hair fell like a silk shroud over her face as she turned away. His stomach fluttered as a schoolboy's would with his first crush in sight, but Mason had lost his naïveté years ago. The uncomfortable sensation reminded him of what he'd read about in books, but he knew better than to utter the most dangerous four-letter word in the English language to Mia.

Love.

He didn't know what love felt like. Desire burned in his veins when he looked at her, and he wanted to make her happy, but could a man like him let his guard down and fall in love? Would Mia even want him if she knew everything he'd done and regretted? Mason doubted it, and he wouldn't give his heart to her or any other woman unless she gave her heart to him first.

No, he didn't love her, but he cared too damn much for her to break her heart.

"If I was smart, I would grab your arm and shove you out the door. I would tell you anything for you to hate me and leave." Pain flashed in her eyes as she looked up, and he swallowed hard to not lose his nerve. "You act so strong and self-assured, but you wear your strength as a mask to hide your vulnerability. God, I could destroy that mask, but I won't play you like a yo-yo. I won't push you away anymore, even for your own good, and we'll deal with the consequences when they come. You wanna talk? Fine. Ask me your questions."

Mia chewed on her bottom lip. "The questions are personal."

"I have nothing to hide, not after the other night." Knots formed in his gut as he lied. "Talk to me."

"Well, you explained why you went to prison but not what happened while there."

"I already feel like shit, Mia. Why the hell would I want to talk about that?"

Damn, he couldn't think straight. Her skirt rode high up her thighs as she sat with her legs crossed. The longer he stared at those tanned limbs, the faster his blood raced. He clasped her chin in his palm, and his arm trembled with the strength he exerted to keep the touch gentle.

Her bottom lip puckered into a succulent pout, and her breathy sigh blew over his face.

"I want you, goddamn it." He growled the sensual

edict against her mouth, his lips hard on hers. "I need all of you." He craved more than just the pleasure her body promised. He needed a compassionate woman like Mia Borden Eddison in his life. Every time he thought about leaving her, a surge of loss and emptiness overturned his stomach and panic blared like a horn in his brain.

I need her.

Mason pulled back at that revelation. He walked across the room and faced a large entertainment center that housed a television, gaming console, and DVD player. The dark screen of the TV mirrored Mia's reflection.

With her hands clasped together on her lap, she glanced at the door and at her purse as though she meant to leave, but then she swung her gaze back in his direction.

He diverted his attention to the air-conditioner window unit beside the TV case.

"Let's have sex. Show me to your room."

Her abrupt words knocked him back. He flipped around as Mia stood and glanced down the darkened hallway that branched off from the living room. Lust throbbed in his groin but his stress won out. "I'm not in the mood for that."

"Ask me a question, then. Anything you want, Mason."

He didn't know what to ask. She'd already told him about the car accident that took her parents' lives. Energy had sparked between them, more than desire or lust, as she cried in his arms. He'd comforted her with words and his body, and their connection grew.

He also knew more about her failed marriage than

he cared to. He shared Borden's hatred for Mia's ex-husband and understood her brother's worry, but Mason still wanted her. If he considered her just a plaything, he wouldn't contemplate ways of forcing agonized screams from her ex's throat if they ever met. At least she never suffered physical abuse. Mason would find and beat Evan Eddison to a bloody pulp if he'd ever struck her, and return to prison without regret.

"Put in a DVD. Maybe you'll feel like talking later."

Her snappy tone irritated the fuck out of him.

She sat back on the sofa, so prim and proper with her chin tilted up at an infuriating angle.

He stood before her like a peasant who displeased his queen. *Shit. Just get it over with, man. Say it and move on.* He sighed. "No one raped me in prison. That's what you wanted to know, right?"

Mia closed her eyes. "Yes. Thank you. I didn't know how to word it."

"There were attempts." Mason rubbed his cheek as the muscle beat in a non-rhythmic tic. "The first night after I arrived at the facility my cellmate climbed into the bottom bunk with me, buck-ass naked, as I tried to sleep. I fought him off, and the guards showed up because of all the noise I made. They tossed us both in the hole until morning and assigned me to a new cell."

She gasped and covered her mouth with her hands.

"I didn't want friends, or enemies, so I stayed to myself. I ignored every nasty, crude comment, no matter how much it bothered me, but I snapped whenever someone touched me. I knew better than to act scared or submissive, so I defended myself no matter what." Mason scrubbed his hand down his face.

"I often threw the first punch. Sometimes I ended up in the infirmary, but I usually sent other guys there and landed in solitary myself."

He glanced at the door and wished Alan would come home. His brother knew about the fights—he'd visited the level-three correctional facility often enough and saw Mason's bruises—but Mason never told him about the attempted rapes. Alan never asked, likely too afraid to know the answer.

"I made a name for myself as a hothead. After a few months, most of the guys backed off when I entered a room, and they left me alone."

He paced between the coffee table and the entertainment center. His nephew's crayons and coloring books cluttered the top of the table. Mia's gaze followed his every step like a death ray, and the courage he needed to look at her seemed like a far-fetched fantasy.

"The last attempt happened in the shower room. Three jockers attacked this scrawny fish, and I defended him. They broke my jaw, nose, and a rib before the guards showed up." He rubbed his jaw and swiped his tongue over the spot where he lost a back tooth. A titanium plate connected his jawbone together, but his gums had grown over it long ago.

"Sorry for the prison lingo. A *jocker* is a macho prick, usually a rapist, and a *fish* is a new inmate. Anyway, the new kid, Douglas, turned out to be the nephew of a lifer everyone considered royalty. Even some of the guards respected Oskar Udell and did what he wanted. No one messed with him, his crew, or his inner circle. If they did, they suffered. Oskar offered protection while I stayed in the infirmary. From then on, I never worried about rape again."

Bile burned his throat as he remembered how the largest of his attackers had pinned him on the wet tile floor and prodded his ass cheeks with his cock. Mason locked his shaky hands behind his back, too embarrassed for Mia to see how much those early events still rattled him.

Several minutes passed as the grind of the AC unit and the whirl of the fridge grated in his ears like the slam and clank of metal bars. Mia finally dropped her gaze. Relief swept over him, but then she maneuvered around the coffee table and blocked his hard track across the carpet. The fevered blood in his veins cooled. Not sure if she would pity him or think him weak, he held his breath until his lungs burned, and he released the pent-up air in a slow exhale.

"You were lucky." She tunneled her hand through his spiky hair and wrapped her arms around his neck. Tears glistened in her eyes. "I'm so sorry."

"Don't." He untangled her arms. "I don't deserve your tears."

Mia struck his shoulder with her open palm. "Well, that proves it. I'm not the only one who hides behind a mask. Why do you think you're not worthy of love, friendship, or just plain compassion? You're not a bad person. It's time you deal with your self-esteem issues and realize you have a good woman in your life who accepts you. I'm sick and tired of petting your ego, Mason, so get off this self-pity bandwagon."

His mouth fell open, as dry as gravel. Mia touched a nerve—hell, she severed the damn thing—but he needed to hear it. He needed to quit living in the past and move on with his life, but he didn't know how. The mistakes he'd made while locked up still ate away at his conscience. Mistakes he *wouldn't* willingly confess to the lovely hellion who'd conquered his every thought and teased him in his dreams. He'd lived with the shame and the regret of his mistakes for too long. How could he just accept and forget everything? He considered every day a miracle if someone or something from his past didn't track him down to bite him in the ass, but after the run-in with his old buddies, he knew to expect the worst.

Mason clasped her face in his calloused palms. "You're so different, so understanding. I didn't know women like you existed."

"I'm a rare breed." Her tears fell as Mia grasped his hands. "I feel complete when I'm with you. My heart somersaults when I'm near you. I'm a fool for saying that, but it's true."

Moisture blurred his vision and he brushed it away on his shoulder. "Maybe we won't last more than a few months, a few years, but I want to try."

"Take me now, Mason. Please."

He couldn't deny her any longer. He craved her like the air he needed to breathe.

Their mouths meshed in a wild tango of tongues and clashing teeth. Mason held her close, her plump breasts pressed against his chest, and her warm body flamed the liquid fire in his veins. Self-hatred burned like a living entity inside him, but Mia soothed his demons and eased his guilt.

Maybe, just maybe, he could be more than a pair of fists.

Like the rev of a car engine, his libido kicked the clutch and shifted into overdrive. Blood hammered through his cock. Every muscle in his body trembled and drew taut. The haze of desire clouded his mind. He wanted to be tender, he needed to shower her with care and respect, but she rubbed her sweet spot along his thigh and almost straddled his leg as though desperate to join their bodies.

She moaned as if the friction teased her clit. As her hands moved over his back, she cupped his muscles and gripped him hard.

Tomorrow. I'll make love to her tomorrow. Tonight, I'll give her what she needs.

He nibbled her lower lip until it swelled between his teeth. Her sharp moan traveled down his throat, and he pulled from their lip-lock to stare into her eyes.

Heat blazed in the dark brown depths. Mia dug her nails into his waist, left the barest centimeter of space between their bodies, and feathered her lips down his neck.

No, not feathered. She kissed and suckled, nipped his skin with her little white teeth, and her hard caresses whipped through him as though she sucked his balls into her mouth.

"Damn, Mia. You're ravenous."

She swirled her tongue over the throbbing vein in his neck. "I haven't seen you since last Sunday. I haven't felt you inside me in far too long."

Five days. Six damn long nights.

"I've missed you, Mason. I need more than just talking on the phone."

The garage closed at five o'clock every weekday. As long as Mia drove him home before curfew, they *could* meet after she closed her store at six p.m., but they couldn't share a romantic dinner or sleep together since he would stink of oil and sweat. The bus ride to Westminster took thirty minutes on a good day and forty-five on a bad one, not to mention his transfer to a local bus if Alan couldn't pick him up at the bus station.

He'd shower and change clothes at the apartment, backtrack to LoDo, and spend maybe half an hour with Mia before she'd have to drive him back home. His sweetheart of a girlfriend offered her shower, but he didn't want to dirty up her bathroom, so they talked on the phone every night and waited for the weekend to be together.

He slid his hands under her blouse and flattened them on her smooth, supple skin. Mia tortured the hollow of his throat with her delectable mouth, and she'd better mark him all over.

He would wear her hickeys with pride.

Mason jerked off her blouse and tossed it over her head. Her ample bosom heaved as she breathed, and her cream-colored lace bra pushed up those kissable mounds. He unzipped her skirt and the soft screech of the zipper rent the air.

The fabric fell down her legs, and she lifted her feet to untangle it from around her ankles.

"Leave on your bra and shoes." He stilled her hands as she tried to free the bra hooks.

Her eyebrows quirked up. "Kinky."

He pushed her toward the sofa. In a mouthwatering pose befit for a lingerie model, she reclined on the furniture and trailed her fingers along the curve of her breasts. Her red-painted toenails peeked out from her strappy gold heels. He stepped back to strip away his clothes, and her eyes seemed to track his every movement until he dropped his underwear.

She licked her lips.

His manhood jutted out through thick, dark hair and moisture glistened on the tip. His heavy balls drew tight to his body, and he strained to hold himself back.

"Should I remove these?" She trailed her fingers down her stomach and tapped at her panties.

"No, I'll do it." His rough voice scratched his throat. Mason knelt on the floor beside her and pulled the lace panties down her legs. Dark curls wound tight at the apex of her thighs, and he hovered over her to lick the fleshy pink nub that shone through the curls. Mia gasped, and he pressed his hand on her chest to keep her flat. "Don't move."

"Wait. I changed my mind."

"What?" His arms shook as she sat up. He grabbed her waist, his hands firm, and plunged his tongue into her belly button. He caged her in his arms as she shivered. "Don't tease me, Mia. We're going all the way."

"I know, but I want to take *you*. Don't you remember? I warned you this might happen." Mia patted his whiskered cheek as though to chastise him. Her legs drew to her stomach, the precious nub concealed, and she shifted free from his hold to stand. Her dark hair fanned her shoulders, and the look in her eyes promised paradise. "Lay back and grab something. You'll need an anchor."

His eyebrows shot to his hairline. Mason climbed on the sofa, propped himself up on a few pillows, and crossed his arms behind his head. A smug smile crossed his face, he couldn't help it, and he flat-out grinned as she settled down between his legs. He bent one knee, his thick package on display, and his cock ached for the taste of her kiss. Mia licked the long length of his snake tattoo instead, and seemed to pay particular close attention to each individual black stripe.

Wrong damn snake, he almost shouted as the muscles in his lower abdomen bunched.

Her wet tongue swirled clockwise around his navel before it dipped inside. Her long, silky hair tickled his inner thighs. His cock grazed her breasts, and he would kiss her feet if she sandwiched it in between her heavy mounds. Again she teased him. She drew her breasts away from his crotch and leaned over him to clamp her lips around his hard nipple.

Pleasure whipped through him with her every touch, and he'd swear a thousand fingers caressed his body if he didn't know better. His manhood jerked as the little vixen claimed his testicles with a firm but gentle grip of her hand. A mouthful of air whizzed out through his clenched teeth. He grabbed a pillow in order to not fist his hand in her hair.

"Good, it's about time you listened." Mia blew warm air across his penis.

He cursed and flung his head back against the upholstery.

She massaged his sensitive balls with one hand and stroked the underside of his bent knee with the other.

"Damn, Mia." He thrust his cock closer to her face as she brushed kisses along his stomach.

Mia stared up at him, her dark eyelashes deepening her sultry stare, and she flicked her tongue across the slit in his head.

He shuddered and slammed the pillow against the back of the sofa. "I'm so damn hot right now. Why do you tease me?"

She circled the shaft of his penis with her hand, pumped up and down, hard and soft, and changed the rhythm again and again until he wanted to scream. His heavy balls smacked against his ass as he thrust his hips.

Mia licked the enlarged head and sucked him into her mouth.

"Fuckin' hell." Mason buried his hands in her hair and pushed her face into his pubes.

She opened her mouth wider and engulfed him. Her lips sealed around the base and her tongue followed every bite of her teeth.

Stars danced behind his eyes. His cock hardened into a stick of granite, so stiff it ached and pleaded for release. He gasped, the pleasure too much, his orgasm on the brink.

Flattening her tongue, she licked to his tip.

The sweet haven of her mouth slid back down, and he screamed. Mason jerked her head up before he lost all control.

His lover blinked away the dazed gleam in her eyes and trailed her nails through the hair on his legs. A seductive smile played over her lips. She reached for the organ that made him all man, but he covered himself with the pillow.

A frown creased her forehead. "Did I hurt you? I'm sorry. I went too hard."

"No, no. You were incredible. Really fucking incredible, but I almost exploded. We don't want our fun to end too soon, right?" Mason sat up and pulled her onto his lap.

She shook her head, relief in her eyes, and the moist lips of her vagina embraced his cock as she straddled him.

"You're so damn wet from giving me head. It aroused you that much?"

She blushed scarlet. "I like giving blowjobs. It's not very ladylike, but I wanted you to explode in my mouth."

"Next time." He ground out the words as he gripped her hips and impaled her. Mia rode him fast, just as he wanted, and her feminine walls dragged him deep inside her. His body heated like a furnace, surely as red as hot coals, and he bet ice would crackle and melt on his skin.

"Oh, God. Oh my God."

"I know, darlin'." He bucked his hips to shove deeper. Sweat gleamed on her skin and moistened her chestnut-brown hair. Desire and tangy sweat sizzled on his tongue as he suckled her neck to darken a few fading hickeys. Too horny and already primed, Mason doubted he could stave off his release for more than a few minutes, but he'd be damned if he came before she did. "Come for me. Be my good little girl and let loose. Spiral out of control for me. If you don't, I'll call you sugar. I swear I will."

Mia yelped as he slapped her ass with his open palm. Pleasure lit her face. "Yes, Mason. That's the spot. Call me whatever you want. Just touch me." She tossed her head back and shoved her cleavage into his face.

Oh, fuck.

A firestorm tore through his balls and raced up his shaft. Lightning arced in his veins. Her soft breasts muffled his curse like a mound of pillows as he shot his seed inside her. Mia's liquid heat rushed around his cock, aided his thrusts, and a deep grunt ripped up his throat.

Her cry of pleasure matched his.

"Ah, shit. We forgot to use a condom." Mason braced his forehead to hers. "Are you on birth control pills?"

"Yeah, to regulate my period. I much prefer this activity to the red one." She panted hard as he chuckled. "I'm clean. Are you? We should've discussed STDs before now."

"Don't worry. I'm a bad boy, but a healthy one."

His semi-hard penis slipped from her vagina as she laughed and rearranged herself on his lap. Mason hissed, the loss of her heat a shock to his system, and he stood with her cradled in his arms. Sleep thickened her eyelids as he headed down the hall for the last room on the right. The full-sized bed welcomed her with open arms, and he fought the urge to stroke her back as she stretched like a sleepy kitten. The ceiling fan spun on low, and he pulled the chain to up the speed.

God, what I wouldn't do for this woman.

"Hold me all night, Mason. Don't let me go."

Joy clutched his heart in a tender grip, her soft plea a balm to his blackened soul. He crawled into bed, removed her bra and high heels, and spooned Mia from behind. Little goose bumps followed the trail of his fingers as he stroked figure eights over her flat stomach.

Her breathing evened out as she fell asleep.

Mason sighed, happy and pissed all at the same time. "I'll never let you go," he whispered in her ear. "Never." He'd reached the point of no return. Mia belonged to him, and he would protect the woman he adored at all costs.

Chapter Seven

"Mason?" Mia reached blindly across the mattress for him and grasped wrinkled sheets. A groggy moan crawled up her throat. She peeled open her eyelids and wiped away the blur. Cool air from the ceiling fan cut across her nipples, and she tightened the sheet around her. They'd made love once more throughout the night. His warm embrace cocooned her for hours, his arm draped over her side and their legs entwined, but now uncertainty struck as she leaned up to glance around the impeccably clean room.

A small lamp, landline phone, and a digital clock that read *7:49* topped the nightstand, and a few books lay stacked on the floor by the bed. Her brow arched as she read the authors—Mark Twain, Edgar Allen Poe, and Louisa May Alcott. *Seriously?* She picked up a worn copy of *Little Women.* She'd meant to read this book for a literature class in college but opted to skim a study guide and see the movie instead. Other than the books, she couldn't find anything like pictures or knickknacks to suggest someone used the room on a daily basis. His lack of décor, or lack of desire to put his personal mark on his bedroom, didn't surprise her.

Deliciously sore all over, she longed for a hot shower to ease the aches and to wash the scent of sex from her skin. Her messy hair cascaded around her shoulders, and she used her fingers as a poor substitute for a hairbrush. Her stomach rumbled. With any luck, Mason woke up early to prepare breakfast, but she knew of a few nearby restaurants they could go to if he wanted.

Dim light streaked under the closed bedroom door, and a faint noise echoed from somewhere in the apartment.

With the sheet wrapped around her body like a dress, she pressed her ear to the door but couldn't make out the sounds. Unease crept up her spine. Mia found her clothes piled haphazardly on a padded chair next to the dresser, her shoes on the floor, and she quickly dressed. Muffled voices drifted closer as she tiptoed down the hall and paused just before the hallway opened into the living room.

"God, Mason. How could you be so damn stupid? We've discussed this." A man grunted in obvious displeasure and chills shot through Mia's veins. "You're lucky Danny isn't here. What if he saw all your clothes scattered about the living room or walked in on the two of you naked? *I* nearly went blind from it. Why didn't you at least tell me?"

Mia flushed hot.

"How could I tell you when I didn't expect this?" A defensive edge lined Mason's deep timbre. "Why does it even matter? Am I not allowed to bring my girlfriend here?"

"Girlfriend?" A noise ricocheted as though a fist slammed down on a piece of wood. "Are you fucking serious? She's your parole officer's sister."

"Damn it, Alan. I'm falling for her. I'm crazy about her."

Alan cursed. "You spent ten years locked away in a

hellhole, and I could only see you through a sheet of bulletproof glass or in a damn commons room with armed guards who watched our every move. You never even met Danny until you came to live with us. I don't want to lose you again."

Mason sighed. "You won't. I would never do anything to jeopardize that. I swear."

"You're doing a great job so far."

"Give Mia a chance. Just talk with her."

"I want her out of here, Mason. If Borden shows up for a stupid inspection and his sister is asleep in your bed, you'll be in the backseat of his car in handcuffs. He won't care if it's legal. Borden will throw something at you and get you in major trouble. No woman is worth that."

"*She* is."

"I'm not." Mia turned the corner and entered the living room.

The men quieted and looked at her from the open kitchen.

If only I could've snuck out before Mason woke or Alan returned home. She held her head high and focused on Mason. "Your brother is right. I should go. I—um—I have some errands to take care of, anyway." Though the errands could wait for later in the week, she headed toward the front door and narrowed her gaze on her purse.

"No, stop." Mason hurried after her and grabbed her hand.

Mia tried to pull back, but Mason drew her into the kitchen and set her in front of his brother like a prize.

Alan's dark-green eyes burned with a coolness she didn't care to fathom.

Her gaze slid down his body. Though tall and handsome like Mason, Alan failed to boil her blood or kick-start her libido. From his wayward dark hair, loose dress shirt, and slacks—and the fact he'd stayed out all night—she imagined his date went well. Too bad he came home so soon.

Mason stood behind her and wrapped his arms around her stomach. "Mia Eddison, Alan Harding. Brother, I'd like you to meet my girlfriend."

Alan hid a cough behind his balled-up hand and offered his other hand to Mia.

She accepted it. "It's good to finally meet you." Benji had accepted her right away, and she expected Alan would too. At a loss for words, she stood a little straighter to not show weakness.

"I'm sorry you heard all that." Alan stepped back. "I'm just protective."

Mia blushed hotter. "I understand. I'm sorry I spent the night. I didn't mean to intrude in your home, and I definitely don't want to cause any problems for Mason's parole."

"Don't do that, Mia." Mason tightened his grip as he glared at Alan. "You promised me when I moved in that this place is half mine. I pay half the bills. You don't have a choice with whom or what I bring into this household as long as it doesn't violate my parole. She stays."

Alan gripped his hands. "You're right, but Borden will probably ban her from returning if he finds out about this."

"It's possible." Mia turned her head to stare up at Mason. "But he wouldn't want to. Jim will have to put my name down on legal documents and probably update his supervisor of this situation. He'd consider that shameful."

Mason kissed her hair before he released her. "We'll deal with it when the time comes."

"My brother can be an asshole." She stepped toward Alan in a plea for him to understand. "I'm not. If you would feel more comfortable if I left, I will. If Jim files the paperwork to legally forbid me from coming here, I won't return. I won't jeopardize Mason's parole for anything in the world. I care about your brother too much to hurt him."

"No. Stay." Alan forced his hand through his short hair and sighed. "We should talk. You're important to Mase so you're important to me. Come, sit down." He headed to the living room without waiting for a reply.

Mia followed and sat beside Alan on the sofa while Mason plopped down in a winged chair. They found a common subject—*Mason*—after a rocky start. She flipped through a collection of old photo albums Alan brought out from the hallway closet as he told her childhood stories. After about an hour, they laughed like good friends.

She set aside a Halloween-themed album to flip through a birthday album. "Your mom is so pretty, Mason. You both look really happy in this one." Mia glanced at him as he fumed, his arms crossed over his chest. Mason ignored her. She stared back at the snapshot of a smiling brunette woman and a rambunctious little boy. A wild mop of dark hair flew up as if Mason shook his head just as someone snapped the photo. A cat-shaped cake waited on the table in front of him.

Alan leaned over to see the picture shielded behind

glossy plastic. "Oh yeah, I remember that party. Mom hated her haircut, and Dad broke the camera right after he took that shot. Mason begged for a cake shaped like a cat's face for his fifth birthday, and it had to be yellow. I ragged him up and down for weeks for that girly cake." He smirked at his little brother as Mason flipped him his middle finger. "Mom always indulged him. No matter what he wanted, he got it."

"So he was a momma's boy?"

"Hell, yeah. It made me sick."

Mia laughed as Mason clenched his hands and avoided her gaze. Tension radiated around him like a cloud. Though she shouldn't look at the pictures anymore, she enjoyed the stories Alan told her with each photo she asked about. Despite her lover's mood, she wanted to know everything possible about Mason Harding, including his childhood. She only wished her parents could embarrass *her* in the same manner. Jim would never do it.

She pushed aside the thought and flipped a few more pages. Mason and Alan's dad seemed to take most of the photos, but the few she found of him answered her unspoken question.

So the Harding boys got their good looks from Daddy Gorgeous.

She silently laughed at her own joke until she flipped to a picture of Mason as a teenager. Her brow lifted. "Wow. You were a little heartbreaker, huh?" With his shaggy hair, spiked dog collar, leather jacket, and ripped denim jeans, he reminded her of the boys she'd always crushed on in high school but never had the guts to talk to.

"Yeah, the sweet kid morphed into a moody prick

after the divorce." Alan leaned back on a fringe pillow, the same pillow Mason clutched in ecstasy last night, but she wouldn't tell Alan that. "Mom had to bribe him to show up to his own birthday party. Mason claimed his friends planned to throw him one, but he caved in after she promised him a hundred dollars."

"Yeah, and she never gave me the damn money. God, I can't remember a more boring b-day party." Mason finally spoke up. "What seventeen year old guy would rather play board games and watch old movies at home when he could drink and sleep around?"

Alan huffed. "Boring? Maybe, but that's not the point. Family and loved ones should be with you on your birthday, but you acted like a dick the whole night and barely spoke to me for the rest of the summer I stayed home from school."

"Thanks for the reminder, college boy, but you're wrong on one thing. I *am* a dick, so watch what you say around my girl."

Mia fought a smile. Her heart fluttered with the "my girl" remark, but she doubted Mason meant it in a sweet way. He tapped his foot hard on the floor and flexed his arms. The sleeves of his T-shirt tightened over his taut biceps. His gaze steel-hard, he looked ready to strangle someone.

Yep, that remark is all hot, angry possession. Her nipples tightened. *Calm down, girl. Now's not the time.*

Alan closed the album as though he noticed his brother's volatile mood, too. "So, Mase, have you thought more about Mom's dinner party? You should bring Mia."

The telltale tic pulsed in his cheek. "No. I already told you I'm not gonna go."

"You've seen her twice in the past six months. She wants you there for her anniversary."

"That's fucking bullshit, Al. It's ten years too late to make amends. Do you know how many times she visited me in prison? None, so I've upped her twice already."

Alan rubbed his eyes and glanced back at Mia. "I'm not sure how much he's told you, but Mom took his arrest very hard. He'd pulled a lot of crap as a teenager, and she washed her hands of him. She calmed down several months after the arrest and visited the prison a lot over the years, but Mason refused to see her every time. Dad never cared to try. Mase won't talk to either of them when they call here."

Mia bit her lip. "You left that part out, Mason."

"I didn't expect my big mouth brother to tell you. I would've eventually."

"What anniversary?" She waited for Mason to answer but looked at Alan as he cleared his throat.

"Mom remarried about five years ago and moved west to Carbondale. Her husband operates a small helicopter service in the mountains. Anyway, he's a great guy and she's happy with him. They plan to have a private little dinner to celebrate in a few months."

She turned back to Mason. "I'd like to meet her."

He rolled his eyes and stood. "Mia, I know we made plans for today, but it's time for you to leave. I need to speak with my brother alone."

Her mouth dropped open but she snapped it shut. Mia fisted her hands and stood as well. "We're just having a conversation. I realize the topic is a little touchy but—"

"Very touchy." Mason stalked to the door, grabbed

her purse from the rack, and held it out to her. "I'll call you later, sometime today."

The air in her lungs wheezed out through her grinding teeth. She forced a smile on her face and turned to Alan as he followed her up with the birthday album in his arms. He flushed red. "It was nice to meet you, Alan." She offered her hand and he shook it.

"And you. I'm sorry my brother is an ass."

A comment that degraded Mason to something far worse than an ass jumped to the tip of her tongue, but she held it back. Mia walked to the open door and snatched her purse. Mason's hard gaze never left her face, and she tilted up her chin. "Don't bother calling."

And she left.

****

Mason closed the door and cursed.

"You're an arrogant prick, you know that?"

"Not now, Alan. I'm not in the mood for a pep talk."

His brother stomped toward him. "I didn't even want her here, but I gave her a chance for you. Guess what? I like her. She's nice, kindhearted, and well-spoken. She's not a skank like the women you saw a few months ago. Besides her relation to Jim Borden, she's pretty damn perfect. I wish *I* met her first."

Mason shoved his brother against the sofa. "Don't even think that."

"Think what?" Alan scowled as he righted himself. He dropped the album on the table. "That she has a great ass and long legs that won't quit, or that she makes you smile and wants to hear stories about you? Or that she wants to meet Mom? What woman in her right mind wants to meet the boyfriend's *mother*? She must be crazy about you to agree to that hell."

Mason fisted his hands and stalked away from Alan before he punched him.

I shouldn't have kicked Mia out. What the hell was I thinking?

He'd wanted to plow his foot up his own ass as she brushed past him with her head held so regally. She'd headed down the metal stairwell outside the apartment without a backward glance.

"Call her cell phone." Alan crossed his arms over his rumpled shirt. "Ask her—beg her—to come back. We had a good time until you ruined it."

"Me? You got out Mom's old pictures. I can't believe you even have some of them. You and Mia had fun at my expense. I kept thinking how the hell is she supposed to see me as a man after she saw pictures of me dolled up like a drag queen with fake boobs and a wig to boot?"

"You were seven years old on Halloween night. I was dressed in drag, too, but I'm not humiliated."

"You're not screwing her."

"God, you're unbelievable." Alan headed toward the hall but paused and turned around to stare at Mason. "You're my brother and I love you, but you've made a ton of mistakes in your life. Don't make another by letting a decent woman like her get away."

He seethed as Alan disappeared down the hall. A door slammed shut. Mason kicked the entertainment center and rested his head on the wood panel. After he filled his lungs with several deep breaths, the pounding in his blood slowed. He hated this up-and-down rollercoaster he rode with Mia. He liked her, he truly did, but he couldn't stop pushing her away. Every time he thought they'd worked things out, something happened to piss him off and he opened his damn mouth.

"Fuck. Why do I do this? Why am I always a fuckup?"

Mason pressed the heel of his hands to his eye sockets. Harsh fluorescent lights flashed behind his eyelids and clanking bars echoed in his head. All the wrongs he'd committed waded around his feet like a river of acid and threatened to drag him under. The faces of the friends he'd left behind in prison and the life he no longer wanted part of laughed at his attempt to become a better man, and the one bright light in his life had just walked out his door.

He headed to his bedroom and paused at the sight of the twisted sheet and blanket on the bed. Mia's feminine floral scent wafted through the air. He tried to ignore it as he jerked off his shirt and kicked away the jeans he'd jerked on after Alan barged into his room a few hours ago. Mason had woken up with a start and Alan glimpsed Mia's juicy bottom, the curve of her back, and the side of her left breast before Mason tossed the sheet over her body. Not that he'd let Mia know how much his brother saw.

After a quick shower and shave, he dressed in a fresh T-shirt, tan cargo shorts, and a pair of worn sneakers. He left the apartment, desperate for fresh air, and caught the bus that catered to the Westminster area. He soon transferred to the Denver southbound bus and walked the streets of LoDo for over an hour before he summoned his courage to stop by Mia's loft.

Mason pushed a small red button on the intercom to buzz the loft, but no one answered his summons or buzzed the door open. The old steel door that led into the stairwell held strong under the weight of his fist— he doubted she could hear his hard knocks anyway— and he stomped to the storefront windows to peer inside. At times like this, he wished he owned a cell phone.

God, he sucked as a boyfriend. He'd promised to visit her store a few weeks ago but never thought to mention a tour when he and Mia indulged in playtime upstairs.

Movement in the back of the store caught his attention. He banged on the window and hurried to the double doors to bang again on the glass. Early afternoon light shone through the windows, and he braced his hands on the door to cup his face to better see inside the dimly lit building. Several tall shelves formed three aisles and occupied the middle section with a long counter on the left and what appeared to be dressing rooms on the right. He banged on the door again.

"We're closed!" Mia shouted from within the boutique.

He banged harder and faster on the thick-plated glass. Pedestrians stared as they passed, but he didn't care.

Mia emerged from the shadows. Her hair was in a loose ponytail, a gray tank top hugged her breasts, cut-off shorts highlighted her legs, and even her sneakers upped her sex appeal.

Or he really just needed to kiss her.

She paused in her fast stride as though shocked to see him.

He held her gaze, willed her to give him a chance

to explain.

She walked to the doors and pushed a few buttons on a mounted panel. A security alarm beeped.

Mason didn't dare breathe a sigh of relief as she cracked open one of the glass doors.

Though she said nothing, her scowl and bloodshot eyes spoke volumes.

I made her cry. What kind of man am I?

He wanted to kick his own ass all over again. "I'm sorry. I'm an idiot. My anger took control of me and I snapped. I knew I made a mistake as soon as you left."

Mia leaned her head against the door. Her eyelashes fluttered, and her lips moved as though she carefully worded her response. "I care about you, Mason, but that temper of yours is a problem. I'm too busy to deal with mood swings and childish bullshit. I asked your brother for stories about your childhood because you never tell me anything good. I'm sorry I upset you, I never meant to hurt or embarrass you, but you can't keep me in the dark about your life." A long sigh parted her lips. She flipped up a few switches on the wall and opened the door for him.

Soothing white lights lit the store as he crossed the threshold. White and purple décor decorated pale pink walls. Scarves and dangling beads adorned the ends of a few shelves. A purple sofa, two cushioned chairs, and a coffee table formed a relaxation area in the corner. A bowl full of colorful gemstones topped the table. Three half-sized doors opened into three small dressing rooms just as he'd guessed. Mia had even painted the checkout counter pink and trimmed it in white.

"You weren't kidding." He turned in a circle to get a good view of the store and noticed a corded-off staircase toward the back that led to the upper story. "I've never seen anything so girly in my life."

"I'll take that as a compliment." She closed the door and reset the alarm. Sadness pinched her delicate features as she turned to head down an aisle.

His grin faded. "Mia, I'm really—"

"Sorry, I know." She stopped halfway down the aisle and straightened a few trinkets on a shelf. At his approach, she continued toward the clothing section in the back of the store. Three cardboard boxes stood stacked on the floor, a few more boxes lay empty, and she grasped the lid of the top box and tossed it aside. "Look, Mason. I'm not sure where this thing between us is going. You don't want to introduce me to your mom. You kicked me out before Danny came home today. You gave me a lot of ridiculous excuses about why I couldn't meet your brother, but now I have. Alan seems like a nice guy." She withdrew a spaghetti-strapped dress from the box and hung it on a nearby rack neatly stocked with summer dresses. "Why don't you want me to meet your family?"

"Because I don't want to lose you. I knew Alan would freak out—which he did—and my mom is very judgmental. I don't want anyone to ruin what we have."

"Only you can do that, hmm?"

"No, Mia, what I mean is… Hell, I don't know how to say this without coming across as a pathetic psycho who traps women in his basement." Mason struck his forehead with his open palm. "Fine, I *am* a pathetic psycho—minus the basement. I learned in prison to guard my belongings with my fists because someone could steal them. I learned not to show off something I prized because someone could damage it.

I'm very protective of my things, and I'm sorry if it offends you, but I see you as mine. I don't want to share you." He flushed hot over his male-chauvinistic words. "You're a sweet, generous person, and I've never had anything so pure. So yeah, I messed up. I'm pretty damn good at pushing away the people I care about."

Mason waited for her to scream and kick him out, and he tensed as she wrapped her hand around his forearm. Air burned through his lungs.

"Take me to your mother's home for dinner."

He grimaced. "Is that the proof you need?"

"No, I believe you. I just want to go."

Mason nodded, prepared to do anything to earn her forgiveness. "We'll probably have to spend the night. It won't be a fun, carefree visit. Expect arguments."

"That's fine. Thanks for the warning."

"All right, but I have to let my PO know about the trip. Your brother may schedule me for some drug and alcohol test or show up at Alan's place for an inspection the day we're supposed to leave. He won't like us taking off together."

"True, I wouldn't put it past him."

"I can't pass state lines, but I can travel anywhere I want within the state and stay overnight for a maximum of three nights, but I bet the privilege is revoked because of the curfew. Again, I have to check with Borden. We'll go if I can manage it." For her sake, he hoped he could. "We also shouldn't carpool with my brother and Danny. Alan says the kid is loud and wild on road trips, and knowing me, I'll be in a mood. His excitement and my temper mix like gas and fire."

Her finely shaped eyebrow rose.

"I want you to meet Danny before then, of course."

He backpedaled. "Will you come over for dinner sometime next week? I make a mean mac and cheese."

She folded her hand into his. "I can do that."

"Are we good?"

"Only on one more condition." Mia nodded at the boxes behind her on the tile floor. "Why don't you help me unload these clothes? I'll be all yours for the rest of the night."

"Until curfew, you mean?"

"Right, you have the cool brother. Mine needs to be knocked down a few pegs."

He laughed and drew her closer. He skimmed his fingers down her smooth cheek and kissed her so soundly she melted right into his arms. Her breath mingled with his and he took it deep into his lungs.

Mason sighed in relief.

Chapter Eight

Mia pressed the *Visitor Pass* sticker to her shirt and headed toward the elevator. She'd called Jim twice over the past two days to see if he would speak with her willingly, but he avoided her calls as usual. Now Wednesday, she had left her most responsible employee in charge of the store so she could bombard Jim at work.

He's gonna flip, but that's why I have muffins.

She tightened her hand around the handle of the small wicker basket at her side. More than ready to take Jim's snide comments in stride, Mia wore her hair up in a clip to show off a string of little hickeys on her neck and to assert her independence. Jim would realize, one way or another today, she wouldn't lie down and let him walk all over her.

A *ding* echoed the arrival of the elevator. Two well-dressed middle-aged men, likely parole officers, and a possible parolee near her age boarded the lift and rode with her up to the second story. One of the officers reeked of cheap cologne, and the stale air in the compartment compounded her nerves. The parolee flashed his teeth at her in a *Baby, I want to eat you* grin as he admired her hickeys. He would be handsome if not for the gold tooth up front and center in his mouth and the way her skin crawled.

Mia bolted out of the elevator as soon as the doors

slid open, and she smiled at a few people she knew during her mad trek down the cluttered, noisy hallway.

As the hall opened into a large cubicle section, she caught sight of her brother's old college friend across the sea of short gray walls and bobbing heads.

Giles Morrow, now a narcotics officer, talked with a heavyset parole officer as a pissed-off looking parolee in baggy pants hunched over in a metal folding chair. Giles glanced up as though he felt someone watching him. Their gazes met. His eyebrows lifted as though in surprise to see her, and he waved.

She waved back. Though Jim said he kept in contact with Giles, she'd lost touch with the tall blond policeman over the past few years. If not for her current mission, she would like to catch up with him, but she needed to focus on Jim and making him see the error of his ways. Another hall branched out from the cubicle section and she hurried down it toward Jim's private office.

Mia hated this office building almost as much as she did her dad's old precinct. Mom would take her and Jim down there as children to visit their dad no matter how much she whined. The place had scared her, but her parents didn't understand. Jim did, and he'd always held her hand and tried to shield her when they passed loud, burly men in handcuffs or strung-out women dressed in clothes better suited for the bedroom than out in public.

The parole building depressed her, but she considered it a step up from the precinct.

Jim dealt with a lot of stress, so she tried to cut him some slack, but his job turned him into a paranoid ass. Even if he didn't deal with dangerous ex-felons on a daily basis, the lackluster beige walls and sterile smell of the office building would drive anyone a little mad.

Mia stood outside his office door and raised her hand to knock. She'd asked the security guard downstairs to not call her brother's work phone and alert him of her visit, and she hoped the elderly man had kept his word.

Be strong. You have to do this, or you might as well kiss Mason goodbye.

She rapped her hand on the door. The air in her lungs stilled until her brother bellowed "Come in" from the inside.

It's now or never.

Mia opened the door and entered.

Jim looked up from behind his cluttered desk, and his face blanched.

She locked the door behind her and strolled up to him in the small office. Noise and chatter seeped through the thin walls in a soft flow of murmurs, but she ignored it.

"I tried to be reasonable. I tried to set up times when we could meet after work, but you wouldn't play ball. I even tried to bribe you with blueberry muffins, and not the kind from the pouch. I'm talking about real muffins made from scratch with fresh berries from the farmer's market. Your favorite." Mia sat the basket on the desk. "Here are a dozen muffins. I saved the rest for me. Call it an olive branch. Cancel your appointments if you have any. I asked Angie to watch the store for me, so I have a few hours free. We need to settle this."

"I know we do." Jim leaned back in his swivel chair. His gaze flickered between the basket and his desktop computer screen, and landed on the latter. He clicked a few buttons on the keyboard and stared back at her. "I'm backlogged on reports, so I don't have any appointments today. We need to talk about Mason."

"We need to talk about *me* first." She ignored Jim's offer to sit down as he nodded toward one of the two chairs in front of his desk.

His law enforcement degree and a few awards hung on the wall behind him, but most of his certificates gathered dust in an old box he'd kicked into the corner of the office years ago. Her brother acted macho sometimes but humility ran in his veins.

"I'm twenty-eight years old, Jim. I made a mistake with Evan and learned the hard way. If Mason is a mistake, too, I'll learn from it and move on, but these mistakes are mine to make. How do you expect me to grow as a person if I don't try?"

"I'm just trying to protect you. I failed with Evan and I won't fail again."

"I'm not a child. I don't need your protection." She struggled to pick the best words to help him understand. "I *do* need your respect. I need you to trust me to make my own choices. If I mess up, I'll deal with it. I don't need you to catch me if I fall."

"What kind of brother would that make me, Mia?" Jim rubbed his temples. "Don't say I don't respect you. Of course I do. You're an intelligent woman. You normally make good decisions, but you have a bad track record when it comes to men." He held up his hand as she tried to argue. "I don't mean just Mason and Evan. The boyfriends you had in high school and in college before you met Evan were only after one thing."

"News flash, Jim. *I* was only after one thing too." She mentally patted herself on the back as her brother cringed. "Sorry, I'm not a saint. I like sex just as much as the next woman, or man, for that matter. Can't you tell by the hickeys on my neck? I've never despised any of your girlfriends, even the bitches. I've always tried to befriend them. You owe me and my boyfriend the same courtesy."

"You're right. I do, but not if he's an ex-con."

"That shouldn't matter." Mia swiped her sweaty palms on her slacks. "I don't care if I choose to date a gang member or a drug addict. That's my choice. You're supposed to respect that and support me in all my decisions even if you don't agree with me."

Jim cocked his head to the side. "You don't know everything, do you?"

Heat flushed her face. "Mason hasn't told me his whole life story, but I know enough. His past embarrasses him. Believe it or not, he does have feelings."

"He knows you'll leave him if he tells you."

"I can deal with his baggage. He accepts mine, and I owe him nothing less." She braced her hands on her hips as Jim scoffed. "Besides, I don't like squeaky-clean men. Evan hid his asshole ways behind a pretty face and a billion-dollar smile. I take Mason at face value. Yeah, he acts like a jerk when he's mad, but he doesn't try to hide from me."

At least not much, she amended silently.

Jim stood so fast his chair knocked into the table behind him. An old-fashioned printer wobbled and a bowl of paperclips fell to the floor. He stomped to one of the many file cabinets that lined the side wall and shuffled through several folders before he grabbed one to toss on the desk. "You don't think he hides from you? Read his file."

Mia stared at the thick folder. A few pages fell out, and she glimpsed Mason's name in a bold black font. "That's illegal, Jim. I'm a civilian. I'm not supposed to read someone's personal file without their approval."

"We'll keep it hush-hush, and I'm sure you'll thank me when you're done." He crossed his arms, and his navy-blue blazer stretched over his broad shoulders. "Or should I just tell you?"

"No. I want Mason to tell me. Documents like that are so impersonal." She nodded at the folder. "I'm not stupid, okay? I've suspected for a while Mason has kept a few things from me, but I don't know why he would. Maybe he just doesn't think it's a big deal. He's a private person. He has a hard time trusting people but—"

"Lay off it, Mia. I feel ready to vomit every time you defend him. What has he told you? I should know so I won't spill any of his dirty secrets by mistake."

His condescending tone set her teeth on edge. "All right, fine. He told me about his parents' divorce that sent him on downward spiral to rob a liquor store. He told me he saved a man's life when his friends ran off. He told me how much he hurt his brother and how ashamed he is of his mistakes. That's what he told me, Jeremiah, and that's what matters to me."

Jim smiled, and her stomach dropped. "Read his file. You'll find a hell of a lot more in there that will matter to you."

"I won't read it."

"Ask him what Sondokes is. Ask him about Onyx. You should at least watch a damn news show or pick up a newspaper now and then, like a normal person. I know you try to avoid them because you don't like to hear about all the violence and misery in the world, but it's childish to live in a perfect little bubble. You're in the dark about a lot of important local issues, Mia." He tapped his foot on the tile floor. "Just watch for reports on Onyx or check out the names online to get an idea of what kind of man you're dating."

Mia licked her dry lips. This meeting definitely didn't turn out as she'd planned. Jim backed her into a makeshift corner with questions she couldn't answer and questions she needed answers to. "You're right. I need to pay more attention to the local news, but Mason will tell me when he's ready."

"He better tell you soon, or I'll do it for him. I don't care if you never forgive me. I will drive your relationship through the fucking mud to keep you safe."

"Safe from what? Mason would never hurt me."

"Maybe not intentionally, but he has a temper. Sooner or later, that temper will result in his fist across your cheek. Sooner or later, his past will haunt his ass and try to take you down too. When that happens, I'll be there to catch you."

A shiver shot down her spine. Mason hadn't told Jim about his run-in with his two old friends last Saturday, and she hoped Mason kept silent. Her throat tightened as though someone squeezed it. She loved Jim, and that made her next words more difficult than she imagined.

"No, you won't be there. That's why I'm here. If you don't rescind these new restrictions, like the weekly mandatory visits and the eight o'clock curfew, you won't have a sister anymore. I don't want to choose between you and Mason, but I will if you force my hand. And you'll lose." She held up her arms as Jim rushed around the desk and reached for her. "I'm serious, Jim. I know you think this is just a fling, but it's not. I'm happy with him. I won't lose interest or forget about him in a few weeks. I want to spend months, *years*, with Mason. He feels the same about me."

"He's told you this?"

"Yes, he has."

Jim shook his head. "You talk big, Mia, but you're full of shit. Mason Harding will keep you around for a while because you're beautiful, but you're nothing more to him than a piece of tail. He's screwed a lot of women since the State released him on parole. He's even gloated to me about it, so don't think you're special to him. You're just a chew toy."

Don't cry, Mia. You'd better not cry. "Thank you, Jim. You sure know how to win me to your side. You insult me in the worse possible way and expect me to fall in line. That's real smart. I'm not one of your parolees. I don't have to follow your rules."

"No, but Harding does. I can make his parole conditions a nightmare if I choose to."

"You'll lose me as your sister if you do."

Silence passed between them, and the temperature in the room seemed to kick up a few degrees. Pain and tension separated them like a canyon.

Jim dropped his gaze. "You don't mean that."

"I mean every word. I don't need my big brother to take care of me. You're not my guardian. If Dad was alive and he tried to control me like this, I'd tell him the same thing and that would hurt me even more than this does now. I have to live my own life." She wrapped her arms around her chest and walked to the window that overlooked the parking lot. People milled about below, and she longed for a warm breeze to freshen the stifling air in the office. "Mason asked me to meet his mom. Well, his brother did, but I still want to. Alan is very nice and Danny's a sweetheart. I met the little boy yesterday. You have no idea how gentle and loving Mason is with that child, or how much Danny loves him."

"I've seen it, but those tender family moments could be an act. Your boyfriend has lied to you. Maybe not flat-out, but he's omitted the truth about things that will shock and disgust you. The sooner you realize that, the better off you'll be."

"You just don't get it." Her hands shook as she wiped at her eyes. "Evan's parents always thought their golden boy could do better than me, and his sister called me a slut more than once. Alan likes me, even though he's worried sick you'll throw Mason back in prison. I want to meet their mom. I want her to like me, too, not hate me because of you."

"I have to do my job, Mia."

"I don't expect you to give Mason a free pass. Treat him like all the others, but not worse."

"Leave him and I'll ease up."

"Why are you like this? Why don't you understand?"

Frustration bubbled like acid in the pit of her stomach. While she and Jim shared a stubborn streak a mile wide, she never thought of him as an overprotective brother and even told Mason that on their first date. She never thought, not in a million years, he would make demands and dictate to her.

They'd built their brother/sister relationship on trust, love, and respect, but he didn't seem to care about that anymore.

"It's not as if I plan to marry Mason, but things may go in that direction. I want to be on good terms with his family, if so. Don't you know how important that is to me?" Mia straightened her back as he rolled his eyes. "Our parents are dead, Jim. Our grandparents are, too, and Mom and Dad didn't have any siblings. I'd love to have uncles, aunts, and cousins, but we're alone. We're orphans. All we have is each other, unless we find another family who will bring us into their fold. I may have that with Mason, and I hope you'll find a wonderful woman whose family will love you too. We deserve that."

"Damn it, Mia. I don't know how to talk to you." Jim closed the distance between them and grasped her arms. "I just can't wrap my head around all this. I don't expect you to join a nunnery or anything like that, but how can you pick someone as messed up as a violent ex-con? What he's done—"

"It's in the past. That doesn't mean he'll do whatever he did again. A few mistakes shouldn't define Mason for the rest of his life."

"You don't know—"

"I'll find out." Mia jerked from her brother's easy hold and stared up at him through a veil of restrained tears. "Trust me enough to know I will nag and bitch until he confesses every dirty secret and sin. If it happens to be too much for me, then I'll cross that bridge when I come to it. For now, I just want to enjoy the ride. I *will* make the right decision, but I need time to do it."

"What if you make the right decision too late? I don't want you pregnant and alone. I don't want you dead."

"His secrets won't get me killed, Jim. He's not a dangerous person."

"Are you sure about that?"

She swallowed the lump in her throat. Mia glanced again at the thick file on the desk. The more and more they argued, the more she wanted to read it. Jim acted as though Mason's mistakes could end the world, and she wished she knew who to trust and what to do.

Just trust in yourself. Do what you think is right.

That's all she could do in a situation like this.

"I don't know the exact dates Mason and Alan plan to visit their mom, but I'll let you know. Or Mason will. I want you to let him go."

Jim ran his fingers through his short brownish-blond hair. While she took after their mother in the dark hair and eyes department, Jim resembled their father with his sandy-brown hair and lofty height. "Fine, but Mason will have to wear an ankle monitor. He's under curfew and I won't rescind it. Under normal circumstances, he can go anywhere he wants within the state without a tracker. He just has to inform me. With the curfew, well, I have to make sure he returns to his mother's residence by eight o'clock every night while he's there, which can only be for three nights."

"He explained the 'three-night out/four-night in at his legal residence' rule to me."

"Good. I'll still call him every night since I can't personally monitor the tracking device. A communications center will handle it. I will, however, get a warrant for his arrest if he tampers with the device or tries to flee the state. I'll call the com center every day for an update."

Mia sighed in exasperation. "Why would he flee? His home and family are in Colorado."

"Who knows why criminals do the things they do?"

She stepped back before she smacked him. "Will you at least push the curfew back to ten o'clock? It's really hard to manage dates with that early schedule."

"That's the point, Mia."

"We need more time together if you want me to break up with him. I can't find out all these supposedly horrible secrets over the phone."

"You have a point too." His mouth twisted on one side. "All right. Ten o'clock it is. I'll fill out the paperwork today, but it won't go into effect until tomorrow. I'll give Harding a copy."

Relief swelled in her chest. "Thank you, but I wish you'd give him a chance. All you know about him is from some biased file, and Mason doesn't know the real you, either." She glanced around the cramped office. "You're more than a state official, Jim. You're the boy who always kicked my ass at video games when we were kids. You still kick it when I drop by your place to play on the old game system. You're the supportive brother who stood at my side through my messy divorce. You never once told me 'I told you so' even though you tried to warn me over the years that Evan couldn't be trusted."

"I've warned you again, but you're too damned stubborn to listen to reason."

"Mason is not like Evan. I want you guys to make peace."

"That will never happen." Tears filled his eyes. Jim braced his hands on the windowsill as though he needed help to keep upright. "Now, if that's all, I have more work to do than I'd planned today. I better get started."

A sob clogged her throat. His cold, gruff voice cut like a shard of ice through her heart. "Okay. I understand." She reached out to hug him goodbye but paused midway. He'd probably take it as a sign of weakness or think she wouldn't cut him from her life as she promised.

Mia tightened her purse strap over her shoulder and headed out the door.

Chapter Nine

"Are you sure you don't want me to clean the bathtub?" Mason licked the tip of her pinky toe on Saturday afternoon. "I don't mind."

Mia drew back her leg. "Damn it, no. Why are you obsessed about that?"

"There's an oil stain around the drain. It's my fault." He crossed his arms as Mia sat up in bed and wrapped the sheet around her naked body. Her breasts plumped up and he longed to bury his face in her cleavage. *Again.* She'd picked him up from Alan's apartment hours ago, and they barely left the bedroom since lunch. "It's okay, darlin'. I'm a neat-freak anyhow. You gotta be in prison or the bacon freaks out. I clean the tub at Alan's place every week or so."

"Bacon? Oh, you mean pigs, like in guards." Blush lit her cheeks. "Some of the lingo you picked up in there is funny."

"Yeah, I don't mean to say it. It just slips out."

"I don't mind." She shifted sideways to lie at the foot of the bed. "We have more time together now, and I don't want you to waste it by cleaning the tub. As I said before, it's okay if you come over to shower after work. In fact, I want you to. An oil ring is a small price to pay if I can see you more often. I just want to be with you, whether or not we make love."

He kissed her hand. After the new paperwork went

into effect, Mia had insisted he come over after work on Thursday to shower while she closed the store. They'd slept together, ordered Mexican takeout, and she took him home a few minutes before the clock struck ten. They'd met up after his anger-management meeting the following night, and she surprised him with a romp in the shower and a slow-cooker dinner.

"All right, Mia. You win. The important thing is we can see each other throughout the week, so I'll shut up."

She twiddled her thumbs. "We could have before Jim pushed the curfew back, you know. You could've come to my place, showered, and waited for me to close the store, just as you did on Thursday. We would've had two hours together."

"No, half an hour to cook and eat, one hour to screw, and another half hour or so in your car." Mason clarified things a little too sharply as she rolled her eyes. "You're more than a quick lay, Mia. I need to spend *hours* touching you. I want to talk and get to know you better, and not keep a constant eye on the clock. Besides, if we'd done that, I would've complained about the oil stain a lot sooner."

Her eyebrows knitted in a line. "That's the main reason you never wanted to see me, isn't it? Not because of the time restraint, but you were worried about the damn bathtub?"

"I should've told you that, but I'll clean up here from now on since you don't mind."

"I told you I didn't mind a while ago."

"Yeah, but now I believe you." He feathered his fingertips over her scrunched-up nose. "I'm still pissed you gave your brother an ultimatum. I'm relieved about the curfew, don't get me wrong, but I don't need you to fight my battles for me."

"*Our* battles. His rules affected both of us."

"It's a man thing, darlin', so don't rip my balls off again. Try to understand that."

But she didn't. He could tell by her narrowed eyes and the self-righteous indignation on her upturned face. Borden had left his updated parole restrictions with Benji on Thursday while Mason took his lunch hour, but the PO didn't stick around for an inspection or to hassle Mason once he'd returned. Mason wanted to talk with Borden, though, and let him know he would never ask Mia to choose between them.

Mia lay flat on her back, away from his touch, but she kept his gaze. "Weekend-only dates were fine, but not fair. The more I stop by your apartment to visit, the more likely Jim will find out and possibly ban me from there. Besides, I'd wear out my welcome with Alan real quick if I stopped by every weeknight. I can't sleep over anyway, not with Danny there." She trailed her fingers over the floral design on the blanket. "Something had to give."

"True, but why did you threaten to cut him from your life? That's a huge threat."

"I don't think it will come to that."

His stomach churned. Who knew what Borden told her the other day, or how desperate and angry the man would become? Mason waited for Mia to question him or to tell him to catch the first train out of her life, but she acted as though nothing had changed between them. He needed to know what she knew, no matter how much it damned him, so he could relax and not worry anymore.

"Is there anything you want to ask me?" His heart drummed like a death metal concert in his ears. "Anything at all?"

Her chest shuddered and her pupils dilated. She didn't blink, not once in the several seconds they continued to stare at one another. Her face flushed crimson and she glanced away.

Shit. Borden did tell her something. He'd seen that nervous look before, but usually on the inmates he had the displeasure of disciplining.

"Uh, yeah. What do you want for dinner? We could order a pizza or go somewhere?"

Poor save, Mia.

He nodded, too gutless to confront her. "Pizza's good."

"Great." She teased her fingers over his thigh, and her gaze dropped to his semi-hard penis. Desire darkened her irises. "Would you rub my back?"

"Sure."

She flipped to her stomach and the sheet twisted to expose part of her apple bottom. He leaned up on his knees and rubbed down the smooth curve of her back, her skin soft under the roughness of his palms. Her muscles were tight like corded rope, so he stroked her gently to work out the tension.

"I won't break, Mason. Rub harder."

His hand automatically lifted to slap her ass, but he stopped it. Her words hinted he didn't please her. Her bossy tone challenged him. He could rub her so damn hard she'd need lotion to soothe the burn, but he didn't want to go all alpha on her. Borden could've told her all kinds of shit, so she needed a strong dose of his tender side, not the asshole beneath the surface.

Mason rubbed just hard enough to draw a moan from her throat. Her muscles started to loosen, and she turned her head to face him, her eyes closed. A smile curved her supple lips.

"I trust you." Her soft words reached his ears on a gasp. "Oh, yes. Harder."

She trusts me? He knew she did, but why tell him now? Did she need to convince *herself* of it? *Take her word, man. Don't freak out on her. You'll just scare her.* Mason slid his hands under the sheet and grasped her firm backside.

She squirmed, a giggle escaped her mouth, and she clutched the blanket into a makeshift pillow.

A strange noise echoed outside the bedroom and drew his gaze to the door.

"Is that the buzzer? Are you expecting someone?"

"No, I don't think so. I—oh, crap." Her muscles coiled again. Mia scooted out from under him and grabbed her underwear off the floor. "I'm a total ditz. My friends and I usually meet for drinks on the last Saturday of the month. It's our girls' night out, but I completely forgot this time."

He glanced at his watch. "It's only six o'clock."

"Yeah, it's early. Shea told me a few days ago Belle's gig starts at seven tonight, but I didn't think to tell her I'd made other plans. It's at a coffeehouse a few blocks away, so we planned to have drinks here first." She jerked on a pair of pajama shorts and a blue top, and scurried around the room to grab his clothes. "I can't believe I screwed up like this."

"My bad, but you like my brand of distraction." Mason waggled his eyebrows at her.

She licked her lips, her gaze dropping to his chest.

"I'll tell them I can't make it." His black T-shirt and denim shorts slipped from her grasp as she turned to leave the room.

"Wait." Mason jumped off the bed and grabbed her hand. "I didn't say that for you to stay. I want you to go. You shouldn't change your plans for me."

"I'd rather spend the next few hours with you." Mia twirled her fingers in his chest hair and ground her lower stomach against his erection. "C'mon, play with me."

Her sassy grin and the bat of her eyelids twisted his body into knots. Desperate to jerk her closer and plow his tongue inside her mouth, Mason locked his hands behind his back.

One of them needed to think straight.

The landline phone rang in the living room, and she pulled back with a sigh. "Oh, all right. I'll go. Besides, they'd blow a fuse if they knew I blew them off for a guy. I did that a lot for Evan since he didn't like them."

"Well, I'm not Evan. I don't want you to give up your girlfriends for me."

Her eyelashes fluttered, and he bet he earned a dozen cookie points for that remark.

The buzzer echoed again. "Do you want to meet them or hide out in here?"

"I'm not shy, darlin', and I don't mind dressing for a meet and greet."

She kissed his cheek and hurried from the bedroom.

Mason rubbed his eyes, grateful for the interruption. Tension spun its fucking web between them and though he could screw her to relieve it, a little space might do them some good.

He dressed and opened the door. Unfamiliar voices rang through the loft.

"Mia, are you all right? What took so long?" A blonde, blue-eyed woman crossed the threshold first. She carried a brown paper bag in one arm and hugged Mia with the other.

"Everything's okay. I'll explain." Mia closed the steel door after her friends entered.

"Oh my God, it's true." A grin split the blonde woman's lips. "Wow."

Mason grinned as she and the other two strangers gaped at him, their eyes wide and mouths open. Mia blushed and waved him toward the living room.

"Mia finally got a new man." The tallest woman in the group whistled as he wrapped his arm around his lover's waist. Model-thin but curvy, the other woman's tanned skin highlighted the reddish streaks in her long dark hair. "It's about damn time."

"Is he Mason? The guy you almost put six feet under?" The petite brunette woman braced her leather guitar case on the floor and shifted her gaze between Mia and Mason.

His ego soared at her friends' comments. "So you've mentioned me? Good." Mason kissed Mia's forehead and introduced himself to the women.

"This is Chanel, Belle, and Shea." Mia pointed first at the model, then the musician, and the freckled-face blonde woman. "We lived in the same college dorm, but Belle and I were roommates. Just to warn you, Mason, the girls are crazy and should probably see a psychiatrist. Don't take anything they say seriously." She leveled her glare at the women as though to warn them to behave.

"Mia told us she met a guy, but I didn't believe her at first." Belle tilted her head to one side. "We've tried for months to hook her up with no luck."

Chanel blew on her manicured nails. "I believed her but thought she exaggerated all those muscles. I'm obviously mistaken."

Shea's gaze traveled down his body. "Do you have a brother?"

Mason couldn't hold back his laugh. Mia stiffened, and he tightened his arm around her. "It's nice to meet you, too, ladies." He flashed them a sexy smile, but reserved his scorchers for Mia and Mia only. "Belle, I'm a hundred percent real. Chanel, you can flick a coin off my abs. Sorry Shea, I do have a brother, but he's dating someone. Some people say he's as hot as I am, but they're delirious. I'm the better-looking one, especially with all my tattoos."

Mia gently elbowed Mason's ribs as her friends swooned like teenagers. "Cocky much?"

"Have you seen me? It's hard not to be."

She chuckled. "Your arrogance levels are through the roof. Bring it down."

He grinned, too cocky for his own good, but he hardly cared.

Mia turned back to her friends. "Sorry, I forgot about our plans tonight. I spent all day unloading boxes, so give me a few minutes to change clothes and we'll head out."

Chanel's eyebrow lifted. Sunlight streamed through the windows and glinted off her dangly earrings. "If unloading boxes is code for 'screaming in orgasm,' I want a job in your store."

Mason and her friends bellowed in laughter, Belle high-fived Chanel, and Mia blushed red. He didn't know why she tried to lie. The scent of sex covered them like perfume. Mia glared at him, and even though he tried to straighten his face and sober up, he failed miserably.

"Why don't you join us, Mason?" Shea offered once she calmed down. She placed the paper bag on the open kitchen counter that separated the kitchen from the living room. "Belle is an awesome musician, but she's going through an angst phase, so she's dressed all in black."

Everyone's attention now seemed to shift to the woman with the bobbed haircut. The girls laughed while Belle frowned and shoved Shea. Shea shoved back.

All we need is a pool of hot scented oil, a couple of string bikinis, and for Mia to join in. Mason smiled as Mia pinched her eyes shut as though annoyed. *Nah, just my girl. I'd slip and slide all over her luscious body and massage every drop of oil into her skin.*

Chanel separated the fighting women. "You really should come, Mason. Mia and I could use some help to keep these chicks off one another. They're friends, but damn, they have short tempers."

He glanced at Mia for approval. She nodded, and he smiled back at Chanel. "Sure, but I gotta leave before nine o'clock. Mornings are always a bitch for me." Since he would rather not spread his past around like dirty laundry, he'd asked Mia to keep his prison stint on a need-to-know basis. His mistakes shamed him, but he accepted and made peace with the past. He only hoped it stayed buried.

Mia pulled from his grasp. "I need to change or we'll be late. Girls, keep Mason company but don't drive him so crazy he leaves here screaming for his sanity."

Her friends dismissed her comment with a few eye rolls and huffs. Belle grabbed Mason's arm and dragged him to the sofa as Mia headed toward her bedroom. He sighed, a little uneasy with Mia gone.

Shea broke out the bottle of wine from the bag and grabbed a few glasses from an overhead cabinet in the kitchen.

He refused a glass, relieved he didn't crave a taste despite his nerves, and they sat in the living room to play a fucked-up version of a party game. A version where he couldn't pick *dare*, only *truth*, or be the player to ask a question or dare someone else.

The bedroom door opened behind him.

Mason peered over his shoulder as Mia hurried into the bathroom instead of rushing to his aid as the savior he needed. Most of her friends' questions revolved around his feelings for Mia, so he didn't have to lie, but a good handful dealt with his sex life *before* Mia. He learned right off the bat her friends would swoop down like avenging angels if he ever hurt his girlfriend. Mia returned as Chanel asked, "How many notches are in your bedpost?" and Mason jumped right off the sofa and rushed to his lady's side.

"Ready to go so soon?" Mia asked as she arched her eyebrow at him. Mischief danced in her eyes, and Mason bet she'd overheard the third-degree he suffered. As Belle guzzled the last of the red liquid from her wineglass, Mia fluffed her friend's hair. "If you're late or hammered, Miss Rock Goddess, the coffeehouse owner won't let you play tonight."

Belle stood and thrust the glass in Mia's hand. "We don't want that. C'mon, you hoochies. Let's go." She pulled Shea off the sofa, slapped her ass, and Chanel followed them up. The girls piled out the door.

Mason escorted Mia from the loft and waited on the small balcony of the stairwell as Mia locked up. Once the locking mechanism clicked into place, he tugged her into his arms. "Your friends are something."

"They're the best." Mia's smile beamed like a ray of sunshine as her friends' laughter bounced off the stairwell walls from down below. "We'd better go or they *will* come back up here and drag us out." She pulled from his embrace and led the way downstairs.

The next few hours passed in a whirl. Women hooted and hollered, incense filled the air, and the strong, rich taste of his Columbian-bean coffee kept Mason grounded as he listened to Belle sing. Though they could've stayed longer and watched another performer, Mason and Mia left the artsy coffeehouse after Belle's hour-long set for a little more playtime.

"What do you think of Belle's songs?" Mia wove her fingers through his as they walked down the sidewalk. "Cynical, right? Most of her stuff is sarcastic and man-bashing."

He whistled. "Oh, yeah. The part about blowtorching her ex's jewels and feeding them to her cat made my own jewels ache. I feel bad for the next poor sap she lines up as her boyfriend."

"Yeah, Belle has issues." Mia bit her bottom lip. "I'm worried about her. She broke up with her guy right before Christmas because he cheated on her, and then she slept with some man at a New Year's Eve party.

She won't tell anyone his name or anything about him, and she probably wishes she'd kept her mouth shut about the one-night stand. Now she's sworn off men altogether." She tightened her grip on his hand. "I've gone through the man-hating stage, too, but the girls helped me through it. Belle won't heal if she doesn't deal with her pain. She's just so angry."

"I hope you don't take this the wrong way, but I itch to track down Evan like the piece of shit he is and beat the living hell out of him."

She smiled up at him. "He's not worth it, Mason. We can tag team and raze his car in our dreams, okay? I don't want to lose you because of him. You're too important to me."

Her confession rushed through him like the perfect summer breeze but flamed his anger even hotter. He couldn't understand why her ex-husband mistreated her. Evan should've counted his lucky stars a sweet woman like Mia chose him.

If Mason razed the car for real, or bloodied Evan's face so bad the prick needed stitches or plastic surgery, no one would know to blame him. He'd learned in prison how to cover his tracks and how to shift the blame to someone else. Evan Eddison wouldn't stand a chance against him.

Mason swallowed hard to push his hatred for Mia's ex to the pit of his stomach. "I can't believe I was the only man there. At the coffeehouse, I mean. Did you notice the way some of those other women stared at me?" He shuddered. "God, if looks could kill."

"I'm sorry about that. Saturday is ladies' night at that particular place. I should've warned you." She tightened her grip on his hand. "Chanel and Shea sneered at those bitchy women for you. I think they see you as a new girlfriend."

"Oh, goodie. I'm one of the gals now."

She laughed. "That's a good thing. They gave Evan a chance, too, but he shot them down so many times. He insulted them behind their backs and called their fun antics immature." She glanced away. "They really seem to like you."

"You act like that's a bad thing. What's wrong?"

"Oh, nothing. Not really. It's just a little insecurity."

"Tell me."

Her lips moved as though she struggled to form her words. She tugged her hand free from his and swiped a lock of hair behind her ear. "Evan slept with one of my employees. We didn't hang out outside of work, but I liked her a lot. Chanel, Shea, and Belle are flirts, but their flirtation isn't real. Chanel loves her boyfriend, and Shea is backward-shy around guys she likes. You should see her around Chanel's older brother. The poor girl can barely string a sentence together. Belle, well, she's not ready for a new guy. I trust them and I trust you, but I'm worried—"

"Hold up." Mason wrapped his hand around her arm and pulled her to a stop. He tilted her chin up with his other hand and stared deep into her eyes. "I'm all about you, Mia. Your friends are beautiful and they seem like good people, but you're my girlfriend. I lose sleep at night because I can't stop thinking about you. When I do sleep, I dream about your sexy smile and long legs." He still sometimes dreamed the past few months had never happened, but Mia's dark eyes and silky hair would always filter through the nightmares and bring him back to reality. He kissed her forehead. "Don't worry about me and infidelity. I'll rent a blowtorch and burn off my own jewels before I sink that low. Okay?"

Her face flamed red, but the tension in her body seemed to fade as she hugged him.

"Thank you, Mason, that makes me feel better."

A peculiar feeling crawled up his spine. Mason pulled back from her and glanced over his shoulder. People laughed and window-shopped as cars passed at a slow but steady pace. He tugged Mia close to his side and they resumed their walk.

Mia filled out her dress in all the right places. The diagonal-striped fabric clung to her breasts, hugged her hips, and reached the tips of her knees at a sharp point. Her oh-so-proper cardigan sweater and low-heeled shoes downplayed the outfit, but his cock still hardened at the sight of her.

He stumbled over a crack in the sidewalk. His stomach clenched and heat flushed his skin. Fuck, he knew this feeling. Someone planned to attack him. Where or why, he didn't know, but he'd fought too many fights to not recognize the signs.

"Are you okay?"

Damn, he'd hoped she wouldn't notice his mood change. "I'm fine." He kept an eye on his surroundings as they stopped at a crosswalk with other pedestrians. Someone followed them, but he couldn't spot the culprit in the mass of people, buildings, cars, and flashing lights. Hues of blue, orange, and purple streaked the evening sky as the sun descended. Lampposts lit the urban neighborhood and outdoor lights from various stores pushed back the shadows.

They crossed the road and he pulled Mia down a side street instead of heading straight for another two blocks to reach her home.

"Where are we going, Mason? You know the way."

He wondered if his stalker also tracked him from Mia's loft to the coffeehouse. He didn't feel on edge earlier, but her friends had distracted him with countless questions.

Mason cast his gaze over his shoulder again as two men in leather jackets turned the corner. The dead-eyed men stared straight ahead and prowled like wolves on the hunt. Their shaved scalps gleamed red with sunburn, or maybe a wanted tan. Several yards separated Mason from the strangers as oblivious bystanders weaved between them.

Keep Mia safe. He drilled the mantra into his mind again and again.

Worry darkened her eyes. As he pulled her farther down the street, she glanced around and tightened the edges of her sweater over her chest. The air in her mouth left in choppy puffs. The blood in her veins surely raced a marathon. She squeezed his hand almost to the point of pain.

"Some guys are following us. I don't know who they are. Stay calm," Mason whispered in her ear. As Mia picked up her pace and kept a better stride beside him, he rolled his shoulders in an attempt to ease his tight muscles.

They turned another corner and headed farther away from the bustling downtown area. Mason paused at the mouth of a dead-end alley and looked up the street. Two cars drove by, music blared from an old sedan, and a homeless man shuffled around a corner and out of sight. The strangers stalked closer from about a block away. He dragged Mia down the alley and pressed her against a graffiti-covered brick wall at the far end. The barrier cut the alley in half and stood too high for them to climb over.

A two-story building stood on the left, and a three-story building with a broken fire escape towered on the right. Shadows cloaked the seedy alley. Onyx gang symbols covered the storefront walls and trash littered the ground.

He clasped Mia's cheek with his palm. "I don't know what's going on, but stay back. Don't talk to them. I'll handle this."

"Let's go to my loft. We'll be safe there."

"I won't let them know where you live." He hoped they didn't know already.

Mason pressed a fast kiss to her lips and hurried to a large rectangular trash container near the fire escape. The dented metal top of the old bin creaked as he pushed it up. The stench of rotting cardboard boxes, wet plastic bags, and maggot-covered food containers struck him in the face like a gale-force wind. He dug through the trash until he found an old lead pipe. He struck the weapon on the ground to check its strength, and the vibration of the metal against concrete shot up his arm.

"Mason, be careful."

Her concern warmed him. No one had ever cared whether he made it through a fight without a scratch. She cared for and respected the Mason she knew. The prison Mason—the hard, unforgiving bastard who demanded respect through fear, intimidation, and his fists—would probably scare Mia to her core.

The two men emerged from the street. A shit-eating grin spread across the taller man's face as he headed down the alley. The other man stayed back and blocked the exit, the nasty scar on his cheek stretching as he pulled his lips back in a snarl. The taller dickhead stopped at the midway point of the alley and cocked his head to the side as though he'd noticed Mason's weapon. His gaze slid past Mason's shoulder, and his broad grin showed a set of stained teeth.

The obvious leader of the two looked familiar, but Mason couldn't place him.

"What the fuck do you want?" Mason refused to cower. Vultures got their kicks when they discovered someone's weakness. Too bad Mason's stood behind him. He braced his feet apart, squared his shoulders, and held his ground. He wouldn't let them near Mia.

"You don't remember me, do ya?"

Mason frowned. *That face, that voice...* God, why couldn't he remember?

The stranger's grin twisted into a sneer. "I haven't forgotten your pretty face. The warden tossed me in solitary because of you and transferred me from that cushy level-three facility to the fuckin' state pen. I spent seven years there, my first three months in the damn hole, and none of that would've happened if not for you."

The neo-Nazi who'd attacked him? Mason rubbed the scar on his chest and collarbone. He never knew what happened to Franz Harper after his transfer, and he didn't care, not then or now. Besides, only an idiot would consider that level-three prison cushy.

Stay calm. You don't have your old crew to back

you up right now. Not that he needed help against two skinheads, but he knew better than to let his anger take control of him.

"Oh yeah, I remember you. I whupped your racist ass after you attacked me from behind like a coward. If I could do it as an eighteen-year-old kid, I'm sure I'll do it again." Mason spread his arms out wide. "Sorry, man, but I haven't thought about you since I got you transferred. I take your resentment for me as a compliment." He didn't have anything to do with the transfer, but he'd take credit for it if it pissed Harper off.

"Who's the babe?" Harper fisted his hands. "The courts locked me up for two counts of rape, but I've pleasured myself with more than just two whores."

He heard Mia gasp but couldn't let her distract him.

Keep it together, Harding. Don't fall for his trap.

"C'mon, ladies. What are you waiting for? You want another shot? Right, Harper? Let's go." Mason focused on Harper even as the shorter skinhead moved closer, his shoulders hunched as though he would launch into an attack at any second. "Is your boyfriend here to watch or help? For your sake, I hope he mans up to guard your pansy ass. You'll need all the help you can get."

"Wait, Elray. He's mine." Harper lifted his arm and Elray backed up a few steps.

Mason shrugged with fake nonchalance. "You're braver than I thought."

Harper roared and rushed him like an incensed rhino, but Mason leapt out of the way.

"Behind you!"

Mia screamed the warning just as Elray grabbed Mason in a headlock. The lead pipe flew from Mason's hands and air whooshed from his lungs. Sun-heated, smoke-covered leather engulfed him. His head swayed and throat burned. He clutched Elray's arms to pull them back, but the limbs held strong. Mia shouted, but her voice sounded far away.

Mason gnashed his teeth as he struggled for freedom. *Don't give up, damn it. You have to save her from these assholes.* Despite his silent decree, the strength in his bones and muscles ebbed away. His blood cooled. His ears buzzed and his starving lungs ached for air. As Elray squeezed his thick arms tighter, spots flashed before Mason's eyes.

Chapter Ten

Mia flattened herself against the wall. Faint moonlight streaked through the alley but barely penetrated the shadows. Harper stalked toward her, his sick gaze traveling up and down her body, and she clutched her purse in her hand to bash over his head if he got too close. Vomit churned in the pit of her stomach. She stared over Harper's shoulder as Elray squeezed his beefy arms around her boyfriend's throat.

"C'mon, Mason. Fight him!" Mia shouted as Mason's head lolled back.

Harper laughed.

She gritted her teeth. "Focus. You have to focus, baby."

His eyelids fluttered as though he might pass out, but Mason managed to stomp on Elray's foot and elbow his stomach. His attacker howled in pain and Mason pried free from his arms.

Harper licked his lips, probably unaware Elray lost his captive.

Mason's chest heaved as he gulped for air. He tackled Harper to the ground. The men grunted and cursed, rolled on the dirty pavement, and the self-proclaimed rapist screeched as Mason straddled him and pummeled his fists into Harper's face.

Mia slunk further down the wall to give them space.

Elray grabbed Mason in another headlock and pulled him back.

Harper shot to his feet and punched Mason in the stomach. He shouted obscenities, his eyes wild and demented.

Mason's discarded pipe lay near the trash bin, and Mia tripped in her rush to grab it. Concrete skinned her knees but the pain barely registered. The grimy weapon felt like it weighed a ton of bricks. The stench of garbage filled her nostrils. She kicked away her shoes, dropped her purse, and forced her body up on her weak legs to stand. She swung the pipe with only one thought in mind. *Save Mason.*

The hard metal struck Harper on the back. He shrieked. His face twisted into a horrible mask of rage.

Mia swung it again and struck his shoulder.

Harper stumbled sideways and hit the wall.

Elray shoved Mason away, snatched the pipe from her hands, and tossed it aside.

Mason pushed her from Elray's path. "Run. Now!" He lunged at the skinhead, but the scar-ridden stranger flipped Mason up and over his shoulder. Mason landed hard on his back, his legs twitched, and his mouth opened as though to scream. No sound emerged. He threw up his arms as Elray sat on his stomach and whaled his ham-like fists against Mason's chest.

Mia refused to run. She couldn't abandon Mason.

Harper groaned several feet away and clutched the spray-painted wall as he pulled himself to his feet.

Mason stretched his arm across the concrete to reach the pipe, but at least a foot separated him from the weapon.

Mia grabbed it and struck it over Elray's back.

"Take that, you asshole," she yelled as Elray screamed and lurched up.

Mason kicked his legs and thrust up his lower body to knock Elray off. He struggled to his feet, grabbed the pipe, and slammed it hard against Elray's chest. The skinhead hit the concrete, knocked out cold.

Harper bellowed and lunged forward with a knife in his hand.

Mason swung the pipe like an expert batter and hit his attacker's arm. The knife clanked on the ground, and a loud snap echoed in the tight confines of the alley. Mason swung again, hit the other man's chest, and Harper collapsed face-first in a pile of trash.

Other than the sound of Mason's hard panting, silence rang in her ears so loud Mia wanted to scream to break the stillness. The air in her lungs burned and the blood in her veins ran hot. Her chest ached from the ferocious pounding of her heart.

Mason dropped the weapon and braced his hands on his knees. His back shook as he hunched over and dragged tainted air into his mouth.

"Is anything broken?" Tears welled in her eyes. "Should we go to a hospital?"

Mason straightened his back slowly, or as much as he could as pain undoubtedly knifed through his body, and he rubbed his jaw with one hand and his chest with the other. Anger swam in the depths of his green irises. His right leg dragged a little as he hobbled toward her, and she wrapped her arms around him to help hold him up.

"I'm so sorry, Mia. I'm fine. Are you?" He kissed the crown of her head.

"No one touched me, thanks to you." She shivered.

"Who—who are they? Why?"

He hugged her close and moaned at the contact. She tried to pull back, but he tightened his grip around her shoulders. "I'll find out. Please don't hate me for this."

"Hate you? Mason, no. I couldn't—"

"Shhh." He pressed his lips to hers and silenced her. "This damn rollercoaster sucks."

Mason turned away before she could question him. As Harper rose to his knees, Mason snatched the pipe off the ground and kicked Harper in the stomach. The stranger shouted a curse that heated her cheeks.

Mia clenched her hands at her sides so as to not grab Mason and pull him from the alley. The nighttime air unnerved her, even with their attackers laid flat, and she needed the safety of her home to fully calm down.

Mason dropped to his knees beside Harper and pressed the pipe against his enemy's throat. The muscles in his arm bulged.

Harper panted hard and clutched his broken arm to his chest. Hatred flared like sparks of fire in his eyes as he stared up at Mason.

Mason patted him down and removed a gun, a few knives, a plastic zipper bag stuffed with cash, and a little baggie of rocks from inside his jacket.

Meth or coke, maybe? She couldn't be sure.

Mia had never used narcotics, not even recreational pot in college. She'd never even seen the hard stuff outside of photos and documentaries. She'd always considered LoDo a relatively safe neighborhood, but she never steered off the main streets alone at night.

He tossed the items out of Harper's reach. "Why did you attack me?" Mason dug the barrel of the pipe against the thug's windpipe as Harper tried to spit on him. The nasty saliva splattered up and back down to hit Harper's bruised cheek. "Answer me, or I'll break your other arm."

Harper's Adam's apple bobbed as he tried to swallow. Mason hauled back his fist and punched the man in the stomach. Harper coughed and lurched up, but Mason used the pipe as a billy club and slammed his former assailant's torso back down.

She jumped in shock. Though she expected violence, Mason's use of force almost froze the blood in her veins.

"I'll enjoy breaking your bones, Harper." Mason backhanded him across the face. "If you don't want that to happen, answer me."

"I-I hate you." The skinhead slurred his speech. "You'd better kill me or I'll come after you again, Harding. I got lots of men."

How many is a lot? Mia wanted to ask, but she'd rather no one focus on her. Her gaze darted to Elray and relief swamped her. Though he still appeared down for the count, his chest rose up and down in a steady rhythm as he breathed. She didn't want anyone to die. She especially didn't want Mason back in prison just for protecting himself and her.

"No one makes a fool of me and lives, especially fucking teenagers." Harper's snarled words drew her attention back to him. "You're just a punk. I bet you would've been a lousy lay."

The scowl on Mason's face knocked her back a step. "Who do you work for?"

"Someone very powerful. He'll be pissed when he finds out what happened to us."

"Did he authorize this hit?"

"No. It's all on me."

Mason struck Harper in the face and leaned back on his haunches. His eyes hardened like emeralds. "Give me detailed information or you'll leave this alley with broken feet."

Although she understood why Mason interrogated him, the sight of it heaved chunks in her stomach. *Did he develop this cruel side as a moody teenager or afterward while locked up?* She suspected the latter. Someone so cold probably wouldn't have fallen for his mother's fake bribe to attend his own birthday party.

"How many of your cronies are here?" Mason growled the words in a low tone.

Harper sputtered as though Mason pressed the lead harder against his windpipe. "J-just me and Elray." He stuttered and gasped for air once Mason pulled back. "I di-didn't even know they let you out of p-prison until I saw you come out of that coffeehouse."

"Who do you work for?" Mason clutched Harper's broken arm and squeezed.

The skinhead shouted in agony. He tried to push Mason away with his free hand.

Mason grabbed that arm and slammed it against the concrete. "Answer or I'll snap your other arm." He raised the pipe for effect or to follow through with the threat.

Harper obeyed. "Scor-Scorpion."

"No fucking way." Shock clouded his features. Mason pressed the pipe back against the other man's throat. "Don't lie to me."

Harper sputtered and struggled to shake his head. "I-I'm not. Look at my arm."

147

Mason dropped the pipe, clutched Harper by the collar of his jacket, and slammed his head on the ground.

A strangled gasp lodged in Mia's throat.

Harper lay limp as Mason jerked the jacket from his body, pulled up his shirtsleeves, and checked each biceps.

She glimpsed a circle design of some kind on the left arm before Mason thrust the sleeve back down.

"Goddamn it." Mason pushed to his feet and stomped toward the other skinhead. Fury pulsated from him in waves, hotter than when he'd fought their attackers. He pressed his fingers to Elray's neck as though to check for a pulse and inspected him as he did Harper.

"What do you see?" Mia clutched her arms over her chest in an effort to fight off a chill. *Don't break down or cry in front of him. Be tough.* Her throat tightened and she swallowed hard to steady her voice. "Who's the Scorpion?"

What's Sondokes and Onyx? The question burned on her tongue. She promised Jim she would nag Mason until he confessed his every sin, but the right opportunity never came up.

That's bull and you know it, girl. You're avoiding the subject like a chicken.

She should've spoken her mind tonight. Mason had opened the door for a long, necessary conversation, but she brought up dinner, instead, which they skipped to see Belle's performance. Uneasiness had settled between them until her friends arrived.

"There's nothing on their arms. I've never heard of the Scorpion." Mason stood, fine lines creased the corners of his eyes, and he kicked at Elray's unconscious body.

Her heart dropped to her feet. He'd never lied to her before. She would rather watch him torture a rapist for information, no matter how much it scared her, than listen to his lies.

"Mia, are you sure you're all right? You hit two neo-Nazis with a lead pipe. It's okay if you're frightened." Mason held his hands up and moved closer to her. He hobbled, but not as much as before. "Don't take offense, but I didn't know you had it in you."

She backed up as he drew closer to her. Though not afraid of him, she would rather he not hold her or touch her as he spat lies through his teeth.

Mason stalled a few feet away. Hurt and shame narrowed his eyes. The air around him seemed to sizzle with his volatile emotions, and he fisted his hands until his knuckles whitened beneath the grime. A long sigh hissed through his teeth. He grabbed an old rag from the ground and wiped down the pipe, Harper's weapons, jacket, and everything else they'd touched.

Smart move to clean off our prints.

"We gotta go, darlin'. They don't have reinforcements—they'd be here by now if so—but we don't want a patrol car to drive by or some random person to see us and call for help."

"Right. 'Bigger the posse, harder the beatdown, and coppers don't mind their own business.' " She ignored his frown as she uttered lingo from the action movie they'd watched on their first date. "What time is it? We don't have long to get you back to Westminster."

He glanced at his watch. "Near nine o'clock. Mia,

I—"

"Don't." She grabbed her purse and leaned against the brick wall to slide her feet back into her shoes. "I'm not mad at you for this. How could I be? Thanks to your street skills, you saved us both, but I don't appreciate your lies."

"I'm not lying."

"Maybe you have good reasons, maybe you don't, but I don't care. Lies are lies."

She stomped from the alley, and Mason followed her. The moon and city streetlights lit the way. Her adrenaline faded, and the cold weight of fear settled in her chest. The temperature had dropped a few degrees, and Mia huddled deeper inside her favorite knit sweater. They reached the bustling downtown shopping area, and bystanders parted like the Red Sea.

Their reflections in a storefront window caught her attention. Neither asshole had touched her, but her rumpled clothes needed a wash and her hair hung wild around her head. She forced her gaze to Mason.

His bottom lip was swollen, a lump almost doubled the size of his left cheek, and scrapes marred his arms and legs. His hair stuck up at odd angles. Bruises likely covered his body beneath his dirty clothes. The limp barely dogged his step, but he probably tried to hide it.

Mason grabbed her hand and pulled her to a stop about a block from her store. She nearly tripped, but he wrapped his arms around her waist and steadied her.

People walked around them.

Mia tilted up her chin and almost dared him to lie some more.

Mason tightened his grip on her waist. "The Scorpion is a dangerous criminal involved with drugs.

Several of my fellow inmates worked for him and spoke about him in hushed whispers. If Harper and Elray are on his payroll, I'm in trouble. The less you know, the better."

"What kind of tattoo was on Harper's arm? One like yours?"

"No, nothing. I don't know why he said to look—"

"I'm not an idiot, Mason. You have a beautiful circle tattoo with two snakes in the middle of it on the back of your neck. Someone spray painted similar O and X graffiti on the alley walls. If I go back there and look at Harper's and Elray's arms, I'm sure I'll find a tattoo like yours." She should've checked before she stormed out the alley. "It's a gang symbol, isn't it?"

He stepped back from her, his arms at his sides. "It's not what you think."

"Then tell me. What's Sondokes? What the hell is Onyx?"

"Where did you hear those names?" He pinched his forehead with his fingers. "That's what Borden told you. I fucking knew it."

She rubbed her hands over her cheeks. "He just told me the names, nothing else. Jim also gave me your state file, but I refused to read it. I want to hear the truth from you. All of it."

"Are those the only names you know? Sondokes and Onyx?" He ran his hands through his hair as she nodded. "Good, that's not too bad." He grabbed her arm and they continued along the sidewalk.

She clenched her fists to stop herself from hitting him. Mason wouldn't look at her, and he walked so fast she had to lightly jog to keep up.

They reached her store and he stared at her car

parked by the curb. "Harper doesn't know where you live or anything about you. That means you're safe for now, but he'll probably search this area to find us. Stay cautious, okay? Drive your car from now on. Don't walk anywhere."

"Why are you avoiding my questions? You can tell me anything."

"Not this. If you trust me, don't ask those kinds of questions." He tightened his fingers around her forearm as she tried to jerk free from his grip. "Listen to me, damn it. You mean a lot to me, but I can't tell you this. At least not right now. That's nothing against you. It's all on me. I just need time to take care of this problem. Okay? I'm fucking stressed, in a shitload of pain, and I don't need you to hound my ass." He dropped his hand from her arm and scowled as though he just noticed the dirt and blood on his knuckles. "I'd like to go upstairs to clean up before you take me home. I don't want Alan to know what happened."

Mia dug through her purse with shaky hands, so angry she didn't trust herself to speak.

He took the keys from her before the little pieces of metal slipped between her fingers, and he hugged her despite the grime on his skin and clothes.

Tears clogged her throat. Her mind screamed at her to push away from him, but the strength in his arms enveloped her and stole her will. His heartbeat soothed hers, and she no longer cared about his lies or if filth caked him.

At least not at the moment.

"I never meant for this to happen, Mia. I will fix this."

"I know, but at what cost?" She pried her face from

his chest to stare up at him. "You're nothing if not determined, but I'm scared and confused. You have answers to my questions, but I won't *hound you for them* as you so eloquently stated. I just thought we got past this. I thought you knew I would never insult or condemn you for whatever it is you did."

"And I thought you knew not to push me too fucking hard." His deep voice sent shivers of unease down her spine. "I have to keep certain parts of my past to myself."

"Whatever." Mia finally pushed against his chest for freedom and stomped to the stairwell door. She waited for him to unlock it and then led the way upstairs.

As he showered, she headed downstairs through the doorway in the dining room, grabbed a T-shirt and a pair of shorts from the sparse collection of menswear she sold, and left the clothes on the bathroom sink as he toweled off. She also gave him a bottle of aspirin and her best liquid foundation to cover his bruises.

They arrived at his apartment a few minutes ahead of schedule but barely spoke on the ride there.

Her brother called Mason every night at ten o'clock on the dot to verify his return home, and he continued to call at various times throughout the night to make sure Mason stayed home. Jim's supervisor obviously didn't approve of an ankle monitor to track Mason's movements, so Jim relied on his cell phone to track him. If they went to Carbondale to visit Mason's mother, the parole supervisor would then have to authorize a temporary monitor.

She would never forgive her pigheaded brother for these restrictions.

153

"Call me when you get home. I need to know you arrived safe." Mason braced his hands on his knees. "Promise me."

"I will."

He reached over and kissed her. His lips feathered across hers in simple yearning, not demand or lusty exploration.

Her anger melted away. *Damn him.* Mason kept her on her toes, knocked her off guard, and hauled her back to her feet to knock her over again. He said he wouldn't play her like a yo-yo, but damned if he didn't.

Maybe this is what he meant by a rollercoaster? We're always up and down.

Mia drove back home, called Mason as promised, and relaxed under the hot shower spray for over an hour. Tempted to power up her laptop and look for Onyx reports online as Jim wanted, she decided she would rather hear the truth from Mason and not read some report colored by conjecture or a so-called expert's opinion. She indulged in the wine her friends had left behind and reclined on the sofa as she called him back. Alan picked up the phone this time, they exchanged pleasantries, and she heard him through the line as he banged on a door and told his brother to answer the phone. After Mason complied, a click echoed and she assumed Alan hung up.

"You persist like a piranha, Mia. You snap and bite until you draw blood."

She scoffed but didn't plan to ask him about Sondokes or Onyx. In fact, she wouldn't ask again until Mason came to *her* with the confession and begged her forgiveness.

For now, she needed to know what the hell

happened tonight. "Those guys attacked you for something that happened years ago. That's crazy, Mason." Her insides twitched like jittery little birds. "What are we going to do?"

"They had reason. At least Franz Harper did. He blamed me for his transfer."

"Do you think Trent and Pedro sent them?"

"Nah, Trent hates skinheads and Pedro's Latino. Harper didn't know I was out until he saw me leave the coffeehouse, or so he said." She heard a squeaky noise over the phone line and assumed Mason changed position on his bed. He always took their personal calls in his room. "Harper claims to run with a huge crew. He wants my balls for a trophy, but he might go after you or Alan if he can't get to me. I won't let that happen." Mason muttered a low curse under his breath. "I need help. The Scorpion has a lot of men under his thumb, assholes bigger than Harper. I don't have any connections on the outside, but I do on the in. I have a friend who could look into this."

Mia closed her eyes. She was desperate to mention the tattoo on Harper's arm or that Mason sported a tattoo similar to the graffiti on the alley walls, but he would just lie to her again. As Jim claimed, Mason hadn't told her everything about his time in lockup, and she almost wished she would never find out. The thought of his *connections* twisted her stomach into a pretzel, but he *did* need help. They couldn't turn to her brother. As Mason suspected, Jim would likely throw the proverbial book at him rather than help him stay out of trouble as his job demanded.

"What can this friend do? Call Harper and say, 'Mason's an old pal of mine. Leave him alone or else.' " Mia toughened her voice to gravel. The menacing tone reminded her of a cranky old man and she coughed to clear her throat. "C'mon. That's ridiculous."

He laughed, but the deep timbre lacked joy. "Yeah, well, that sounds about right, but he'll speak to whoever Harper answers to. Not to Harper himself."

"The Scorpion?"

"No, someone under the Scorpion but above Harper."

"That's so confusing."

"You shouldn't know anything anyway."

"Don't start that crap with me, Mason. I didn't ask two strangers to ruin our evening. I don't want you to contact anyone in prison for any reason, but I know you gotta do what you gotta do." She slammed her fist against a pillow. "You're keeping secrets and lying to me. I'm more pissed than you know, but fine, I'll deal with it. Even if you did tell me everything, you know better than I do the kind of people we're up against. I'm involved in this whether you like it or not, so you better suck it up." He growled but she ignored him. "I trust you to take care of this, but I know you don't trust me if you keep the facts from me."

"I *do* trust you." A strange *whoosh* traveled through the line as though Mason blew air through his teeth. "The lifer I told you about, Oskar Udell, told me to contact him if anything bad happened to me on the outside. The State doesn't allow former inmates to visit current ones, but I can still call him."

She rubbed her temples. "Aren't phone calls monitored? Do you know Oskar's extension? Does he even have one?"

"He has a cell phone. Cells are illegal on the inside, but that means squat. He's one of the top dogs in the inmate community, remember? The guards suspect he has one, a few of the guards even know it for sure, but they wouldn't confiscate it even if Oskar flashed it in front of their faces."

Mia should've realized she would have to throw her morals out the window to date a man with so much baggage. She cared for him too much to let someone hurt him, especially for a useless reason like revenge a decade after the fact, so she would lie and back him up if needed.

Not a stranger to illegal activities, she'd poured sugar into the gas tank of Evan's beloved sports car and kicked his three-thousand dollar camera around like a soccer ball after they broke up. During their divorce hearing, Evan couldn't prove she damaged his property, and the thrill that she actually got away with it had whipped through her like a high—or at least what she imagined a high felt like.

She one-handedly poured herself another glass of wine. "I'd hate it if someone *did* take away Oskar's cell and found your brother's number in it. You need a prepaid phone, so no one could trace the call, but you'll have to ditch the phone when you're done with it."

"Good idea. I'll stop by a store tomorrow and pick one up. I'm sorry about this, Mia."

"I know, but it's not your fault."

Her brother would call her a fool. Maybe she was, but she wanted to give Mason the benefit of the doubt. For all she knew, Sondokes and Onyx could be the names of some evil people Mason knew in his cellblock, and not something gang-related.

Perhaps she was blowing up this skinhead problem or connecting dots that didn't exist?

Yeah, sure. Because I'm so prone to panicking and making up elaborate stories.

She fisted her hand and cursed. "What did Alan say about your bruises? Did you get a bag of frozen peas? It'll help reduce the swelling."

"Alan didn't notice. Danny was running around the apartment wet and naked when I got home, and Alan chased after him. I think Al came by my bedroom door the first time you called, but he left. Probably realized I was on the phone. Anyway, I found a cold compress in the freezer for my face. Sorry Mom, we're out of peas."

She huffed as he made light of her concern. Mason's protective big brother would definitely hit the roof when he saw those fight marks, as would *her* protective big bro. "What will you tell Jim? You have a stupid weekly meeting on Monday, and he'll notice your bruises."

"I'll just say Alan and I got into a fight because my brother wants me to dump you."

"That won't work. I already told Jim that Alan likes me."

"All right, fine. I'll say Al changed his mind because he's worried about my parole, which is true anyhow. I don't think your brother will be a problem."

"Not a bad plan, though I'm grateful Alan *does* want me to stick around."

"Me too." He yawned. "I won't call you with the new cell phone, and I won't stop by your place until I settle this thing, just in case someone decides to follow me. It's bad enough I could lead the skinheads back here if they spot me in town or on a bus, and I didn't shake the tail. I have to stay vigilant." A short bark of laughter escaped his mouth. "After I talk to Oskar, this whole situation probably won't seem like a big deal anymore."

Mia rolled her eyes. *Not a big deal?* The lifer or anyone else who helped Mason deal with the skinheads might demand he do something in return for them.

Why can't Mason escape his past? He doesn't deserve this.

"Call me tomorrow from Alan's phone. Okay, Mason? I want to know what this buddy of yours says. You owe me that much."

"That's fine, but don't worry. I'll take care of everything."

She glanced at the clock across the room. "I'm sorry, but I'm exhausted. I need to hit the sack. I'll talk to you tomorrow." Mia hung up the phone before he could say goodbye, and she replayed the conversation in her mind as she finished her glass of wine.

Mason had most likely joined a prison gang. If she nagged him too much for the truth, he would probably leave her high and dry. Though, after what had just happened, that might not be a bad idea. In all honesty, she should probably break up with him and wash her hands of this whole situation before it was too late.

Shame washed through her.

Despite everything, she didn't want them to go their separate ways, but she *would* leave him if he didn't confide in her soon. She'd give him time to get his head straight and work through the Harper and Elray problem the best he could, but she wouldn't wait forever.

Mia curled up on the sofa, almost afraid to go to

sleep. Anything could happen in the following days and add to this nightmare. With few allies and lots of questions, she needed to bide her time and wait it out, but she couldn't stop thinking about the future.

And whether she and Mason would survive it.

Chapter Eleven

"Okay, Mase. It took a lot of phone calls, but I found out some interesting shit," Oskar Udell said as soon as Mason answered his cell phone. "Bad news first: Franz Harper and Virgil Elray *do* work for the Scorpion. Harper met a boss in the state pen and joined up with another set after the State released him. His loyalties lie with Dowitcha, the Fort Collins and Loveland set, but he's first and foremost a Scorpion drug dealer."

Mason braced his back against the wall and slid down to his ass. His phone had rung a few blocks from Union Station, and he hurried down a back alley to answer it. His gaze shifted back and forth from the mouth of the alley to the rear exit. Someone had parked a gorgeous black convertible at the far end, and he would love to look under the hood. A large trash receptacle rested against a graffiti-free wall, and a steel door likely led to the sports bar he'd passed on the street. A few beer bottles and plastic cups littered the concrete pavement, but the alley didn't compare to most he'd seen.

He'd called Udell for help on Sunday afternoon and kept a close eye on his surroundings for the last four days. Mia's foundation concealed the bruises on his face and arms, but the makeup washed away as he sweated at work. His leg still ached, but he no longer limped. Borden believed the lie about Mason's fight with Alan and scheduled mandatory therapist visits on Wednesday in addition to the Friday ones. Mason just hoped the PO didn't call Alan to verify.

He rubbed his stiff neck. "I could really use some good news, sir."

"Lucky for you, kid, I got it." The lifer whistled as though pleased with himself. "I spoke to Iversen, the Fort Collins captain, and informed him a few members of his set attacked my former employee. Iversen didn't give a damn until I told him the Scorpion himself authorized your release from Onyx and wished you his best. I then told him Franz Harper sold drugs to someone in LoDo."

Mason smiled. "You've always said a drug dealer from one turf can't sell or peddle on another captain's turf without permission, and I doubt Harper had it. I bet that got Iversen's attention."

"Yep. Iversen promised to investigate the matter and that Harper and all of Harper's friends will leave you and yours alone. I'm sure Iversen will punish him and Elray for the business deal they did. He might even kill 'em over it. That stupid shit could start a turf war."

True. Even though the Scorpion monitored and supplied various areas with the needed products, the turfs operated separately. "So it's done? That's all?"

"Pretty much. Don't go out of your way to thank me or anything." His former mentor huffed, but he didn't sound too irritated.

"No, no. Thank you. I mean that, but it just seems too easy." Mason leaned his head back to rest his eyes for a few seconds before he looked up and down the alley again. "Franz Harper hates my guts. He's angry, humiliated, and focused on revenge, probably even more so now. He won't leave me alone just because his captain ordered it."

"Think about it, Mase. Don't you remember the things you did for me even though you didn't want to? You obeyed. Plain and simple. You knew the consequences for defying a captain's orders and so does Harper. Otherwise, he wouldn't be a dealer. He'll listen, or he'll be in a body cast for six months or in the ground for eternity." Oskar tsked. "You worry too much."

Mason tunneled his hand through his spiky hair. "Shit, you're right. I'm just paranoid. I don't want this racist prick to screw up my parole."

"Or mess with your girl, huh?"

His blood ran cold. "How do you know about her?"

"Through the grapevine. Harper vowed to have his way with a sexy brunette bimbo before he killed her. I heard she beat him up pretty bad."

"Yeah, she's a tough one." A headache pounded in his temples. "If Harper comes near her, I will kill him."

"I wouldn't recommend it. You're a civilian, and that will give Iversen legit reason to come after *you*. Let him handle Harper his way. Beat up the skinhead if you gotta, but don't cross the line. I can't pull any strings if you do."

Udell was right. The old man understood the drug business better than anyone else Mason knew, even though Udell had spent the majority of his life behind bars. He rose through the prison ranks quickly, and as far as Mason knew, the mysterious Scorpion preferred Oskar Udell to the other prison captains under his command, even though the state pen boasted higher profits and a larger number of gang members.

"What do I owe you for this? Information and pull like yours—"

"Stop right there."

Mason obeyed the abrupt order. He could easily imagine the shit-eating grin likely curling on the robust, gray-haired inmate's face as easy silence spread between them. Udell had taken him under his wing when Mason needed help the most, and though Mason swore loyalty to the captain of Sondokes, an Onyx prison set, he still thought of the captain as his friend.

"You don't owe me a thing, Mason. I promised you an out and you got it, but I'll back your re-entry if you want it. It'll be with Thorn, the captain of Capularia."

His mouth slackened. "Wow. I'm shocked. Thank you, sir, but I don't want a re-entry."

"You kept my weak-ass nephew out of trouble more times than I can count. You're the nephew I wish I could call my blood, you know that. So, yeah, just forget this damn Franz Harper situation ever happened and get back to your life. Just do me one favor, hmmm?"

"Sure."

"If you have kids, name the first boy after your good ol' Uncle Oskar. Oskar Harding, that has a good ring to it."

Mason burst out laughing. "I'll try. Who knows what the mother of my kid will want."

Oskar chuckled. "It's good to hear from you, even under the circumstances."

"Likewise. Thanks." Mason flipped the cell phone shut to end the call. He'd memorized Udell's cell number before he left on parole but never intended to use it.

"Everything's fine." He spoke the words aloud to strengthen them, but dread still packed his stomach like lead. Trent and Pedro hadn't contacted him, but he doubted his two old friends would forget him. Unlike Udell, they didn't respect or care for him. They just wanted to use him as they did when he was a foolish teenager. Mason considered calling Udell back, but he refused to whine about his other problem. Udell had done more for him than he would for anyone else who left Sondokes and needed help. Mason had to handle this on his own.

He flipped the phone back open and punched a few buttons to open the Settings page. He'd struggled for half an hour to activate and install minutes on the damn thing after he bought it. He wanted to keep it, but he'd have to register it with the State if Borden found out he owned a cell phone, and Big Brother would track his calls. Mason removed the battery, twisted the device with his hands until it snapped in two, and dug through his backpack to find the phone charger. He tossed the items in the trash bin. He'd stuffed the backpack with clean clothes, soap, deodorant, a toothbrush, and other toiletries, and carried it with him to work since he didn't have a car to store his belongings in and never knew when he might need it.

Mason left the alley and headed down the street, his gaze watchful, but he didn't check over his shoulder quite as often as he did before Udell called him back. Only a fool threw all caution to the wind, and he stayed on guard for the sake of his sanity. People passed him, but no one sneered or gave him a wide berth. He'd instilled fear in his fellow prisoners when he used his fists to protect himself or others, or to get what he wanted, but he would rather not hurt or scare anyone in the civilized world—not that he considered the outside very civilized.

Two women smiled at him and fluffed their hair as they window-shopped. Mason paused at an intersection, and the heat of their gaze traveled down his body like sunbeams. Before he met Mia, he would definitely have chatted up the hot little numbers and taken them to the nearest motel, but now he couldn't imagine anyone but his girl in his arms.

While in lockup, he had never imagined he would enter into a serious relationship with a respectable woman. Hell, he never thought he would have more than flings once he finally got out. After a few weeks with Mia, he didn't know if he could ever return to meaningless sex.

Every fiber in his body demanded he see Mia. Just the thought of her coiled heat in his veins. They'd last talked on Sunday night, and he'd dreamed about her every night since. Before he would fall asleep, however, he would have to stroke the monster between his legs and climax with her name on his tongue. If not, he would toss and turn in bed for hours, unable to relax enough to sleep.

Mason crossed the street and turned right at the next intersection instead of heading straight for Union Station. The 86X regional bus would take him to Westminster, but he'd ask Mia for a ride or take the B-line bus to Alan's apartment later that night. Even after seven months, he still didn't think of the apartment as his home. Alan set too many damn rules, and sometimes Mason felt as though he walked on eggshells around Danny, but he'd always lied when his parole officer asked about that.

On the flipside, Mia welcomed him in her home without excessive rules and demands. She cursed, walked around naked, and threw popcorn at him during movies, and expected him to do the same. She only wanted one thing from him—to act himself.

God, he couldn't imagine being so comfortable and free with anyone else.

He imagined all the places on her body he wanted to kiss. He would start with her lips, eyelids, and temples before he trailed his tongue down the curve of her throat. He'd suckle her nipples into hard beads, leave teeth marks on her stomach, and tease the supple underside of her knees with his mouth. He'd nip at her thighs until she begged him to go higher.

Mason walked half a block past her store and reached the next intersection. With a laugh, he backtracked and glanced through the storefront windows. Mia folded a few dresses and placed them in a pink paper bag at the checkout counter, and handed the merchandise to a woman whose breasts he assumed cost a few thousand dollars. He held open the door, his gaze glued on Mia, as the buxom woman headed for the exit. The customer huffed as though in indignation that her breasts didn't draw his attention, and she left the store.

Mia hurried away from the counter and a smile stretched her lips. Though he expected her to jump into his arms, she stalled a few feet from him. Worry flashed in her eyes, and she clasped her hands behind her back.

He glanced down at his oil-stained clothes and cursed.

"I didn't think I'd see you for a while." She glanced around the store as though to make sure her customers had left before she locked the double doors.

Mason checked his watch—a few minutes before six o'clock—as she set the alarm and dimmed the lights.

Mia turned back to him. "What happened? Are you okay?"

"I'm fine, as are you. I just talked with Oskar, and he took care of everything. Franz Harper and his friends won't look for us."

"Just like that?" She snapped her fingers to illustrate the point. "What did Oskar do? Does he want anything in return? C'mon, Mason, I need a little more info."

Mason hesitated. She would probably look down on him if he told her he'd joined a gang—her rejection would crush him—so he glossed over the facts.

"Oskar talked to a man named Iversen and told him about the drug deal. Iversen's pissed Harper sold to someone in LoDo, and he promised Oskar that Harper won't come after me or mine as payment for my information. Harper has to obey this order, or he'll be in even more trouble with his boss."

"That seems too simple. Can this Iversen person be trusted?"

"I think so. Oskar trusts him, so that's good enough for me."

"So that's it? We're safe?" She dropped her gaze and wrapped her arms around her waist. "I've been so worried about you. About us. I don't see how everything is okay."

"Oskar has a lot of pull and friends in the right

places. He doesn't want anything from me because we're friends, too. I know you're unsure, but I promise you on my life you're safe."

Not that he put much value on *his* life. After all the shit he'd gone through and the things he'd done, his life could end up in the trash with a few wrong moves. He would lose all chance for redemption and land in the lowest pits of Hell if he dragged Mia down with him.

Mason pulled her close, hating the tears glistening in her eyes. "Push this whole damn thing from your mind, Mia. I came here as soon as Oskar told me the news. I didn't call you much over the past few days because I didn't know what to say."

"You're here now. That's what's important."

"Let's go upstairs. I need to be inside you, darlin'. I need to feel close to you."

"I'd love to, but I gotta close the store." She sniffled and pulled back to pat her flushed cheeks. "I'm sorry. I'm just a little emotional with all this going on."

"Don't be sorry."

"You're probably tired, so I hate to ask, but could you vacuum the floor while I count down the register and finish the closing paperwork?" A shy, small smile curved her lips. "I've managed the store alone since two o'clock because my second-shift cashier couldn't come in, and I'm a little behind. It's time I fire a few people."

"No problem, boss lady, but wouldn't you rather we shower first?"

She brushed her fingers over his stubbly chin. "It'll just take fifteen minutes. I don't like to leave the register and safe uncounted at night, security reasons and all."

He sighed. "All right, where are your cleaning

supplies?"

Mason followed her to the restroom area where she pulled a cordless vacuum from a small utility closet. It was lightweight with a thin frame, so he didn't see how this thing worked, but he kept his opinion to himself. He vacuumed the tile floor and found out other things he'd keep his mouth shut on. Mason knew zip about Mia's clientele and the way she operated her business, but the high prices on some of the merchandise shocked the hell out of him.

He stored the vacuum back in the closet just as Mia exited her office.

"Ready?" She leaned against the wall as she smoothed her hands down her slacks.

A growl rumbled in his throat. Her perfume surrounded him like a cloud. The soft floral scent teased his nostrils and clung to the back of his throat. Mason swallowed hard, desperate to taste her. He would take her right there on the floor in front of her security cameras if he thought she'd allow it.

He followed her to the back of the store, stepped over the red-velvet cord that blocked the stairs, and waited a few steps down from her as she pressed a code into the security panel. After they crossed the threshold into her loft and she reset the alarm, he grabbed her hand and dragged her to the bathroom. Mia's laughter died as he slammed the bathroom door closed and pushed her against it. He jerked off her blouse and dipped his face in the swell of her breasts.

Too long. Too fucking long.

He unbuttoned her slacks, his fingers a little stiff, but he managed to push them off her hips. The fabric pooled around her ankles.

"Mason, wait. Get in the shower." She fisted her hands in his T-shirt. Her chest heaved as she breathed. "I want to bathe you."

His cock sprang to life. He dropped his backpack and stripped off his clothes as she finished undressing. Steam wafted from the shower and fogged the glass doors as she stepped under the spray. Water darkened her hair, the lengthy locks clinging to her skin, and her nipples hardened as water sluiced over her curvy, tanned body.

Mason joined her in the tub, closed the door behind him, and hot water pelted his back in a rough caress. Tension eased from his shoulders, and he glanced at Mia as she gently rubbed a sudsy body puff over his pecs. Several bruises still marred his chest and stomach, and she looked ready to cry.

"The bruises look worse than they feel." He clasped her cheek. "I'm a fast healer, and I've been through worse than what you witnessed on Saturday. When I say I'm fine, I mean it."

She kissed the hollow of his throat and rubbed slightly harder. Tempted to jerk her against him and prove he could handle it rough, he gripped his hands in his hair to let her go at her own pace. Her soft, reverent touch eased his aches, burned through his hard shell, and pierced his dirty soul.

He'd done so many bad things in his life, and he didn't know why she accepted him.

Because you haven't told her everything, you asshole.

She already knew too much and asked too many questions. He'd expected her to grill him about Onyx and Sondokes as soon as he walked through her door, but she only asked about Udell and Harper. She didn't seem angry with him anymore, and he didn't know what to make of it.

Mia scrubbed the puff over the bulging biceps of his right arm, past the elbow and forearm. She swiped it over his fingers and moved to his left hand to scrub all the way to his shoulder. She darted her tongue out to lick a few scars on his chest. The muscles in his back flexed as she scrubbed the puff down his spine. Her wet breasts pressed against his chest, her nipples hard like diamonds, and she pulled back to lather a bar of soap in the puff. His erection jutted close to her face as she knelt. She cleaned his thighs, knees, and calves, and cupped his balls with the puff still in her hand.

He gasped and dropped his arms to grab her hair.

"Keep your arms up. I want you at my mercy."

A shudder coursed through him. "Yes, ma'am." He locked his hands behind his head again and closed his eyes as she bathed him. Her sensual touch brought tears to his eyes. He couldn't remember a time in his life when he felt so clean and whole, and not because he showered. The water washed away the embarrassing tears, and he held himself rigid as she cleaned the hard length of his penis, the sensitive band of skin that connected his testicles to his ass, and then his anus. He involuntarily clenched his cheeks. Although shocked she touched him there, the pleasure she gave trumped his hesitation and he relaxed.

A soft little murmur left her mouth. Mia trailed her fingers over the wet hairs on his thighs and massaged his ball sac again.

He cleared his throat. "I have to ask you something. It's nagged at me for days." Mason forced his eyes open and met her gaze. Her hand never left his balls. "You called me 'baby' the other day in that alley. Why?"

"You heard that?" She bit her lip. Water beaded on her eyelashes and clumped the strands together, but she didn't look away. "You always call me darlin', and I love the way you drop the *g*. It's much better than *sugar*, by the way. I thought you would like a pet name too. That's fine if you don't want one or don't like it. I can call you—"

"I like it. A lot. I'm just surprised. I don't think I've ever had a pet name."

"Well, you have one now, baby." The grin she beamed up at him weakened his knees. "I'm happy you like it. I thought it might be a little too feminine for you."

"Nah, it makes me feel precious."

Mia laughed as he winked at her. "You are precious, but right now you're solid as a rock, and you're all mine." She licked his mushroomed head as though to claim him.

Yes, claim me.

Her mouth opened and she took him inside.

The air in his lungs rushed out. Mason thrust his hips and braced his hands on the wall to keep upright. Mia didn't seem to notice or mind that he dropped his arms. Her magnificent tongue licked and prodded him. She tickled his balls with one hand and kneaded her fingers against his ass cheek with the other. Then she scooted closer to him as she moaned.

The vibration of that sexy sound shot through his cock. "Yes, Mia. Hell, yes." Mason buried his hand in her hair and forced himself deeper into her mouth.

She dug her nails against his thighs.

The deep mewling sounds she made rocked him to his core. He pushed in and out of her sweet haven, teased the back of her throat, and tried not to choke her.

A surge of liquid fire filled his cock. A sweltering burn sizzled through his veins. He thrust harder and faster, gripped her head with his palms to steady her, and shouted in release. His ego skyrocketed as she swallowed his seed.

She gripped his thighs harder and likely broke the skin.

Fuck, he wanted to bleed for her.

Mason eased back from her after the last of his orgasm ripped through him. The shower wall supported his weight and kept him on his feet. Spots dotted his vision, but his penis throbbed for more. He loved his cock. The damn thing led him into trouble so many times, but he suddenly realized he'd only practiced with his hand and with other women in order to learn the ropes and to become the best he could be for Mia. She stared up at him, her large brown eyes so naughty and tempting. He fisted his semi-hard erection, feeling the pulse pounding along the velvety length like a live wire.

She crawled forward on her knees and licked his heavy ball sac. Though the water pounded like a rainstorm, her soft moans reached his ears. She nipped his pubic area and finally took him back into her mouth.

Pleasure spiraled through his body so hot it hurt. He tried to push her away, but she clamped her lips around him and kneaded his waist with her fingers. He could die from ecstasy and didn't care.

"Goddamn it, Mia. You'll turn me blue."

She drew back and chuckled. A devious glint lit

her eyes. "I already told you I like blowjobs. If you can't handle this, well, we got a problem."

He arched a brow. Mason fisted her hair and she engulfed him again. His scream bounded off the walls. His body seized up, every muscle and tendon tightened, and his heart sped so fast it might burst. His orgasm surged from the darkest, deepest part of him and he shot off like a pistol. He pulled back before he strangled her. His seed swam in her belly, and he wanted to love her like this for the rest of their lives.

Unclenching his hand from her hair, he helped her stand. "I'm speechless, Mia. Really. Wow."

"Good, I like my man tongue-tied. That means I'm in control."

Surprise stilled the air in his lungs. *He* jerked off in *her* mouth. He controlled the whole damn experience. Then he thought about it. Mia gave him what she wanted to give him. She could've stopped at any time, and he would've used his hand to relieve himself. That resulting orgasm would've paled beside the one that still sent tremors through his body.

Damn, is she right? Did Mia take me with her mouth?

A laugh bubbled up his throat. He kissed her forehead. "Tongue-tie me whenever you want, darlin'. I'm yours to control."

Chapter Twelve

"Dad, I want cake." Seven-year-old Danny Harding clasped his hands together and pouted the best pitiful face Mia had ever seen.

"For the last time, we have to wait for your uncle."

Mia bit back a smile and relaxed in an overstuffed chair as Alan argued with his son. Although she was a little irritated Mason neglected to tell her about his birthday, she should've remembered since Alan showed her the Harding Family birthday photo album not too long ago.

Alan had called her yesterday morning and invited her to a spur-of-the-moment birthday party he decided to throw for his little brother. After ten years in prison without his family to celebrate with him, Mason probably needed this more than he realized.

Mason had called her later that afternoon. Jim scheduled him for a sobriety test on Saturday—she believed her brother purposely scheduled it on his birthday—but Mason wanted to meet her for lunch after the appointment. Though she normally would've agreed, Mia claimed she and Belle had already made plans to go shopping, and she couldn't get out of it.

"What about ice cream?" Danny flipped around on the sofa and leaned up on his knees as his father paced from the front door to the mouth of the hall. "Just a bite? A few little licks?"

Benji laughed as he stood by the window that overlooked the parking lot. Mason told her Benji had sided with Alan when his sister, Meghan, divorced him, rescinded all maternal rights to her infant son, and skipped town. "C'mon, Al. Let the kid have some ice cream."

Danny's head bobbled up and down. "Please, Dad. Uncle Mason won't mind. Would you, Uncle Benji?" He turned to the handsome man in question. "Would you care if I ate some ice cream if you were late for your birthday party?"

"Nope, not at all." Benji folded his arms across his broad chest as Alan scowled at him.

Mia laughed behind her hand, unable to contain it.

Benji winked at her, and Danny now pleaded with her to help him on his quest for ice cream.

Alan ceased his frantic pacing across the carpet. "You're siding with them, Mia?"

"Sorry, but yes."

"Can I, Dad?" Danny piped up again.

"No."

Danny growled, his bottom lip puckered out, and he plopped back down on the sofa.

Mia's heart twisted, and she wanted to race into the kitchen and grab the ice cream from the freezer for the adorable little boy.

Alan resumed his pacing and spoke to no one in particular. "Where is he? Mason said he'd probably leave the testing center at noon, so that meant he should be home at around one p.m. It's now two o'clock. I'm gonna kick his butt."

Mia glanced at Danny as he rolled his big green eyes, a few shades darker than Mason's, but dead-on with his father's. Alan curbed his language around his son, but his anger permeated the room. Alan's temper reminded her of Mason's, though not nearly as volatile, and she blamed their genetics for that infuriating trait.

A ripple of unease shot down her spine as the minutes passed. Although she believed Mason's prison friend took care of everything, she wondered if Franz Harper refused to follow orders and sought Mason out. Mason probably didn't tell her everything the other night. Lies and secrets still burrowed between them, but she tried to not let it bother her.

Her stomach churned over her little white lie about Belle.

Mason's not the only liar, but at least I didn't lie to him about something important.

Though she did lie to Alan.

He'd asked her about the bruises on Mason's arms and face.

Backed into the proverbial corner, Mia claimed she and Mason ran into her ex-husband and the men brawled on the pavement after Evan called her a dirty name. Then Mia reassured Alan that her brother didn't document the fight since Jim wished *he* could've been the one to beat the shit out of Evan. Alan and Benji seemed to buy the lie and she needed to tell Mason this before Alan questioned him.

"Hey, hey." Benji clicked his tongue and gathered everyone's attention. "He's coming down the sidewalk now with a fast-food drink in his hand. The inconsiderate A-hole went to lunch."

"Okay. It's game time. Everyone hide."

Danny grabbed Mia's hand at his father's announcement. Alan lit the candles on the huge chocolate cake he'd picked up from the grocery store as she hunkered down on the floor between the large sofa and the coffee table. Laughter bubbled up from her chest, and Danny pressed his finger to his lips. Mia laughed harder and bit the inside of her cheek to control herself.

Alan flipped off the lights and Benji closed the window blinds. Several flickering bands of orange light lit up the living room as the men hid. A few minutes passed until the doorknob shook and the door opened. Outside light streamed inside, and Mia ducked further behind the sofa. Danny bounced like a kid at a carnival but somehow managed to stay hidden.

"Alan?" Mason shut the door. "What the hell is that? A cake?" He flipped on the lights and Danny jumped up first.

"Surprise!"

Mason jumped back against the door and everyone else followed the child's lead. His plastic cup hit the floor, and Mia chuckled as his eyes bugged out.

Danny hugged his uncle's legs. "Happy birthday."

"Thanks, buddy. What a surprise." A smile spread across his face as he grabbed the cup and hoisted his nephew into his arms. "Was this your idea?"

The little boy shook his head and pointed toward his father.

Mason glanced at Alan who stood by the dining room table. His brother's mouth twisted up at one corner. "Really? Even after I said he shouldn't bother?" He smiled back at Danny.

"Yep, but I'll tell you a secret." Danny leaned in close to Mason's ear but spoke loud enough for everyone to hear. "I think he wanted to have this party for a long time."

Guilt flashed across Mason's face but quickly disappeared. "You're probably right." He kissed Danny's forehead and sat him back on his feet as Alan approached him. The brothers hugged, Mason shook Benji's outstretched hand before his friend and boss pulled Mason into a big bear hug, and then Mason's gaze landed on Mia.

She tried to give him a small peck on the cheek, but his lips claimed hers in a fiery kiss that should be illegal. Her heart leapt to her throat. Her knees weakened like melted butter, but then his strong arms snaked around her, holding her close. She pressed her hands to his chest and pushed back to stand on her own.

Mason grinned at her. Mischief flared in his eyes.

Her cheeks heated. "Learn some tact, Mason. We're not alone."

Benji chuckled. "Really? Did you forget you backed this guy up against your car a few weeks ago? A dozen-plus men watched and hooted like monkeys."

"Ben told me you tongue-lashed him good." Alan fist-pumped his former brother-in-law. "I would've paid to see that."

Danny frowned as the three men shared a chuckle at her expense. "Hurry up. Blow out the candles before yucky wax covers the cake." Danny grabbed Mason's hand and pulled him toward the dining room. Balloons and streamers decorated the apartment. Blue paper plates, napkins, plastic utensils, and cups bordered the cake on three sides.

Mason sighed as though he didn't want to. His eyebrow arched as he peered down at the cake. "Is that twenty nine individual candles?"

Alan shrugged. "Overkill, I know, but the store had sold out of the 'Nine' candle. So, unless you wanted to be two years old again, you got this."

"This is good." Mason sat the cup aside, braced his hands on the table, and blew on the candles. Only half burned out.

Danny giggled. "They're trick candles! Those were my idea."

Mason pulled Danny close and tickled him. "Help me with these, huh?"

The boy nodded, and they blew together until all the candle flames died. Danny gave Mason a high-five and looked at his father. "Can we have the cake now?"

Alan laughed. "Sure. Go wash your hands before you grab the ice cream and milk."

Danny ran toward the kitchen.

"You're late," Alan whispered to his brother. He picked itty-bitty candles and melted wax off the cake.

"I should've realized you'd planned something since you asked me three times this morning and twice yesterday when I'd be home today." Mason forced his hand through his hair. "Thanks for not inviting Mom. That definitely would've ruined the party."

His brother sighed. "I figured as much."

Benji clapped Mason on the back. "Did you get the new Big-Mister burger with the wood-smoked bacon, grilled jalapeños, and three kinds of cheese?" He nodded at the plastic cup.

"Oh yeah, talk about greasy heaven. I'll add a few extra sit-ups to my workout tonight and tomorrow, but the burger and fries were worth it."

"You're not supposed to bring that stuff home with you."

Mason cocked his eyebrow at Alan. "Seriously? It's one thing you won't let me eat junk food here. It's another if I can't bring home my drink which I finished on the bus."

"It's not healthy. Danny needs to know good eating habits."

"I do, Dad." Danny peeled open the low-fat ice cream container and smiled at Mia. "I love family events. I get to eat whatever I want and today no broccoli."

Mia smiled. Danny's presence seemed to ease the tension between the brothers. "Don't you like broccoli? It's so good."

Danny scrunched up his face as Alan cut the cake into squares. "Stop, Dad," he cried out. "You gotta light the candles again. We forgot to sing. Uncle Mason's wish won't come true if we don't sing."

Mia reached to hug him, but Mason beat her to it.

"Don't worry, buddy. I already got my wish." He tousled the boy's dark hair. "This party is awesome."

Danny perked up and hugged him back.

They sat at the table and indulged in the cake and cookie-dough ice cream. Alan and Benji laughed and spoke with one another as though truly brothers.

She noticed a fair amount of jealousy in Mason's eyes, but he stayed quiet, laughed when everyone else did, and ate his food. That was why he probably didn't want a party. Though he loved Alan and liked Benji, she bet Mason didn't get along well with either man. How could he? The life Mason led differed drastically from theirs, and she doubted they understood him.

Mia grasped his hand under the table. His gaze shifted to hers, and a small smile curled his lips. She wanted to apologize for her part in this, but she'd had no idea he probably dealt with this sense of alienation on a daily basis.

Mason opened presents after everyone finished a few pieces of cake. Danny gave him a ceramic coffee mug with the words *I Love My Uncle* painted in big bold letters on one side. Alan had bought him an MP3 player, a few dozen songs already installed, and Benji coordinated his gifts with a few T-shirts from some hard rock bands Mason loved back in his youth.

Mia handed Mason a small box, and he tore off the red wrapping paper. His eyes bulged. "Wow, a camera."

Excitement fluttered through her. Mason had mentioned a few nights ago that he wanted to take pictures of her naked and tape them in bed together. Though his request shocked her, she found the risqué act intriguing. Evan had begged her to do the same, but she refused since he wanted to use the photos in his portfolio. This camera signified her trust in Mason. Hopefully, he understood that.

"You're incredible, darlin'."

Heat bloomed in her privates. She avoided Alan's and Benji's perplexed stares, drained her cup of milk, and the liquid nearly spewed from her mouth as Mason's hand traveled up her thigh. She swallowed hard, her eyes and cheeks burned, and she coughed to clear her throat.

Mason drew back his hand to hide his chuckle.

Alan told Danny to play in another room.

Danny grumbled as he left the table and headed down the hall, but he returned to play on the sofa. Action figures overflowed from his arms.

"Sorry," she said to Alan, but he waved his hand in the air as though he didn't care. The birthday boy grasped her leg again, and Mia sealed her lips to cut off a gasp.

Mason smiled at Alan. "Thanks, man. I'm having fun after all."

Mia pushed his hand off her leg as Alan gave his brother a knowing look.

"Well, I'm damn good at throwing birthday parties. When I throw Danny's party in a few months, I want all three of you to help me corral him and his crazy friends." Alan rubbed his forehead and smiled at Mia. "Last year, Benji skipped out early because some kid squeezed glue in his hair, but that's really my fault. I never should've let them play with arts and crafts. Anyway, he straight up left me, my mom, and my stepdad—who are both in their mid-fifties, I might add—all alone at a busy skating rink to deal with thirteen screaming little monsters."

Mia laughed. She definitely planned to attend the upcoming party.

"I had to chop off my long hair because of that brat. I couldn't get the glue out." Benji patted the wavy auburn locks that reached his ears. "I should've squirted glue back on that kid."

Laughter rang around the table. Even Benji offered a small smile, and the next few hours passed in what seemed like twenty minutes.

Alan cursed as he looked at his cell phone. "I'm supposed to be at work at six o'clock. It's now half past five. I'm lucky my boss likes me."

"Likes you?" Mason scoffed. "He's made you work strange hours all week. Like today. You don't work nights or Saturdays."

"Sometimes I have to. I'm behind on an evaluation and the boss wants it done ASAP. I gotta pull more hours."

"Evaluating what?" Mia asked as Alan picked up the cake tray. She gathered the used cups, plates, and utensils. "I'm sorry, but I don't even know what you do for a living."

"I work for a security firm, Denver Alerts Plus. I usually just monitor high-end businesses via their computer systems, but sometimes I evaluate and review those businesses every year before their renewal period."

"Oh, yeah. The company I use called me about six or seven months ago because someone used a stolen credit card to buy a two-hundred-dollar item."

Alan whistled as he carried the leftover cake to the kitchen. "Did your bank and insurance company get involved?" A roll of aluminum foil lay in wait on the counter, and he tore off a long piece to wrap over the food. "Oh, the trashcan's in the pantry closet."

She opened a narrow door across the room and tossed the trash in the bin. "Yeah, they did. Everything worked out fine, but talk about a headache." Mia bit back a startled squeal as Mason came up behind her and pinched her butt. She popped his arm, but he unabashedly winked at her as he stacked the unused plasticware on a shelf.

"Let's go, sport." Benji clapped his hands as though to get Danny's attention. "Grab your bag."

Mia glanced up as Danny jumped off the sofa and hurried down the hall.

Mason frowned. "What's going on?"

"Happy birthday from both of us," Alan said as Benji followed them into the kitchen. Both men grinned like jackasses. "Benji agreed to babysit Danny and I'll crash with them for the night, so you kids have fun."

Mason glanced at Mia and she shrugged.

Alan rolled his eyes. "Do I gotta spell it out? The stupid curfew cuts into your overnight sexy time, right?"

She blushed as realization dawned.

"You're welcomed to stay the night, Mia. You two have the apartment to yourselves."

Mason playfully punched his brother on the shoulder. "Best birthday party ever."

Alan laughed, and left the apartment with Benji and Danny in tow a few minutes later.

Mason grabbed the camera box from the table and held it up in the air. "Well, it's time to give this thing its first test run."

"I knew you were gonna say that."

He wrapped his arm around her waist. "C'mon, darlin'. It's my birthday."

"Really? What if I say no?" He tightened his grip, and a squeal lodged in her throat. Mia pressed her palms to his chest and faked an overdramatic sigh. "Oh fine, but only because it's your birthday." She blew him a pouty kiss and lightly patted his whiskered cheek.

A deep, triumphant laugh left his mouth before he kissed her. She tasted chocolate on his breath and wanted to scrape the icing off the remaining cake to rub it on Mason's chest.

Food play can wait, you bad girl, Mia chastised herself. *Stripping for a camera is naughty enough for one night.*

Mason released her to rip open the cardboard box and pull out the camera. The box and instructions fell to the floor. "Are batteries included? What about a memory card?"

"Included and installed. It's ready to go."

"Perfect, but give me a moment to figure out how to work the video setting. Go to bed, and I'll join you in a moment."

"Bossy, bossy." Mia sashayed her hips as she headed down the hall and pulled off her blouse to drop on the floor. His lustful groan reached her ears, and his gaze scorched her back like lasers. Her skimpy black bra fell to the floor next, and she turned to the side to show the feminine curves of her profile. "Don't take too long, baby. I might start without you."

His mouth fell open.

She opened his bedroom door and strode inside like a tease, then giggled after she closed the door. A deep breath filled her lungs. She flipped on the bedside table lamp, left the overhead light off as she turned on the ceiling fan, and finished undressing.

Her lover's comfy bed welcomed her like feathers, and his rich, spicy scent engulfed her as she relaxed. Mia moaned as though in the throes of pleasure, loud enough for Mason to surely hear. She pinched her nipples into hard peaks, teased her fingertips around the entrance between her legs, and a shiver coursed through her as she pushed inside herself.

A genuine gasp escaped her mouth. Her eyelids fluttered closed as she inserted a second digit and twisted her hand in a circular motion. She kept a slow, steady rhythm and imagined she gripped Mason's shoulders as he probed inside her with his long, limber fingers. A groan left her mouth as she curled her fingers so her knuckles pushed against her G-spot. Mia lifted her hips off the mattress for a better angle and wished Mason knelt between her legs.

A flash of light filled the room and vanished. She collapsed on the mattress. Air ripped through her lungs and heat flushed her body.

Mason stood naked at the foot of the bed, his new camera in hand.

She licked her lips as he stroked himself. "Good, you're here." She withdrew her fingers and wiggled them in the air. "I'm talented with these things, but I prefer yours."

"Keep using them. Act natural. Forget I'm here." Mason focused on the camera. "Touch yourself. Turn me on." Desire swam in his eyes as Mason snapped photo after photo.

She played with herself with one hand and crooked her index finger at him with the other.

A liquid pearl glistened on his erection. The thick organ jutted up and down as he moved. Mason placed the camera on the nightstand and grabbed a condom from within the drawer. "Don't stop, darlin'. You're so damn hot. Moan for me."

Goose bumps covered her skin. Mia thumbed her clit and moaned as the bed squeaked.

He hovered over her, the condom sheathing his bulging cock, and he grabbed her knees to push them farther apart. As he settled in the crook of her body, he braced his arms on the pillows beside her head and pushed himself deep inside her.

"Oh, God. Yes." A sharp moan tore up her throat. Her breasts bounced and her pulse hummed as she gyrated in rhythm to his every stroke.

He rammed his hips into the apex of her thighs. The slapping sounds of their joining bodies echoed in her ears. She circled her legs around his waist and followed the rise and fall of his hard body. Her vision blurred every time he slammed to the hilt. A ball of need coiled in her womb like a ticking time bomb. Her feminine muscles milked and suctioned him so tight she burned from the force.

Mason pulled from her vagina's tight grasp, lifted her bottom with his hands, and drew her legs over his shoulders. He licked away her salty tears. Thumbing her clitoris, he kissed her and drew little mews from her mouth.

Mia clasped his sweaty chest for a lifeline. Lightning zipped through her blood as he pistoned his hips, filling her with his shaft. Her liquid climax pushed against his steel, and she shouted in release.

A hoarse cry left his mouth. His orgasm took over and he joined her in paradise.

Mia panted for air as he collapsed beside her. "I love when you talk dirty, Mason."

"I know, naughty girl." He flashed her a wicked grin before he grabbed the camera and turned it off. "Shower time. I hope this device is waterproof."

She laughed softly. "I don't think so."

He pressed a kiss on her shoulder. "Thank you for today, for every day we're together. You make me happy, Mia."

His words brought a fresh round of tears to her eyes. Despite his problems and secrets, Mia knew she could easily fall in love with him. Maybe she already had.

Chapter Thirteen

"It's permanent. You sure about this?" Mason asked Mia as they left her car in the parking lot on Thursday afternoon and walked up a short ramp to the tattoo parlor.

"Yep. I've thought about this for years, and I'm ready for it." She pulled him to a stop by the glass door. "Thanks for coming with me. I'm a little nervous."

He kissed her cheek. In preparation for the outing, she'd closed the store early and cooked dinner while he showered in her bathroom. Mia talked about nothing but the tattoo she wanted as they scarfed down the spaghetti, and he couldn't wait for the tat to heal so he could bathe it with his tongue.

"I wouldn't want you to go alone. Besides, it's my treat, as I promised." He half-expected her to offer to pay for it as though he couldn't afford it, but she never brought it up. "Angie said this place is reputable, right?"

"Her cousin co-owns it. Angie called Lars yesterday to let him know about us."

"Okay, but we'll leave if you feel uncomfortable or if you change your mind." He'd never heard of L and R Tattoo Parlor. The store operated in a rundown neighborhood surely ripe with Capularia thugs, but Mia seemed to trust her employee's judgment, so he backed off.

A rush of cool air hit them as they crossed the threshold. Though the old building could use a remodel on the outside, someone obviously had shelled out a lot of time and cash to fix up the inside. Tattoo and rock band posters covered forest-green walls, a leather sofa and armchairs bordered a coffee table on three sides, and several photo albums lay scattered on the table.

Early evening sunlight streamed through closed window blinds as an episode of some tattoo show played on a flat-screen TV. Two large jewelry cases sectioned off a corner of the waiting room, and a register, a desktop computer, and a printer topped the table in the makeshift office. Two small rooms branched off from the waiting area, and a dimly lit hall led deeper into the building.

A man with long dark hair exited one of the adjacent rooms and pulled off his latex gloves. "Hey. Are you guys here for a piercing or a tat?"

"Tattoo." Mason nodded in greeting. "Are you Lars?"

"Nah, I'm Randy. Have a seat and chill. I'll get Lars for ya in a minute." Randy and a heavyset man with at least a dozen hoops in his eyebrows and lips headed to the register. The customer bought a few barbell piercings, and Randy hurried down the hall after the big guy left.

Mia walked around the furniture to look at the posters.

Mason stood out in the open, no furniture in the way in case he needed to move fast, and he noted the possible exits in the room if someone compromised the main door. Randy seemed friendly, and Mason liked the airiness of the interior environment, but an underlying current of shit probably ran deep in the business. Footsteps echoed down the hall as Randy and another man headed toward him.

"Hey, I'm Lars. Randy says you're here for a tattoo." Lars slapped Mason's outstretched hand in a firm shake. Tall and lanky, he was probably no older than his early-thirties. His bleach-blond hair rose in liberty spikes and tattoos covered his arms.

"I'm Mason. This is Mia." He wrapped his arm around her waist once she reached his side. "Angie called you about us."

"Yeah. Glad you guys could come by." Lars shook Mia's hand and smiled at her. "I only see my cuz around the holidays or when she's cravin' the needle. I've inked all her tats. You run a clothing store or something down in LoDo, right?"

"I do, Shadow Rose Boutique." Mia glanced around the room. "You have an awesome place. I want a blue-and-black butterfly on my shoulder blade, but I don't know if I want curved or pointed wingtips. Could I look at some pictures to get a better idea?"

"Sure can." Lars headed toward the coffee table and shuffled through a few albums. "Feel free to look around. I always take snapshots of my artwork if the customer doesn't mind, and all the insect photos are in this one." He handed Mia a thick leather-bound album.

"Perfect. Thank you." Mia sat on the sofa and opened the album.

"Nice tats, man." Randy nodded at Mason's arms and waved Lars over. "Where'd you get them?"

"Different places." Mason lifted his shirtsleeves so the guys could see the phoenix and skull tats better. "They're a few years old."

"I got a phoenix too." Lars pulled his T-shirt up to his pecs and showed off a large black-and-orange phoenix on his stomach. "You want some tats?"

"Always in the market for more customers, huh?"

Lars grinned. "I'm runnin' a business, ya know."

Mason laughed. He should have gotten full sleeves in the slammer. The best tattoo artist on his block had left on parole a few years into Mason's sentence, however, and he trusted no one else to step up to the plate. A thousand-dollar sleeve on the outside cost no more than a hundred or two on the in, so he wished he had sucked it up and let the other guy ink him. He eventually wanted to cover up the gang sign but could always grow out his hair. He'd picked the back of his neck so everyone could see it and think twice before they fucked with him, but he no longer needed that kind of protection and intimidation. Mia's tat would probably cost him a few hundred bucks, so he couldn't splurge on himself right now.

"Maybe, but let's worry about my girl today."

"Fair enough." Lars clapped him on the back. Mason turned and covered three steps in Mia's direction before Lars's sharp inhale drew him to a stop. "Fuck, man. Why didn't you say something? Who do you run with?"

Mason frowned and pivoted back around as the tattooist patted the back of his own neck. *Shit. He saw my Onyx tat.* His gaze darted to the exit, but Mia would bitch if he tossed her on his shoulder and ran out the door.

Or worse, she'd demand an explanation.

"Don't know what you mean." Mason nodded toward one of the small adjacent rooms. "Why don't you guys show me where you work your magic?" He headed straight for the room closest to the exit without waiting for their response.

Upper and lower cabinets lined one wall, a few bottles of ink lay on a metal tray beside the sink, and a black leather massage chair stood in the middle of the room.

"What's up?" Randy asked as he and Lars joined Mason in the room. "You look pissed."

Mason glanced through the open doorway and caught Mia's gaze. A little frown creased her forehead. He smiled at her, trying to give off the impression he just wanted to inspect the tattoo materials, and she turned back to the photos.

He swung his gaze to Lars and Randy and lowered his voice. "Mia doesn't know about Onyx. I want it to stay that way."

"Oh shit, my bad," Lars whispered. He lifted his shirt again to show two crisscrossing snakes inside an intricate woven circle on his upper chest. "Don't worry. We'll keep quiet."

Randy turned, lifted his hair into a sloppy ponytail, and jerked back the collar of his shirt to reveal a similar tat on his right shoulder blade. "We're with Capularia. What about you?"

Mason figured that. The profitable Onyx set operated in Denver, Aurora, and the neighboring towns and suburbs. Every Onyx member who lived and worked in those areas pledged allegiance to Capularia and answered to Thorn.

"I ran with Sondokes, but I'm out."

Lars's eyebrows knitted together. "A prison set? That's why your tats are so wicked black. Some SOB did a great job. I couldn't tell they weren't professional."

Despite his nerves, Mason couldn't stop his smile. "My guy used a motor from a CD player, and he filed down a spring from a staple gun to make a needle. The ink's made of baby oil and cotton ball soot. He knew his shit."

"Badass, man." Lars laughed.

"You lookin' to buy?" Randy hooked his thumbs in the belt loops of his jeans. "We got some hardcore shit in the back, if you catch my drift."

Mason definitely caught it. "Nah, I'm clean."

Stay calm, Mase. You'll probably make enemies out of the dealers if you tell them to take their drugs and shove it up their asses.

"Cool. No prob." Lars turned as though to head into the waiting area, but he whipped back around to face Mason. "Wait a minute. Are you Harding?"

"That's my last name." A cold tremor shot down his spine.

Lars slapped his hands together, his eyes wide in surprise. "Mason—fuckin'—Harding. Goddamn it. I heard about you. Word on the street is an ex-Sondokes bodyguard beat up two Dowitcha dealers."

Mason bit back a curse.

"Is your girlfriend the one who beat that dickhead Harper with a pipe?" Randy cocked his head toward Mia in the other room.

Mason nodded.

Randy whistled his praise through his teeth. "Damn, man. She's a badass chick."

"Who would be stupid enough to sling drugs on the wrong turf?" Lars grinned from ear to ear. "Racist pricks like them, I guess. Iversen met with Thorn and smoothed things over. Who knows what Iversen plans to do with Harper and Elray, but they're up to their neck in shit. God, can you imagine the blood bath if Thorn's men and Iversen's guys attacked each other?"

"At least Thorn wouldn't call us to fight." Randy crossed his arms. "We just peddle shit."

"Keep it down." Though he'd used his fists to protect dealers like Lars and Randy in the slammer, Mason didn't know or want to know how bloody a turf war could be. "Mia has enough questions, and I'm not sure how much longer I can keep her in the dark."

"Word of advice, man—*don't* keep her in the dark." Lars scratched his chest, right over the gang symbol. "I haven't told Angie or anyone in my family about this crap, but I wouldn't lie to my chick if I had one. Women are nosy and bound to find out your darkest secrets sooner or later. It's best to come clean before she kicks your ass into the doghouse."

Lars's candor aggravated the hell out of him, but Mason knew the truth when he heard it.

"Is this the *boys only* club or can I join?"

Mason jumped and turned to face Mia as she stood in the open doorway. Her cool, unblinking stare unnerved him. "Hey, darlin'. Have you found something you like?" As she lifted her eyebrow at a haughty angle, his stomach dropped to his feet. The air in his lungs stilled. Not sure how much she'd heard, he clenched his hands to not drag her from the building.

She turned to Lars and smiled. "I picked two butterflies, but I can't choose between them. Do you think you could combine them?" She held the album in her arms, her fingers wedged in between a few pages.

"Sure, show me which ones you like." Lars left the room with Mia at his side, and they sat on the sofa to discuss the tattoo.

Mason stayed with Randy.

"I say keep your mouth shut about Onyx for as long as you can." Randy fiddled with the spiked balls on his eyebrow ring. "I told the last chick I had. She slapped me in the face and left."

"Mia would probably do the same." Why he discussed his love life with two strangers, Mason didn't know, but he liked Lars and Randy. They could be friends in another place and time, but he preferred his life drama-free and under the radar from cops and criminals alike.

A huge smile lit Mia's face as she and Lars returned.

"Okay, all non-boyfriends hit the road." The blond artist smirked as Randy flipped him his middle finger and left the room.

Mia shrugged off her overshirt. A long black tube top hugged her breasts and bunched up a little around the waistband of her capri pants.

Mason swallowed a groan. As his penis thickened against the zipper of his ripped jeans, he backed away from Mia before he pulled her into his arms and made love to her mouth.

"You can take a load off in that chair, Mason." Lars indicated a nice padded chair in the corner with a nod as he rearranged the massage chair so Mia could straddle it. To the man's credit, Lars didn't drool or drop to his knees at the sight of his latest customer's body. "This will probably take about an hour, so you guys should get comfortable."

Mason grabbed the chair and parked it in front of Mia.

She brushed her hair over her left shoulder and rested her head on an oval-shaped, cushioned headrest that exposed her face.

He ducked his head so he could make eye contact. "Just say something if you need a break."

"I'm sturdier than you think." Irritation flared in her eyes. "Oh, and for the record, I agree with Lars. I'm a lot nosier than you realize."

He straightened in the chair. His temples throbbed, and his skin crawled as anxious energy zapped through him like a lightning bolt. Mason jerked his gaze to Lars as the tattooist pulled a few bottles of blue ink from an overhead cabinet. Not sure if Lars heard Mia's statement, Mason bit his nails into his palms in an effort to stay calm.

Lars slipped on latex gloves, squirted black ink and different shades of blue ink into little plastic cups, and ripped open a new needle package. "Let me know if you feel queasy or need some fresh air, Mia. I know some three-hundred-pound bikers who can't handle the chair for more than half an hour, so it's no big deal to take a breather." He sat on a short stool, rolled to her side with a marker in his hand, and drew the outline of a butterfly on her shoulder blade. "Look in the mirror and tell me what you think. Good location? Good design?"

Mia stood and glanced at the outline in the full-length mirror bolted on the wall. "Wow, that's awesome. Great location, and I love the sharp wingtips." She straddled the chair again, closed her eyes, and clutched the armrest.

Mason covered her shaky hands with his. Determined to comfort her whether she wanted him to or not, he didn't know what he would do if she scorned his touch.

Her eyelids fluttered open through the hole in the headrest. A small smile lifted her lips as she squeezed his fingers.

The tattoo gun roared to life. Her face tensed, and she gripped him like a clamp as Lars brought the needle down on her skin. The first few dots of black ink stained her skin, and she hissed.

Ready to tell Lars to ease up on the pressure, he kept his mouth shut as she eased her grip on his hands and the tight muscles in her face smoothed out.

Lars tapped a foot pedal that powered the gun through an electrical wire. The pedal reminded Mason of the old sewing machine his grandma used to have before she died.

Half an hour passed in silence, if he didn't count the grind of the tattoo gun, and Mason reached out to stroke her hair. "Are you okay?"

"Fine, I guess. I'm a little tired but the pain's not bad." Mia blinked open her sleepy eyes. "How does it look?"

"Freakin' sweet. I'm proud of you. You're handling this like a champ."

Lars had finished the black outline and the inner design of the wings a while ago, and now he colored it in. "I'm with Mason on this one." He dipped the needle into a cup of blue ink. "I didn't say anything earlier to not jinx you, but most of the women I've tattooed can handle the needle better than the men. I don't get it. Maybe chicks think they have somethin' to prove, but they sit down and take it non-stop without a single tear. Some of my male clients cry like babies and have to go to the bathroom to find their balls."

Mason chuckled.

"What about you, Mason?" A grin spread across his face. "How clean and painless were your prison tats?"

"Clean, man. I sterilized the needle myself and watched my artist create the ink. When it came to stuff like that, I trusted no one. And painless? No way. They hurt like a bitch."

"You cry?" Mia winked at him. "Don't tell me my baby cried."

Her playful tone rolled through him. Lars flat-out grinned and Mason wanted to kiss her. He opened his mouth to deny any and all tears, but someone coughed out in the waiting room. He stood and poked his head through the open doorway.

Two skinny, fatigued-looking men waited by the register, and their hands trembled as they looked around the room. Dressed in baggy clothes, their greasy hair lay flat on their heads and dark circles plagued their glassy, anxious eyes.

Meth heads coming down from a high. Fuck, why now?

Even with a surveillance camera in the corner of the room, pointed right at the register, Mason wondered if the men would still try to jack it open.

The air behind him stirred as Lars approached.

"You're early." Lars narrowed his gaze at the newcomers and jerked off his gloves. An apologetic smile turned up his lips as he faced Mason. "Give me about ten minutes and we'll finish up. Watch some TV if you like. Make yourself at home." He waved his hand toward the addicts, and they headed down the hall and entered one of the back rooms.

"What's going on?" Mia joined him at the doorway and grasped his hand. She stared down the hall.

"Drug deal. We should go."

"My tattoo's not done."

"We'll go somewhere else to finish it. I'll throw some money for the tat on the counter."

She grabbed the doorframe as he tried to pull her from the room. "No, Mason. I won't go. Maybe we should, but I think you feel at home here. Well, you might if not for me."

"What the hell does that mean?"

"It means you're no stranger to drug deals." She braced her hands on her hips. "I have damn good hearing, Mason, and I overheard a lot of crap when you guys talked in your little *boys' club*. I didn't understand all of it, a few parts whooshed right over my head, but none of it surprised me. I'd already suspected you have some gang-related ties."

He held up his arms. "I can explain."

"Damn right you will, but I want to finish this tattoo first. So after Lars finishes up with me, we'll grab some Chinese takeout and talk. I'm tired and famished. I think the pasta we ate for dinner evaporated from my stomach with the first needle prick."

A scream echoed down the hall. Mason shoved Mia behind him as someone shouted from behind a closed door.

Mason gripped her arm. "Stay here. I'll be right back." He stomped down the hall, so angry and confused he could barely breathe, and thrust open the door he'd seen Lars open earlier.

Lars and Randy stood with their arms in the air as the meth heads pointed 9mm guns at them. Stacks of money and several little baggies of crystal sat on an old desk.

Mason knew this scene, had been there too many times with the addicts and dealers in prison, and instinct took over.

He kicked one meth head in the stomach, knocked the weapon from his hand, and punched him in the face. The man hit the floor hard. The other addict raised his shaky arm, his gun leveled at Mason's chest, but Mason grabbed the man's arm and twisted his hand backward.

A pop echoed in the room, the addict's wrist dislocated, and the gun clattered on the hardwood floor. The wide-eyed addict collapsed on his knees.

Lars and Randy grabbed the fallen weapons as their customers writhed in pain.

Mason leveled his hard glare at Lars. "Is this how you run your fucking business? You let meth heads get the upper hand and rob you? You always need some kind of weapon on you during sell-and-trade transactions."

Lars scowled. "They're loyal customers. We didn't think they'd turn on us."

"They're addicts in need of another hit. Just look at their eyes. You can't trust someone who's this messed up. You should know that or Thorn never should've hired you." Mason itched to punch the dealers, but he turned back to the addicts and grabbed one of them off the floor. "Get out of here. Consider your guns confiscated and don't ever come back to this establishment. You want drugs? Go somewhere else."

He shoved the man toward the door.

The addict stumbled, but the other injured man grabbed him, and they pushed past Mia to flee the office.

Shock filled her eyes as she stood in the doorway.

He dished out apologies so often Mia probably took them with a grain of salt, so he ignored her and faced the dealers.

"I think the cat's out of the bag." Randy nodded toward Mia, his face red.

Lars stored the guns inside a desk drawer, and his arms opened wide as he skirted the desk to stand in front of Mason. "Thanks, man. Things just got out of hand. You saved our asses, the money and product too. Thorn would flip his lid if we lost his shit. How can we repay you?" He nodded toward the stacks of bills on the desk. "I'm not sure how much the average Capularia bodyguard makes but—"

"I'm not with Capularia, and I don't want your damn money. Just finish Mia's tattoo so we can go."

Lars nodded. "Sure, no prob. Consider it on the house. If you or your girl ever want anything else, piercing or tat, just come by and it's free."

Mason bit his tongue to not refuse the generous offer. Lars would probably take offense, and Mason didn't want to piss him off before he finished the butterfly. If the dealers followed the standard Onyx rules for robbery and theft, they would notify their main contact in Capularia who would notify one of Thorn's lieutenants, if not Thorn himself, so Mason didn't bother to ask them to keep their mouths shut.

He forced his gaze to Mia and closed the distance between them. "You still want the tattoo? We can go.

It's no problem to go somewhere else."

"Let's just finish it."

Mason sighed as Mia headed back down the hall. "Okay, I'll guess we'll take that free tattoo." He left the office and Lars trailed right behind him.

Half an hour later, Mason and Mia left the parlor. Birds twittered overhead, and a billowing oak tree shaded their picnic table in a densely wooded public park. The sun steadily descended in the cloudless blue sky. Mia scarfed down a quart-sized box of egg foo yung as though she'd starved herself all day, and he guzzled his lemon-lime soda to settle the waves in his nauseous stomach.

"Sondokes is a prison gang." Mia jabbed her chopsticks in the box. "Right?"

"It's a prison *set*, not technically a gang, but let me start at the beginning." Mason rubbed his eyes and tried to form the jumbled words in his brain. "I already told you Oskar Udell granted me protection for saving his nephew from an attempted rape. I didn't tell you Oskar revoked the protection after I left the infirmary. He worked for this organization on the outside, but acted as their lead contact inside the prison. He wanted me to work for him, for *them*. I agreed."

"That's when you joined Onyx?"

"Yeah. Prison politics control everything. Without Oskar Udell's network, some asshole would've cornered me again with his cock reared and ready to go." He slammed his fists on his knees. The incident in the shower room rushed through his mind like tar. "Besides, I didn't want Oskar as my enemy. I didn't have a choice, but that's a cop-out. I could've kept my honor for as long as possible, and then just dealt with the pain and humiliation after some jockers raped me."

Her throat bobbed. "I wouldn't call that the better option."

Mason shrugged. "Oskar accepted only a privileged few into his personal fold though he controlled a large group of men in various cellblocks. I guarded the Sondokes members who dealt drugs or peddled some other contraband. Oskar's outside contacts smuggled it all in. I made sure no one attacked or took advantage of anyone under the captain's protection. Other guys protected me in return." He'd made friends among them, men who took punches for him and vice versa, and he wished he didn't miss them. "A few years before my parole, I realized I needed to behave or I'd never make it out early. Oskar understood. I still watched out for the crew and stopped fights before they started, but I didn't beat up anyone anymore. Backup did it for me."

"You said you rehabilitated in prison. Why didn't you tell me this?"

"I did clean up, and I'm telling you the full truth now." He scratched the gang symbol on the back of his neck. "The captain wanted me to continue working for Onyx on the outside, but I refused. Onyx controls the largest methamphetamine production in the American Southwest. Some guy known as Z heads up the whole thing. Since he distributes to five states, he divided Onyx into five territories and enlisted other people to monitor them. Colorado is one of those territories." He popped his knuckles, and the sharp pain in his joints relieved the tightness. "The Scorpion is the general of the Kondorro set. He controls the trade all throughout Colorado and keeps in close contact with the captains of the smaller sets in his domain. Sets like Sondokes, Capularia, and Dowitcha."

"It's run like the military?"

"Kind of, but it's more like a hierarchy. From captain to kingpin, all the leaders have councilmen or lieutenants to help them make decisions. If the councilmen disagree with the leader, they can overthrow him through a vote and a bloody fight, but that rarely happens." He pushed a long sigh from his lungs. "I don't know much more than that. The less I knew about the shit I fell into, the better."

"Were you a lieutenant?"

"No, no. I didn't pay enough dues for that privilege. I was just a bodyguard."

She shifted on the hard, firm bench and glanced down at the grass.

"I made some money with Sondokes over the years, but I didn't see a dime until I left on parole. It's chump change, really, since I would've made a lot more for the same work if I did it on the outside. No one outside of Onyx knows this, not even your brother." Mason licked his dry lips. "Oskar hired a bank manager to monitor his outside funds, so this guy showed up on Alan's doorstep a few days after I moved in. He gave me a bag full of unmarked bills. I assume Oskar gave him my address, but I don't know how Oskar found that out unless he knew someone who could look at my release papers. I didn't deposit the cash in my bank account because Borden checks it to make sure I don't live above my means."

"How much? Where's the money now?"

"Thirty grand. There's a loose piece of drywall behind the water heater in Alan's apartment, so I stuffed the bag in between the walls." Her eyes bugged out but he barely paused. "I haven't spent a single dollar. I want to live and struggle like an average guy to make ends meet, but I'll put the money in my bank once my parole is over."

"You earned this money by beating people up?"

He flinched. "Yes and no."

"Right, you just beat people up who tried to attack or rob your drug dealer associates? People like Lars and Randy?" She fisted her hands. "Are you out? Really out?"

"Yes, I'm out. Oskar vouched for me, and the Scorpion released me since I didn't know anything instrumental about the way he ran his operation." He forced his hands through his hair, more than a little agitated, as she scowled at him.

A warm breeze wafted around them and swiped a few strands of Mia's hair over her face. She hooked the strands behind her ears and diverted her gaze from his. A few people jogged by the secluded table—the asphalt path wove through all sections of the park—but they didn't seem to pay Mason or Mia any attention.

He sealed his lips until the strangers rounded a curve. "As far as I know, the police and feds have just a basic working knowledge of how Onyx operates. The criminals in charge run everything below the radar and rely on expendable pawns like Harper and Lars to sell their products. From what I've heard on the news and read in the papers, the media can't seem to get their facts straight. They don't often report on Onyx because they don't know enough to begin with, but when they do, they report bad info and half-truths, and leave the clueless public in fear."

"Sounds plausible."

"It's true. You now know more than most people. Don't spread any of this around."

"Of course not."

"I'm serious, Mia. Keep this to yourself." Mason reached across the planked table to grasp her hands. "I want nothing to do with Oskar Udell, his bosses, or anyone else in Onyx. I don't know why I helped Lars and Randy. They deserved to get their asses whupped, but they could've died. I'm good at defusing bad situations, and my instincts kicked into gear."

"Those addicts need rehab and the dealers should face jail time." She stared at their joined hands. Pain narrowed her eyes. "I appreciate Lars's offer for free tattoos, but I won't go back there. I won't tell Angie or anyone else what her cousin does on the side. She probably wouldn't believe me anyway, and I don't want to hurt her."

"Just as I didn't want to hurt you."

"That's different. I'm your girlfriend and you owe me the truth, no matter how much it might hurt." Mia pulled her hands free and braced them on the table. "I'm not mad at you for stopping the drug deal gone bad. I don't think I'm mad over anything, but I am disappointed. Did you think of me as some high-and-mighty bitch queen who would shun you or look down on you? You strung me along for weeks with bits of information here and there, but I tried to give you time to tell me everything of your own free will. A relationship can't stand on half-truths."

"You're not a bitch queen, but it *is* high and mighty of you to expect me to blurt out all my mistakes when you know I don't trust people easily. I trust *you*—don't misunderstand me—but women have stabbed me in the back before, so I took the safe road." Her disappointment struck him hard, worse than her anger could have, and her gentle reprimand reduced him to feeling like the worst type of shit. "It goes against everything I believe in to tell you about my past."

"Why?"

"Because I love you." The words spilled from his mouth. As her eyes widened, he swallowed hard to soothe his rough voice, but he couldn't take back those stupid words. "I love you, Mia, and I know you'll stab me in the back any time now."

"I won't hurt you, at least not intentionally." Tears streamed down her cheeks. "How—how can you love me? We've only known each other for maybe a month and a half."

"A lot can happen in a short amount of time. Does it seem like just six weeks to you?"

"No, much longer."

"That's how I feel. When I first met you, I saw a sexy babe with long legs. During our first date, I realized you were more than a chick to play with for a few weeks. You're intelligent and stubborn. You have a knack for understanding, and your quirky sense of humor drops me every time. You see through my bullshit like nobody's business." He grasped her hand again. "I don't expect you to say you love me back. In fact, I don't want you to. I want you to think of what I've said today and let me know if you can handle it."

"I can handle it as long as you no longer work for Onyx. Your captain let you go, and I don't want anyone to drag you back in."

"I promise that won't happen, darlin'."

"Everything's fine, then. We still have to deal with Jim. He'll shoot through the roof when he finds out I won't dump you over this."

"I wish I could hold you in bed tonight."

"Dream about me. I'm sure I'll dream about you. I usually do." Mia wove her fingers between his and thumbed his knuckles. "Thanks for Fly-Baby. I really like her."

"What?"

Blush filled her cheeks. "I named my tattoo *Fly-Baby*, and it's a girl."

Mason grinned as the tension eased from his shoulders and stiff muscles. "As I said, you have a great sense of humor." He leaned across the table and kissed her.

Chapter Fourteen

"Done." Mia pressed the send button and smiled at the picture of a delicate trinket on the computer screen. The last whimsical blown-glass angel had sold out hours earlier, so she emailed the local artist who created them. She should've ordered a new shipment the previous week after she took inventory, but Mason distracted her in the best and worst ways.

She leaned back in her swivel chair and swept her gaze across the small office. Lush flower swags hung over the door and over two bookcases, her favorite knickknacks decorated a few shelves as dust coated several business books on the bottom, and a collection of framed certificates hung on the wall. An eight-by-twelve photo hung in the middle of the *Best Small Business in LoDo* and *Most Stylish Boutique of the Year* awards. She left her desk and stroked her finger down the protective glass of the picture frame.

"I wish you could see this place, Mom. The business is thriving. I miss you and Dad so much." In the photo, she and her mom had lifted their arms and sashayed their butts like showgirls to present the new sign above the boutique doors. Her brother had snapped the photo as her father rolled with laughter. Mia tried not to think about her parents, the pain still too raw, but sometimes she just needed to talk to her mom for the sake of her own sanity. "I met a new guy and I'm crazy about him. The way he looks at me, the way he touches me, I feel like I'm the only woman in the world. Mason doesn't suck up to people or pretend to be someone he's not. He's definitely dealing with some personal demons, but I trust him. We had a relationship breakthrough the other day, and I believe he's finally and totally open with me."

She rested her head on the wall. Jim had called her a few hours earlier and told her he hired Giles Morrow, his recently suspended cop buddy, to track Mason's whereabouts. Jim knew she and Mason visited a tattoo parlor and a park, and that she shared dinner with Mason and his family twice throughout the past week at his apartment. He *didn't* know about the drug deal Mason sabotaged, what they talked about at the park, or her overnight stay with Mason on his birthday. He also didn't know two skinheads attacked them in an alley, so the tracking probably started a day or so before they met Lars and Randy. Her brother filed the paperwork to ban her from Mason's legal address as Alan had expected he would, and Jim used delivery-certified mail to send her copies of the ban notice earlier that day.

My junkless brother needs to grow a pair of balls and confront me in person. She pinpointed the official Colorado Parole Division envelope on her desk and wished it would shoot up in flames. *I should kick him in what 'nads he does have and ruin his chances of ever having kids.*

She'd hoped Jim would let up after their talk in his office, but her new tattoo seemed to set him off. Mason had told her that his and Jim's meeting yesterday nearly ended in a fistfight at the diner. Since Jim was POST certified, he could arrest his parolees if needed, but she doubted he would follow through with his threat and call for someone to arrest *her* if she stepped one foot in Mason's apartment.

No, of course he wouldn't. He'd probably just throw Mason in the backseat of his car.

Mia struck her fist against the wall. A knock rapped against the open door and she turned to see Angie in the doorway. Though the spunky twenty-five-year-old psych major sported a lip ring, short green hair, and tattoos, Mia would never consider her dangerous or a bad person.

Not like her drug-dealing cousin, whom Mia still halfway liked.

"Two really hot guys are here to see you. They're out front by the register." Angie wagged her eyebrows. "You never said your new boyfriend has a hot Latino friend."

"He doesn't, not that I know of."

"Well, it's about time I meet this mysterious Mason."

"Okay, I'll be out in a minute." Dread pooled in her stomach as Angie left the doorway. Mia straightened the blouse she'd tucked into her plaid pencil skirt and applied a layer of red gloss to her lips. Near six o'clock on a Tuesday evening, only a few customers remained. She reached the register area and looked around for Mason.

"There you are!"

Air lodged in her throat. A tall, handsome man with piercing blue eyes and short blond hair strode toward her. She recognized his deep timbre. A second man with long braided hair and skin kissed by the sun emerged from behind a shelving unit.

Oh, crap. This is so not good.

Mia locked her hands behind her back as they joined her at the checkout counter. "Trent. Pedro." She nodded to each of them. "I'm surprised to see you here."

"You remember us? Good." A cocky grin spread across Trent's face. "That rude-ass man of yours didn't introduce us a while back."

"I don't think he even mentioned my name. How did you find me?"

"You're not much for pleasantries, are ya?" Trent shrugged. "All right, one of our employers wants to see Mason. They're old friends. We stopped by his apartment and the garage, but he wasn't there."

"How do you know where he lives and works? How did you know to come here?"

"The *chica* asks too many questions." Pedro flashed a wolfish grin. "Just answer, *sí*?"

She dug her nails into her palms and grit her teeth to silence her sharp tongue.

"Easy, man. Don't scare the babe." Trent popped Pedro on the arm but never took his gaze off Mia. "Mason says he's out, but the talk all over town says otherwise. He beats up skinheads and stops robberies. How can he be out?"

Pedro tsked. "He can't, *hombré*. Just can't."

"That's what I think." Trent's voice lowered an octave. "In case you haven't guessed, Mia, we have a few mutual friends. They told us Mason's sexy little girlfriend runs a shop in LoDo, so here we are as a last resort. We need to have a powwow with Mason, or at least get a message to him." His gaze traveled down her body. "Don't suppose you'd lift your shirt and show us your new tattoo?"

She stepped back and hit the counter. A deep breath filled her lungs but barely soothed her nerves. "So you know Lars?" Another question, but she didn't care.

"And Randy." Trent winked at her and chills shot down her spine. "Where's Mason?"

"I don't know. He's out with his brother to buy a car. We don't have plans to meet tonight." Mia glanced at the art-deco clock on the wall behind her. They'd probably take offense and break something if she told them to leave, but she couldn't stand to look at them with a fake smile on her face. "The store closes in about ten minutes. Since you guys came here all the way from Aurora, you might as well pick up something pretty for your wife or girlfriend to make the trip worthwhile."

Trent chuckled. "No wives, and our chicks ain't worth the price of this froufrou stuff. Besides, we're happy to talk to you for a while."

She forced a light laugh. Tension throbbed behind her eyes and seeped into her face. The overhead lights shone too bright to accommodate her budding headache and reminded her of an interrogation lamp. She longed to relax in her dark bedroom, safe and warm in her bed.

A small group of middle-aged women headed toward the checkout, so she ushered her unwelcome visitors toward the doors. They walked ahead of her, and her gaze landed on the back of Trent's neck. Crisscrossed snakes in a small circle tattooed his skin. Pedro's thick braid hid his neck and possibly a similar tattoo, but she knew he could have inked the Onyx gang sign anywhere on his body. The men paused and turned to face her—*Why can't they just leave?*—and she forced her smile to stay in place.

Angie hurried to the counter from somewhere in the back of the store, and Pedro's gaze shifted toward her. Her employee smiled at Pedro as she rang up a few items—a flirty smile, not one of civility—so Mia doubted Angie overheard her conversation with the gangbangers.

Mia stepped to the side to block Angie from his sight.

Pedro cocked his eyebrow at Mia and his wolf grin lengthened.

"Udell wants Mason to stop by our party next Saturday." Trent crossed his arms. "You gotta come too. We won't take no for an answer."

"We're busy. Besides, his PO ordered a curfew."

"Change the plans. Break curfew."

Her temper snapped. "It's time for you guys to go." No one ordered her about or threatened her, especially not in her store. As the customers walked toward them and raised their eyebrows at the grungy men, Mia stepped aside so the women could leave.

"Mason knows where to go. He better obey Udell's orders or he'll face the consequences. Tell him to meet us there by eleven o'clock." Trent headed out the doors.

Pedro clicked his tongue at her and followed Trent out.

Angie hurried to her. "Are you okay? That blond guy wasn't Mason, right?"

Mia nodded and locked the double doors. "Let me know when you're ready to leave. I'll drive you to the bus station."

The men drove away in a blue sports car, music blasting from their stereo speakers.

She withdrew the drawer from the register and returned to her office as Angie sprayed a cleaner on the glass doors. Every fiber in her body told her to call Mason, but he wouldn't return home for a few hours. The landline phone on her desk snagged her attention every few minutes as she counted down the sales for the day. Once she recorded the total sales on her computer, wrote up a bank deposit slip, and locked the money in the safe behind her desk, she grabbed the phone and dialed Mason's number. As she'd expected, Alan's recorded voice reached her ears after a few rings and she hung up the receiver. She couldn't tell Mason, at least not over the phone. Her boyfriend would flip out, and then Alan would ask a lot of questions.

"I'm ready." Angie knocked on the door. "Do you mind telling me what's going on?"

"I wish I could." Mia grabbed her purse from the bottom desk drawer. "I just know those guys are trouble. They're not welcome here, so I'll call the cops if they come around again." They left the store and took refuge in Mia's car. She started the engine. "I don't have the right to say this, but you should stay away from them if you happen to see them around town, especially the Latino one, Pedro. I think he likes you."

"He's definitely a hottie, but he creeped me out." Angie buckled her seatbelt. "All the looks in the world can't make up for bad manners."

Good. She drove toward a nearby bus stop as Angie asked her a dozen questions. Mia wished she could give her straight answers, but she wouldn't purposely involve her in this mess.

Now she better understood why Mason had kept secrets from *her*. He just wanted to protect her, as Mia wanted to protect Angie.

They parted ways once the southbound bus arrived.

With the security alarm set in both her store and home, Mia paced the length of her adjoined living and dining rooms for almost an hour and decided to not tell Mason what happened.

The secret ate away at her, and three days later, she couldn't keep quiet any longer.

Mia breathed deep as a breeze wafted through the open windows of her car and pushed out the stifling heat. The sun blazed hot in the late June sky, and she missed the beautiful spring weather from just the week before. For the past half an hour, she'd waited outside a large brick building that housed several psychiatrists' offices. Her temples throbbed and her stomach cramped. People passed on the sidewalk and cars sped by. She tried to prepare her words, but nothing sounded right.

The front door opened and Mason left the building. Sunlight bathed him in lush, golden tones. His wide shoulders and tall frame curled her toes. As he hurried down a short flight of stone steps and headed down the sidewalk, she grabbed her purse and rushed from the car.

"Mason, wait!" She waved her arm just as he reached his new vehicle, an older model four-door SUV.

He whipped around and his lips curved in a smile. "Hey. What are you doing here?" Mason held up his hands as she tried to hug him, and he pecked her cheek. "Aren't you supposed to be at an art exhibit? I thought Chanel roped you into going with her tonight."

"She did, but I promised her I'd go tomorrow

instead. Would you like to come?"

"Sure, it could be fun."

She grinned as he kept her at arm's length. "C'mon, Mason. I want to hug you."

"No, you don't. Trust me. I stink of sweat and oil. A car backfired today so I'm also covered in exhaust." He glanced down at his blackened cut-off jeans and T-shirt. Now that he mentioned it, he *did* look dirtier than usual. "I forgot my backpack, and I don't have any clean clothes in my new ride to change into."

"You could've washed up before you left the garage."

"I did, but a sink doesn't compare to a hot shower. My therapist is a dick, so I didn't care if I stunk up his office a little." An admiring gleam lit his eyes as Mason looked her up and down. "I'm happy to see you, but why are you here?"

"We need to talk."

He backed up. "Is everything okay?"

"I—I don't know. I should've told you sooner, but I knew you'd probably blow a gasket."

"Are you breaking up with me?"

"No. God, no." She wrapped her arms around his neck despite his attempt to keep her clothes and body clean. His chest brushed hers, but the oil and exhaust on his work clothes and the smudges on his skin had already dried. "I'm happy with you, baby."

"Let's go for a walk. I'm so relieved I don't have to take the bus unless I want to, or wait on Alan to pick me up." Mason leaned back to pat the passenger door of the green four-wheel-drive. "And I can finally take you on a proper date."

She rolled her eyes. "You know I don't mind if I

drive or pick you up."

The muscles in his shoulders tensed beneath her hands. "What's on your mind, darlin'?"

Mia pulled back and walked down the sidewalk to gather her thoughts. A few businesses occupied the street, and a concert poster of Jimi Hendrix in a record store window drew her attention. A blue-and-white striped awning sheltered her from the sun and the vinyl edges flapped in a light breeze. Goose bumps covered her arms as she wrung her hands together.

He hurried up beside her. "Mia, you're scaring me."

"Some people visited me at the store a few days ago."

"Who?" Mason grasped her arm.

She turned around to face him. "Those guys from the Chinese restaurant, Trent and Pedro."

Air hissed through his teeth. "When? Why didn't you call me?"

"Last Tuesday. I—"

"Three days ago?" He snatched his hand back as though her skin caught fire. Anger screwed his face into tiny lines. "So that's why you acted so weird at the restaurant yesterday. Alan, and even Danny, could tell you were upset about something."

She swiped strands of hair behind her ears. "I couldn't mention it in front of them."

"No shit, but why didn't you tell me when we talked on the phone for hours every night this week like damn teenagers?" He stepped back and clenched his hands at his sides.

"Mason, please." She smoothed her fingers over his face as the muscle in his right cheek twitched.

"Keep your voice down. There are people across the street." She nodded at an elderly couple who left a pharmacy and then at a few twenty-something-year-old kids near a bookstore.

"Did they hurt you? What did they say? Tell me now."

"This is why I didn't tell you. You're angry."

"I'm not angry. I'm furious. I don't want you near them. You can trust me with anything, especially if it deals with me. Don't you know that?"

"Of course I do." She rubbed her sweaty hands on her skirt. "They want us to swing by their party tomorrow night at eleven o'clock. I told them about your curfew, but they don't care."

"Fuck them. We're not going. Even if I planned to, you sure as hell aren't."

"Trent said you had to obey Udell or face the consequences. He even has an Onyx tattoo on his neck. Pedro probably has one, too, but I didn't see it."

His eyes widened as though in panic. "Trent knows Oskar Udell? Why the fuck is this happening?" He fisted his hands in his hair. His chest heaved as though he would hyperventilate at any moment.

She gripped Mason's T-shirt as he backed farther away from her. "Trent told me to give you this message. I've done that, better late than never. Tell me what it means."

"It means I have a party to go to."

"Mason, no. I—"

"You aren't going, Mia. I don't care what Oskar demanded. I won't take you there."

"What about the curfew?"

"Screw it. If your brother wants to throw me back

in prison, so be it." He glanced at his watch. "We should go. I shouldn't chance missing curfew tonight since I'll do it tomorrow." He wrapped his hand around her wrist and dragged her back along the sidewalk.

"It's not late. You have a few hours 'til curfew."

He didn't seem to hear her.

Mia freed her arm from his grip as they reached her car. "This is a mistake, Mason. Don't act impulsive." She nodded up at the brick office building. "Maybe you should speak with your therapist?"

His eyebrows shot up. "Damn, girl. Never bait a rabid dog." Mason jerked her close and pressed a hard kiss in the crook of her neck. "Go home. I don't have a choice in the matter." He released her and stalked back to his SUV.

Mia clasped her neck where he kissed her and stomped after him. As he climbed into the driver's seat, she yanked open the passenger side door and settled inside the roomy compartment. "We're not done. If you want to drive, fine. I'll take the bus back here to get my car."

He scrubbed his hand down his face. The key ring clanked in the plastic cup holder as he dropped it in, and he rolled down the driver's side window to air out the stuffy vehicle.

"I'll go with you tomorrow. You could get hurt there all by yourself."

Mason scoffed. "It's a party with people who think I'm just like them. I'll be fine."

"You've changed."

"They don't know that and wouldn't care anyway."

"Trent also said he knows Lars and Randy. Lars told them about my store and where to find me, but I don't think he knew it would be a problem for us."

He cursed and stared out the window. "Oskar promised me no one would contact me after I left on parole. With the exception of his bank manager, that's how it's been. I don't know what changed, unless he decided I owed him for the Franz Harper situation after all, but I don't think he'd do that. His word is absolute. None of this makes sense."

"Why do you want to go to this damn party?"

"I don't want to. I *have* to. When a boss summons, you obey. End of story."

She gripped his forearm until her knuckles whitened. "I'll go, too."

"I won't let those bastards near you." He snatched her hand and yanked her closer. "Don't you get it? I have to protect you. You may know what's going on now, but you're not a part of it. I don't want to be knee-deep in this shit myself." He shuddered and clenched his fist as though another wave of red-hot anger poured through him. "Lars needs to keep his damn mouth shut. I should stop by the parlor tomorrow and punch him in the face. Fuck it. I will."

"News flash, Lars already blabbed. Trent and Pedro's *connections* found out where you live and work. They went by your apartment, Mason, and the garage." She jerked her arm as he squeezed harder. "You're hurting me."

A frown creased his forehead. Mason glanced down as he dug his fingers into her skin and bent back her pinky finger. He dropped her hand like a hot chunk of coal.

She fought back a grimace and cradled her sore appendage between her thighs.

"I—I'm sorry, Mia. I didn't mean to hurt you, or yell, or scare you. I don't know what the fuck to do." He gripped her chin, his touch gentler, and feathered his lips over the tears on her cheeks.

"I've always wanted a badass boyfriend with a soft side. You know that, right?" Pain tore through her heart like a wrecking ball, and she chuckled softly to hide it. "I love your wicked sense of humor and possessive streak. In public, you treat me like a lady. In the bedroom, you spank me and pull my hair. I even like the little tic that beats in your cheek when you're angry. It's so damn sexy, until now." Mia picked at her beaded blouse. "Delete the videos and pictures you took of me. I don't want those to fall in the wrong hands."

His eyes closed as though in disappointment. "I'll want to make more when this is over."

"Of course, but how will we replace them if you die or go back to prison? Please, don't do this. You're not a puppet. You belong to yourself and no one else. Don't obey Oskar and do his bidding. You're better than this." A deep breath expanded her lungs. "I'll call Jim before I let you dig your own grave. I won't lose you to them."

Fire sparked in his eyes. "Don't speak that bastard's name to me, and don't you dare call him. We'll both be in a shitload of trouble if you tell him what's going on."

"He's my brother. I understand you don't like him, but—"

"My feelings for your *brother* go deeper than dislike. Borden's a chauvinistic prick who's too chicken shit to go after the woman he craves. He bends the rules in his favor and will screw over anyone to get what he wants."

"And you're different?" Mia didn't know what woman he meant. "You tried to dump me a few times because you were too chicken to fight for me. Now you're ready to break the rules and screw me over to run back to your pathetic, gangbanger friends."

"Oh, believe me. I'm different. When I did illegal stuff, I didn't hide or lie about it. Yeah, I sometimes threw the blame on someone else, but I manned up and took the consequences if they came. Borden hides behind a plastic ID badge and a diploma. He convinced a damn cop to follow me around. Can you believe it?" Mason looked in the rearview mirror as though he searched for the cop. "Crap like that can't be legal."

"I'm upset about the tail, too, but you're handling this completely wrong. You promised me nothing and no one would drag you back in. If you do this, you're not the man I thought you were." Air sawed through her lungs as he scowled at her. Determination set his features into a hard, implacable mask, and she realized she couldn't persuade him from this suicide mission. Her anger kicked up a notch. "Damn it, Mason. What the hell is wrong with you? Right now, it looks to me like my brother *is* a better man than you are."

"Get the fuck out of my car."

Mia thrust the door open and got out. Her heels clanked as she stomped toward her sedan down the street. The SUV engine revved and he sped off behind her.

She didn't look back.

Chapter Fifteen

Mason sat in his SUV outside a rundown apartment complex in northern Aurora. Several vehicles lined the street, and music drifted from open windows on the third story of the large building. He never wanted to come back to this rat-infested place. Whores, addicts, and dealers, scum that preyed on other people, lived and worked there. Even the landlord accepted drugs and used women's bodies as rent payment. The police watched the area but did nothing.

Or at least that's how it used to be.

Mia didn't belong here.

He loved his brother and nephew. He appreciated his job and liked the work. He'd adjusted to life outside of prison better than he expected, but lived in perpetual darkness until he met Mia. He'd told her the truth when he said he loved her, and he would never willingly subject her to the trash that frequented places like this.

Mason pried his hands from the steering wheel and forced his legs to exit the vehicle. A wave of nausea washed over him. He didn't belong here either, not anymore, but he knew better than to ignore a summons from his former captain. He'd acted like a hothead in prison—he snapped at the slightest touch and whaled his fists into someone's face rather than express an ounce of fear—and he needed that hard, out-of-control persona to retake him.

To survive in a world of criminals, he needed to act like one.

He hurried across the street after a car sped by. Trash littered the high grass and the untrimmed bushes near the building. Surrounded by drunks, crackheads, and women painted up in tacky, barely there clothes, he finally admitted the truth.

Mia's right. Her brother is a better man than I am.

He walked up a flight of stairs and ignored the people passed out on the stairwell and those who shot up or screwed in shadowy alcoves. The stench of alcohol, drugs, and body odor cloaked the warm night air. He coughed from the fusion of smells and reached the third story. The strong scent of whiskey stopped him in his tracks.

A woman dangled a bottle over the balcony rail. Delicious amber-colored nectar swished back and forth in the glass and begged him to take a drink. Mason stepped back and shook his head, far too tempted to grab the half-empty bottle from her grimy hands. Even though he'd violated two conditions of his parole— breaking curfew and crossing the Denver/Aurora border—he refused to indulge in a drop of alcohol. He'd never surrendered to temptation in prison, and he wouldn't start now.

Noise thrummed behind the closed door of apartment B10. With four units per level, this particular one brought back fond memories and hated ones alike. He'd played video games in the living room, drank on the same balcony where the hooker was now, and screwed girls in a back bedroom. He'd partied hard here and enjoyed every moment of it, and made a mistake here that changed his life forever.

Mason clenched his hands. He had been at least five years younger than all his former friends, so Pedro, Trent, Joe, and the others took advantage of him more times than he could remember. It took years for him to admit that, and he did so only with the help of a prison shrink. He should've moved far away from Aurora to a small town in the middle of nowhere, not just to the neighboring city of Denver, but he couldn't hide if Onyx wanted him back. Whatever deal he made tonight, he'd probably end up stuffing another bag of cash behind the water heater in the next few days.

He opened the door, not bothering to knock. A heady whiff of alcohol and sex bombarded him as he entered the apartment.

Metal music blared from a nearby stereo and shook the walls. The yellowed ceiling fixture lit the living room in a sickening glow. A few men about his age crowded together on a leather sofa and played a video game on the large flat-screen TV that hung on the wall. Two women made out in the corner while another woman and two men played cards at a cluttered dining room table. Plastic cups and junk food littered the carpet, and the burning rubber smell of black-tar heroin churned his stomach.

After all these years, Mason had thought Trent would've leased a new apartment, perhaps one in a better neighborhood. The man could certainly afford it since he worked for Onyx, but at least he'd upgraded his furniture from the worn hand-me-downs that once filled the rooms.

"Mason, you're here!" A loud voice boomed from down the darkened hall. Pedro strode toward him with his arms spread open for a bear hug. "Right on time."

Mason knocked his arms aside. "You fucking bastard. Why am I here?" If not for Udell's summons, he could've joined Mia and her friends at some art show. Instead he'd paced the length of his bedroom for hours that morning, cussed out the dealers at the tattoo parlor a few hours ago, and returned home to answer his PO's phone call. As Alan and Danny slept, he'd snuck from the apartment and drove here.

He didn't even know why he tried to better himself with dainty things like art.

No, he knew why. He wanted to better himself for Mia.

God, I'm pathetic.

Pedro glanced over Mason's shoulder. "Where's your sexy *señora*?"

"Not here. I'm not stupid enough to bring her to this shithole."

"Shithole?" Pedro crossed his arms over his bare, muscled chest. The Onyx sign darkened the bronzed skin between his pecs and blended with a collage of violent tattooed images. "Easy, *amigo*. I might take your insult personal and kick your ass. Trent definitely would."

"Try it." He'd love to bloody his fists on his old friend's face. "Answer my question. Why the hell am I here?"

"Because I wanted to see you." A voice rang out behind Pedro. "I knew you'd show."

Mason knew that voice. His heart stuttered and his gaze jolted down the hall.

Douglas Udell?

The lean, dark-haired man left a back bedroom and stuffed his loose, button-down shirt into a pair of tailored slacks. A striped tie hung loose around the collar of the shirt.

Mason glanced inside the room to see Trent screwing a woman on the bed and assumed they'd indulged in a three-way minutes earlier.

His former cellmate shut the door and headed toward him.

"Well, I'll be damned. I never thought I'd see you again, Doug." Despite his anger, Mason grinned as Douglas laughed and opened his arms. They hugged. Relief and shock whipped through him. Mason grasped the shorter man's shoulders and looked him up and down. "You look good. You kept up with the weightlifting."

"Hell yeah, I did." Douglas stepped back and pulled up his shirtsleeve to flex the muscles in his arm. The Onyx tat bulged on his biceps. "I expected once you got out on parole you'd find me and beat the shit out of me if I'd stopped. You always protected me."

"I just showed you what to do. You needed to know how to protect yourself in that viper pit and back in the real world." Three years had passed since his friend left on parole. "I'd hoped you moved on with your life, away from the drugs and all that trouble. Looks like you didn't."

"I never wanted to. You knew that. Besides, I didn't have much of a choice. I committed the heinous crime of grand theft auto, crashing the vehicle, and resisting arrest while drunk off my ass." Douglas laughed. "My humiliated family disowned me just as they did my uncle years before. They'd always talked about Uncle Oskar as though he played golf with the Devil, and I never met him until the State locked me up.

Hell, I'm damn lucky he accepted me as his nephew, but you already know all that. Anyway"—he nodded toward Pedro—"we met at a party last year. I recruited him and Trent to the business. When they told me about an old friend they ran into a while back, I nearly shit my pants. *You?* Ha, I couldn't believe my luck. It's high time we catch up."

"So this is a social call?"

"Yeah, isn't your girl here? I wanted to meet her."

"Wait," he turned to Pedro, "Douglas demanded I come here tonight? Not *Oskar Udell*?"

"*Sí*, but Doug told his uncle we found you. The captain's *muy* excited."

"Oskar promised me I'm out."

Douglas slapped Mason on the back. "You are. We just want a little favor. After all, my uncle did one for you. Remember Franz Harper?"

"The boss said to forget about that." His blood pistoned like hot fire through his veins. "I've already violated parole by coming out tonight. I won't take any more risks."

"Curfew sucks, man, but you brought that on yourself. Never bang your PO's sister, no matter how hot she is. That's stupid even for you."

Pedro laughed. "And you're not supposed to hang out with old pals, right? We got copies of your paperwork." He exchanged a sly glance with Douglas. "A couple of Denver cops and parole officers are on Thorn's payroll. Doug convinced a PO to fax him your files."

"So that's how you found out where I live and work." He'd half-suspected Oskar Udell's crooked bank manager had ratted him out, but he couldn't think of a sensible reason to warrant it. "What about my PO? Is he dirty?"

"Nah, not him." Douglas cracked his neck with his palm. "You'll get paid big if you do a little job for us."

"How the hell can I go straight if I do something illegal and accept gang money?"

"C'mon. Let's talk shop outside. I need some peace away from this damn music." Douglas headed toward the door as Pedro flipped him off.

Mason followed him out, more than ready to escape the dirty hovel. Stagnant air wrapped around him, and he yearned for a fresh breeze to blow away the stench.

Douglas avoided the hooker and strolled to the far side of the balcony. Shadows cloaked him like a shroud, and his voice barely rose above a whisper. "I called my uncle a few days ago and told him my associates found you. Oskar said you called him for a favor. It's true he said to forget about payment, but be real, Mase. You know you can't do that. All of us— Trent, Pedro, me, and anyone else who's involved— will forget about you after you complete the job, unless you change your mind and wanna stay on."

Mason tightened his jaw until it ached and struggled not to hit his former cellmate. He tried so damn hard to break away from the bastard he'd been, but shadows from his past kept creeping closer to taint every inch of progress he made.

"If not for you, I'd probably be dead by now." Douglas sighed. "You saved my ass in prison, literally, and you always looked out for me like a big brother for almost seven years. I'm sorry about this, but Uncle Oskar, the Scorpion, and the captain of Capularia think you're perfect for it. Thorn promised to pay you a couple g's at least."

"What kind of job?" He couldn't believe he asked it. "I worked as a bodyguard. I protected our people during business transactions. I bloodied my knuckles when idiots tried to cheat or steal from us. I didn't peddle contraband or collect revenue. I won't start now."

"I know, and you were great at it. You scared the fuck out of people."

"I was a damn bully. I hated it."

Sick as a child and weak as a man, Douglas craved strength and power. Under Mason's guidance, he'd worked out heavily to build his small physique, but he still shied away from fights. He recorded his uncle's in-prison finances but never collected the money due or bartered goods with fellow inmates. He likely continued the profession under Thorn. Mason had taken responsibility for him since that day in the shower room, but now he wanted nothing to do with the misguided young man.

"One of our Aurora-based operators refuses to pay his protection fee. Thorn doesn't want to blow up his store—they sell some high-end shit for us—but the old man and his son are cocky little bitches. They want free protection since they sell drugs for us." Douglas fisted his hands. "We want you to knock them around a bit. Make them pay the fee, seize all the profit from this month's drug sells to penalize them, and break a few things just for fun."

"How much profit does Thorn normally take? The usual?"

"Yep. Eighty percent."

"No wonder they refuse to pay. Eighty percent plus extortion fees are outrageous." Though the Sondokes set claimed the same amount of profits from the dealers, they didn't bother charging the dealers for protection. Apparently, the captains on the outside operated things a little differently from what he was accustomed to. He narrowed his gaze. "Why do you want me to handle this? From what I've heard, Capularia's membership is through the roof. There are plenty of guys to pressure them."

"Yeah, but don't you want revenge?"

"What are you blabbering about?"

"Jeston's Liquor? The assholes who sent you up shit creek without a paddle?"

That shocked him. His mind zipped back in time. *Fear ripped through him. Glass shattered and liquid pooled. His friends shouted. Guns fired. Pain hit him and blood gushed from his shoulder. He shook uncontrollably and pressed his hands to the clerk's wound.*

Vomit rose in his throat. Mason headed toward the balcony beside the hooker.

Her thin lips peeled back in what she probably considered a flirty grin. Her stained, flattened teeth needed a dentist's touch, pronto. She eyed Mason as though he'd magically turned into a large bag of meth, and she would beg at his feet if he promised her a little pick-me-up.

The idea repulsed him.

He grabbed the bottle from her hand and wiped the brim clean with the bottom of his shirt. The amber liquid teased and taunted him as a beautiful woman would in a pair of high heels and a nightie, and he pictured Mia in the sexy lingerie.

The hooker slid her cracked, red nails up his arm and grasped his biceps beneath the sleeve of his T-shirt.

He shoved her hand away and hissed.

"You heard him." Douglas strode up beside the addict. "Beat it."

She cursed them both before she walked down the stairs and out of sight.

"Again, why me? I'm not an enforcer." Mason leaned against the rail, brought the bottle to his nose, and sniffed the contents. A deep shudder coursed through him.

"Were you always this dense?" Douglas grabbed the bottle and took a swig. "Oskar Udell volunteered you for the job. He offers revenge. Thorn offers payment and he's a rich man to have on your side. Does the name Rieger ring a bell?"

Mason shook his head. "Should it?"

"Nah, never mind. My point is, the courts locked you up but you shot no one. You stole nothing. You took a bullet and stayed behind to help one of those fuckers. You're a better man than me." He swigged from the bottle again and smacked his lips. "I understand the DA had to charge you with something, but Walter Jeston and his redneck son Ronnie should've spoken up on your behalf. What kind of asshole father wouldn't show some damn gratitude for the man who saved his son's life?"

"I never deserved their gratitude."

"Be serious, Mason. Don't you wanna walk in there, grab a bottle of whiskey from the top shelf, and chug it down right in front of them?" He handed Mason back the bottle and pulled a gun from the waistband of his slacks. The black weapon gleamed. Douglas touched it with reverent fingers as though he caressed a woman's body. "Wouldn't you love to shove a gun to their heads and hear them cry out for mercy? They owe you a damn apology."

Mason regretted that night more than any other night in his life. He'd deserved his punishment and never harbored ridiculous fantasies of revenge. He just wanted a future.

With one last sniff of his drug of choice, he turned the bottle upside down and watched in sick fascination as the warm liquor splattered on the concrete three stories below. His heavy heart lightened as every drop poured from the bottle. He chose self-respect, honor, a chance to do something better with his life—for Mia and Alan—but mostly for himself. He dropped the empty bottle by his feet.

"Goodbye, Douglas." He clasped his friend's shoulder. "I don't belong here. I wish you happiness and safety, but don't ever contact me or my girl again." Mason turned away before Douglas could respond, and he headed down the stairs. Once behind the wheel of his SUV, he closed his eyes and breathed deeply of the clean air inside the vehicle.

Mason prepared a bullshit speech as he drove home in case Alan waited up for him. Since Borden's cop friend always stopped tailing him after ten o'clock, he didn't have to worry about Morrow notifying Borden of Mason's misconduct and then having his PO issue an arrest warrant. He did, however, hope with every fiber in his being Borden hadn't called and found out on his own.

Once he walked into the living room and his angry

brother approached him from the kitchen, Mason chickened out and hurried to his bedroom. He propped the corner chair under the doorknob to bar the door.

Alan cursed and pounded on the barrier until Danny cried out for him from another part of the apartment.

Mason barely slept as he replayed the night's events in his mind, and he twice answered his PO's phone calls. As soon as the clock struck six, the earliest he could leave his residence without breaking curfew, he bolted out the door while Alan slept. Though he should've called Mia before he showed up unannounced at her home, Mason cut the ignition to his vehicle and hurried toward the security door to push the buzzer.

Air stilled in his lungs. The door stood ajar in the frame and screeched as he pushed it open. Worry washed through him.

No way. Mia wouldn't act so careless.

He raced up the stairs and stumbled to a stop in the open doorway of the loft.

A few artsy wall hangings, pictures, and knickknacks lay smashed on the floor, the sofa stood a few feet back from its usual spot as though someone had knocked into it, and a bundle of mini-blinds hung bent over a window. Cold air circulated as always, but the overhead AC unit chugged as though it struggled to keep the loft cool with the door wide open. The security alarm and intercom panel appeared undamaged, however, which didn't add up.

He hurried through the mess, broken glass crunching under his boots, and searched the bathroom and bedrooms.

"Goddamn it, no." He kicked her bedroom wall and a few pictures rattled. Bile rose in his throat. Sweat slicked his skin. Mason stomped to the dining room and checked the second metal door. It held secured. Spots dotted his vision as he stared around the loft.

"She's gone. She's fucking gone." He gripped his hair with both hands and spun in circles. Fear tore through him like sharpened claws. "Oh God, what have I done? Why didn't I protect her? Fuck, I knew better than to get involved with her. I knew better than to try for a normal life." Tears burned in his eyes, and he rubbed his jaw to ease the tic in his cheek.

He wanted blood. He needed Mia in his arms. He would never forgive himself for this.

He would fucking butcher them.

Trent. Pedro. Douglas.

No one else had reason to take her. *A gun. I need a gun.* He could probably buy one with no paperwork required with the money he'd stored behind the water heater. They still outnumbered him—Onyx versus just him—and Mason knew he wouldn't survive a gunfight.

"What the hell happened?"

His spine snapped straight. Mason flipped around to find his parole officer by the door. *Damn it, I don't need this right now.* Jim Borden would probably shoot him first and search for Mia second. He met Borden's scowl and flexed his hands.

"Where's Mia, Harding?"

"I don't know. I got here a few minutes ago and found the place like this." Mason held out his arms to encompass the large living area. "She's missing."

Borden's gaze traveled around the room and then zeroed back in on Mason. His voice deepened. "What did you do?"

Panic clogged his throat. He swallowed hard and explained everything—his fight with the skinheads and his resulting phone calls to Oskar Udell, his chance meeting with Trent and Pedro, their visit to Mia's store, and the party he attended hours earlier. He even mentioned the incident at the tattoo parlor to segue into Mia's refusal to leave him after he laid the full truth in front of her.

The officer stomped past the sofa and punched Mason square in the face. Borden grabbed him by the collar of his snug T-shirt and thrust him against a wall. "You son of a bitch! How dare you do this to my sister? She's in danger because of your worthless ass."

Pain shot through his jaw and up his back. His vision swam, but he didn't bother to throw out his arms in self-defense. "I'm sorry. I know that means shit to you, but it's the truth. I never meant for this to happen. I swear I will find her."

"Find her? It's because of you someone barged in here and grabbed her." He released Mason, grabbed his cell phone from his blazer pocket, and punched a few numbers on the screen.

"No." Mason knocked the phone from his hand. "Don't call anyone."

Borden shoved him face-first against the stucco brick wall and jerked his arms behind his back. "You're under arrest, asshole. Anything you say can and will—"

"Arrest me later. You need me. I have to make a deal with the bastards who took her."

The incensed PO flipped him around, a pair of plastic cuffs in his hand. "Who? These old buddies of yours? Trent and Pedro?"

"Maybe, but they're just stooges. My old cellmate, Douglas Udell, is probably behind all of this. He asked me to do a job, but I refused. That's why someone took Mia." He cracked his stiff neck as Borden stepped back. "Doug's a lower-level associate of the Scorpion and—"

A bark of laughter escaped Borden's mouth. "You claimed you wanted out, but you still associate with the Scorpion's fucking pawns."

Mason bristled with the reminder. "Listen, Douglas works for Capularia and answers to Thorn. Have you heard of a man named Rieger? I think Thorn and Rieger are the same person."

"The only Riegers I know of are descendants from one of Denver's founding families. The current head honcho owns a few luxury resorts and donates to charities, hospitals, and the like." Borden shook his head. "Tell me about the Scorpion."

"Tell you what? No one even knows that damn insect's real name." Mason rubbed his throbbing jaw. "The Scorpion and my captain in the joint let me go because I didn't know anything important about Onyx."

"Goddamn it. I told Mia you were trouble. She wasted time and tears on you, gave you her body and her trust, and you just let this happen? Why didn't you tell me this sooner? I'm your damn parole officer, Harding."

"I wanted to. Every time I picked up the phone to do so, I slammed the receiver back down. How the hell could I tell you without you tossing me back in prison on a technicality?"

"Well, you're going now."

"No, shit. I'll slap the cuffs on me for you when the time comes, but we have work to do first." Spit thickened in his mouth at the thought of a team-up with the prick. "Don't mention this to anyone. I have it on good authority there are dirty cops in a few Denver precincts and POs in your office."

Borden snorted and thrust the cuffs in his pants pocket. "I trust the people I work with and my friends who work in Patrol and Narcotics." He snatched his phone off the floor.

Mason grabbed it. The PO lunged for him, but Mason shoved him back. "Don't chance it. Doug said there are cops on the take."

"Unlike you, I keep better company than lowlife scum. I won't endanger my sister by calling this in, at least not any more than you have already. Besides, this is a crime scene. The cops have to investigate and start a search." He clenched his hands. "A judge will add time to your sentence for every little wrong thing you say or do, like shoving me, so watch it."

"Mia means more to me than my freedom. Add on years. I don't care." Mason stared hard at the background picture of an orange cat on the smartphone. "Mia is collateral. I'll do anything they want if that means we get her back in one piece. If you alert the wrong people, she could be dead. If you lock me up, you'll lose your only bargaining chip. Why are you even here? I thought you and Mia weren't talking."

"We're not, but she called and left me a message last night. I ignored it until this morning." He rubbed his eyes, then stared at the floor. "She cried through the whole thing. The only words I could make out were 'Mason might die' and 'We need to talk about him.' I called her back this morning, but she didn't answer the phone. Now I know why."

"Damn, I didn't think she'd actually do it." He shoved his hand through his spiky hair. "She called to tell you everything I just told you. Mia begged me not to go to the party. I didn't want to go, but I needed to tell those assholes to stay away from her."

A shrill noise filled the air. Mason whipped his gaze to the living room as Borden rushed toward the upturned end table and grabbed the cordless telephone off the floor. Mason followed him and scowled at the restricted caller ID.

"What?" Borden barked into the receiver and held out his hand as Mason leaned in close to overhear. "Fine, we'll do it." He smashed the end-call button and dropped the phone back on the floor. The fine lines at the corner of his eyes deepened as he growled. Tension pulsated around him. Borden stalked to a window that overlooked the street. "Look at this, Harding. Recognize it?"

Mason jerked aside the bent blinds of the other window. A short black limousine waited out front. "I saw it parked down the street when I got here." He looked for a silver sedan with a dent on the side door but only spotted Mia's car and a handful of other vehicles on the street instead. "Your buddy, Morrow, acted like a thorn in my ass until this morning. He should've followed me over here. Where the hell is he?"

"I'm wondering the same thing myself."

"Who just called?"

"The assholes that kidnapped my sister." Borden grabbed his cell phone back and jabbed it against Mason's chest. "They want us to go for a little ride. Stay out of my way, Harding, or I *will* take you down."

He pivoted at a sharp ninety degree angle and headed out the front door.

Mason cursed and hurried after him.

Chapter Sixteen

Sunlight assailed him as he breached the mouth of the brick stairwell. Mason closed the steel security door that, like the door upstairs, had a lock that didn't appear damaged or tampered with. Mia probably buzzed her kidnapper in, which explained why no one smashed the alarm.

It also means she knows whoever took her.

A short, beefy man dressed in black waited by the open limo door. Shades covered his eyes. He likely performed the same task Mason had in prison, but Oskar Udell never provided snazzy suits for his bodyguards.

The anger in Mason's veins burned like wildfire. He closed the distance between them, and the muscle-bound brute grabbed him by the shoulder and thrust him against the vehicle. Air slammed from his lungs. Alone on the quiet, peaceful street, Mason bit his tongue and grasped the hood in order to not flip around and deck the guy.

Stay calm, man. Wait for the right moment to strike.

The guard frisked him and shoved Mason inside the limo. The carpeted floorboard cushioned his knees like a sheet of granite.

Borden grabbed his arm and helped Mason onto the seat beside him.

The guard entered, shut the door, and sat opposite of them.

Mason faced Douglas Udell.

A smug smile stretched the skinny man's lips. Douglas tapped the tinted window behind him, the limo pulled onto the street, and he thrust Borden's confiscated gun and smartphone in the inner-lining pockets of his blazer. Two grim-faced guards flanked his sides and their parted jackets revealed their holstered guns.

"You little bitch." Venom laced Mason's voice. Rage shuddered through him. "I should've let those jockers rape you the first day we met. I have a damn metal plate in my jaw and a facial tic because I helped you. Why the hell did you do this? Sooner or later, I will kill you. I will bloody your face beyond recognition, and I won't stop even when you beg me for mercy. Mercy I won't have. You know what I'm capable of."

Douglas blanched and coughed to clear his throat. "My colleagues, Stokes and Decker." He nodded to the brunet man on his right and the blond man on his left respectively, and opened his arms wide as though to make amends. "I'm sorry it came to this. I gave you the option to work willingly for the Scorpion and his favorite captain. You refused. You chose a woman over money, loyalty, and revenge. You're a fool to think you could say no without consequences."

"Have the terms changed?"

"Of course. You'll get your girl back instead of money as payment." Douglas tapped his fingers on his knee. Dressed like the perfect gentleman in black slacks, a white shirt, a dark tie, and a blazer, he'd even tamed his short hair and slicked it back over his head. "My guards will act as your backup. They are my eyes and ears to make sure you do the job right. If you fail to prove your loyalty, you're dead, simple as that."

"Oh, it's that simple, huh? I'll make damn sure to put your guards through the wringer if they try to off me. They'll have to work hard for their paycheck."

Douglas rolled his eyes. "You wanted a different life—my uncle wanted it for you—so the Scorpion released you. Jeston refused to pay his protection fee, and your old friends found you a few days later. Plus, you asked for a favor. We all believed you'd jump at the chance for good old-fashioned revenge." He tsked. "Since you live in the Denver area, you work for Thorn. He'd planned to cut ties with you after you fulfilled your debt with this job, but now he wants you for a longer term. You shouldn't have cast aside his generous offer."

Mason scrubbed his hand down his face. *What choice do I have? Mia's life depends on me.* He cocked his head toward his parole officer. "Why is he here?"

Douglas shrugged as Borden's gaze jumped to him. "We didn't expect him to show up at the woman's loft, so we had to bring him along or kill him. You took a long time to visit your little girlfriend, Mase. We expected you hours ago." He fingered the cufflinks on his sleeve. "You see, I figured you wouldn't bring Mia to the party, and you proved me right. I ordered my driver to pick her up shortly after you left. He was already watching her place and waiting on me to call him if you refused the offer."

"I swear to God, if she's hurt—" He paused as Stokes, the guard who frisked him, pulled his gun from its holster. Mason leaned back on the beige leather seat and held up his hands. "Fine, I'll do the damn job."

"No, you won't." Borden gripped Mason's arm and dug his nails deep.

The second thug, the beefier man with the blond crew cut, withdrew his weapon and shifted in the seat.

Borden didn't seem to notice or care. "Don't give these jackasses what they want."

Mason ignored the officer's outburst and jerked his arm free. "I'll do it on one condition." He seethed as an arrogant grin spread up Douglas's face. The shy, backward man he once knew had turned into a monster. "I want Jeremiah Borden and Mia Eddison released, unharmed, and they'll keep their mouths shut about this whole thing."

"Fuck that." Borden's face reddened. "You pricks won't get away with this."

"Don't act fucking superior and get yourself killed, Borden. Think of your sister. Shut up and let me handle this."

Douglas clicked his tongue. "I'll make the arrangements to keep them quiet."

His stomach twisted. "So be it. Just think of me as a puppet. Thorn can pull my strings for as long as he wants." Mason leaned forward, ignored the way the guards shifted, and offered Douglas his hand to seal the deal.

His old cellmate shook it.

Almost an hour later, the limo pulled into the parking lot of a decrepit factory. Abandoned warehouses and factories dotted the old industrial section of northern Aurora like a ghost town.

Mason exited the slick black vehicle behind one of

the bodyguards and Douglas. The sun dispelled the morning chill and beat down on the back of his neck. A soft breeze carried the stench of old oil and musk. He shaded his eyes with his hand and stared up at the large, two-story factory.

Wood planks boarded up several windows while shards of glass protruded from a few uncovered window frames. Rust spread over the metal roof in patches. A smaller building stood off to the side, deserted and worn as well.

Mason moved aside as someone grunted behind him.

Borden exited the vehicle, sunlight glinting off the blond strands in his brown hair, and his lips curled into a sneer as he stared around the lot.

The second guard followed him out and slammed the door shut.

They followed their captors across the broken asphalt toward the factory. With Stokes ahead and Decker behind them, Mason considered half a dozen ways to get out of this mess, but none of the ideas ended well for him.

Stokes opened a set of metal doors, a few flakes of rust drifted to the ground, and they crossed the threshold.

Streaks of light shone dull through the dirty, cracked windowpanes and through gaps in the planks. Shadowy darkness enveloped them. Thick stone pillars rose from the concrete floor and connected with steel beams to support the lofty ceiling. Old paint flaked off the walls. Onyx and rival gang graffiti stained the stone. Trash and tattered blankets littered the floor.

Decker shoved him forward.

Mason stumbled a few steps, gained his balance before he fell into a dirty puddle, and whipped around to face the guard.

Don't hit him. Not yet. Find Mia first.

Mason walked a few steps behind Borden and headed down a wide hallway. A few doors likely led to former storage rooms and offices. During his stupid teenage years, he and his friends would sometimes sneak into buildings like this to spray paint the walls and have parties. Now his skin crawled with every step he took. His nerves raw, he fisted his hands and tried to mentally prepare himself for whatever he might find.

Stokes stopped in front of a thick-plated metal door and groaned as he lifted the lever to unlock it. His right arm trembled and his face flushed red.

He's injured. Mason tucked that piece of information away for later.

Stokes pushed the door open, and a loud creak echoed through the sprawling factory.

Borden gasped and every muscle in Mason's body tensed. His gaze shot over the PO's shoulder. Musty, stagnant air stilled in his lungs.

Mason shot into the room just as Borden did.

Decker grabbed him by the collar of his T-shirt and wrapped his arm around Mason's throat.

Stokes shoved the officer against the nearest wall.

Anger swept through Mason like a wave of lava. He struggled to escape the headlock until Decker pressed a gun to his temple. Mason froze. His heart thundered to a stop and sped up again as he stared at the woman he vowed to save.

Gagged and tied to a chair in the middle of the small room, Mia screamed through the gag and shook

249

her head. Bruises marred her pale face. Tears welled in her eyes. A line of dried drool trailed down her chin, and the cut on her swollen left cheek probably needed stitches. Barefoot other than filthy white socks, she was dressed in ripped pajamas bottoms that concealed her long legs and a dirty tank top that hugged her chest. Sweat matted her hair and glistened on her skin.

The sight of her punched him in the gut. He wanted a do-over for the previous night, this morning, and especially the horrible night a decade earlier that set all this into motion.

"Mia, I will fix this. I'm so sorry." His words rumbled from his throat as Decker squeezed harder against his windpipe. He clutched the meaty arm and strained to pull it back.

"Ease up, Decker. He needs to be able to speak."

Decker obeyed Douglas's order and relaxed his grip, but then he flexed his arm, ready to squeeze Mason's throat again at any second.

Mason dragged air into his lungs and swallowed hard to soothe his bruised throat as Decker shoved the gun barrel harder against Mason's skull. Mason dared a glance at Borden who was struggling to break free from the cage of Stokes's arms. For all the training and experience the PO likely possessed, Mason knew the law couldn't save their lives.

He had to play dirty.

"We made a deal. Let them go." Mason growled like a rabid wolf as his former friend walked behind Mia's chair and placed his hands on her shoulders.

She shuddered but didn't cry out or whimper.

"Where's my money, Mason?" Douglas glanced around the room. "I don't see any bags or briefcases. I haven't watched the surveillance footage of those little pussies pissing their pants." He leaned down and whispered loudly in Mia's ear. "You should be proud of him. Your ex-con boyfriend agreed to extort tons of cash and send two meth dealers to the hospital to save you. You still think he's a good and decent man now?"

Shame flushed his body hotter than a furnace. Mason gripped Decker's arm tighter as Mia yelled into the gag. He couldn't make out her words and suspected Douglas couldn't either since he ripped down the twisted bandana from around her mouth.

"Asshole! You're going to pay for this and all your lies. You—"

Douglas laughed and jerked the gag back over her lips.

She continued to scream and rock forcefully in the wooden chair.

Douglas cupped her chin in his palm, pressed the back of her head on his stomach, and ground against her. Her bra strap fell from her left shoulder and he snapped it with his fingers.

Mia stilled, now silent.

"So feisty. I love potty-mouthed women." He released her chin and stroked his fingers down her messy hair. "I'm not kidding, Ms. Eddison. I never joke about business." His gaze flicked to Mason. "Tell her."

At a loss for words, Mason jerked his gaze to the dim yellow light bulb overhead. His insides churned and his empty stomach rolled. Every fiber in his body screamed in rage and betrayal. He forced his gaze back to hers.

Trust swam in her tearstained eyes.

Mason hardened his voice. "It's true, Mia. He'll

hurt you and your brother if I don't."

Her eyes widened and she stared at her brother.

Trapped in Stokes's hold, Borden managed a slight nod as though to confirm Mason's statement.

Mia shook her head again, dark hair flew about her face, and she shouted into the gag.

Mason swore he heard her scream "No" and "Don't you dare," but he couldn't be sure.

"Mason also agreed to work for my captain for an indefinite amount of time. You'll still see him, screw him, and act as if everything is normal. I don't want any of you to change the way you live, at least not to the outside world." Douglas stared pointedly at Mason and Borden before he leaned down to sniff Mia's hair. "I'll release you and your brother after Mason performs the job. Our employer ensures the silence of witnesses by killing them, paying them off, or through more lucrative, creative means. You and Mr. Borden are in the perfect position to distribute Thorn's product in the Capularia area."

"Just try it." Borden grunted as though in pain. "I know too many people for this little scheme to work. You'll be behind bars so fast you'll shit yourself."

Douglas swiped his tongue over Mia's earlobe. She shivered, and her brother thrashed harder for freedom. "We'll bug your homes, workplaces, and vehicles. We'll monitor your calls," he continued as if Borden hadn't interrupted him. "Your boutique is your greatest asset, Ms. Eddison. You'll receive a shipment from us every week or so, which you'll sell. We'll send you a few loyal customers to get you started, and they'll spread the word. If you don't sell it, expect a few broken windows, a fire, or a number of other accidents.

It just takes a little tweaking with some electrical wires, a busted water line, and *BOOM*."

She jumped and tried to scoot away.

He snatched the back of the chair and steadied her. "We also demand you pay a little protection fee—an *extortion* fee, as Mason likes to call it. Our competitors will seek you out if you sell our drugs. You'll need our manpower in your corner. If you don't pay, you're on your own with the street thugs. If you don't pay, expect accidents from us." He straightened from his lean and clasped his hands behind his back. "Onyx demands loyalty and obedience in all matters."

Douglas paced behind Mia's chair and stared at her brother. "The same applies to you. Sell to your parolees and bring in new customers. If not…" His words trailed off as he sliced his finger across his neck and made a ripping sound in the back of his throat. Borden cursed him as Douglas turned back to Mason. "Does that sound like a good bargain to you?"

The hot, feverish blood in Mason's veins ran cold. *Mia and Jim are good people. Honest people. I can't let criminals blackmail them.* But what could he do? Though it probably wouldn't be too hard to break a few bones and extort money from the Jestons, especially with the guards' aid, he didn't want to ruin Mia's life. Not even her cocky brother deserved this. Outnumbered and outgunned, Mason needed to keep his cool and bide his time.

For now, he'd play along.

"Yeah, it does. A damn good bargain."

Mia grunted and whipped her head to the side as though to stare at Douglas.

Mason doubted she could see him, even with her

peripheral vision, but it didn't matter. Pride swelled in his chest. Except for a few minor outbursts, Mia kept relatively calm when other women would probably panic or break down in useless sobs.

Douglas waved his hand in the air. The guard released Mason and holstered his weapon.

Mason rubbed his sore neck and moved a few feet away from Decker. "When do you want the job done, Doug?"

"Tonight. You'll come back here once it's over."

"Do I have your guarantee you'll release them afterward?"

"Yeah, after I send in a few men to bug their homes, work, and cars. So, by morning."

He clenched his fists. "I guarded people when I worked for Oskar in the joint, usually his *scrawny, pathetic nephew*." He bit out the last three words. "I never acted as an enforcer. I never hurt anyone who didn't deserve it. What you demand I do, I'm not that sort of person. I'm not a cold-blooded monster."

Douglas scoffed and rolled his eyes skyward. "Acquire their surveillance videotape for proof. Leave no prints. Report back here. It's very simple."

Decker made a slurping noise and licked his lips.

Mason stiffened as he followed the guard's line of sight. Despite her bra, Mia's nipples showed through the clingy fabric of her pajama top, and Mason wanted to gouge Decker's eyes out.

Mason tore his gaze away from Mia. Stokes pinned Borden to his chest with both arms, and Mason wondered why the bodyguard didn't use his gun to subdue Borden. Shorter than the officer by half a foot, Stokes forced Borden to bend at the knees. The guard seemed to ignore or not notice Mason's scrutiny as his unblinking stare followed Douglas around the room.

He caught Borden's gaze. Fire sparked in the PO's eyes. Camaraderie and knowledge passed between them, unspoken and just a feeling, but it struck Mason hard. No longer enemies, they stood a fighting chance if Jim stepped up to the plate as his ally.

Mason rushed Decker like a rampaging bull. The brute groaned as he fell on his back, his eyes wide, and Mason pinned him to the floor, grabbed the gun from beneath his suit jacket, and fired it at the other guard. Stokes shouted as blood sprayed from his leg.

Jim twisted free, grabbed the guard's injured arm, and bent it backward. Bone snapped. Stokes screamed and fell to one knee.

Mason dropped the gun. Red flashed in his eyes and overshadowed every sane thought in his mind. He whaled his fists in Decker's face. The blood on his skin soothed and riled his temper all at the same time.

Decker thrust his fist in a swift uppercut and knocked Mason backward.

His jaw burned and vision blurred. Coppery liquid pooled in his mouth. Decker's thick, gorilla-like body trapped Mason on his back, and the brute's knuckle-fisted sandwiches hurt like hell. The rough floor scraped his skin, and he'd definitely need a tetanus shot after this.

He tried to knock the asshole back, but Decker weighed too much. At the mercy of the other man's hamlike fists, Mason spotted the gun scant feet away.

The snarling guard fisted his hands together, struck Mason on the shoulder, and stood up to pound Mason's stomach with his foot.

A gasp of pain lodged in Mason's throat. His body trembled and he struggled to stay alert.

Decker grabbed a knife from his belt, pure hate raging in his eyes, and he stomped on Mason's stomach again. Twice, three times now.

Mason feared he'd pass out if this kept up. With the gun in sight, he lunged across the floor, snatched it up, and squeezed the trigger. The echo of the blast rang in his ears. A glassy sheen invaded Decker's eyes. Blood bubbled from his chest and gleamed like ink on his dark clothes. The knife fell to the floor, and Mason rolled to the side just before the lifeless body landed on top of him.

A muffled cry reached his ears. Mason jerked his gaze to Mia.

Douglas pressed his black gun to her temple and wrapped his arm around her chest as though to hold her still.

She trembled and tears slid down her cheeks.

Decker's gun weighed like solid rock in Mason's hand, and he laid it on the floor. He slowly rose to his feet, his arms up, and stepped back to avoid the thick pool of blood that spread around the body. His stomach twisted and coiled, but he managed to steel his spine and stand up straight.

Jim caught a punch to his chin and stumbled back, but he ducked another swing and rammed Stokes into the wall like a professional linebacker.

Stokes hit his head and slipped to the floor, unconscious.

The tough-ass PO stole the guard's gun and whipped around to face the others.

Mason shook his head and urged his unlikely

partner to calm down.

Jim's brown eyes widened as he spotted Mia. The weapon clattered on the floor as Jim lifted his arms.

"You goddamned fucker!" Douglas pushed away from the chair, his face a mask of fury. He shook the weapon, cursed and shouted, and the gun fired.

A bullet slammed into the wall behind Mason. His ears rang, gray concrete dust billowed and entered his lungs, and his stomach cramped as he coughed. Shock spiraled through him like white-hot lightning, and the old bullet wound in his shoulder ached. Not sure if Douglas meant to shoot, Mason doubted the poor excuse of a man would care one way or the other if he shot Mason right now.

He fisted his hands to concentrate. "These people mean too much to me, Doug. We used to understand each other. Understand this. I won't let you ruin Mia's life or the life of anyone she cares about, so take your demands and shove them up your ass."

The criminal dug the gun barrel against her temple again. "You sure about that?"

He couldn't look at Mia. Anger and fear surely burned in her eyes, and he would grovel on his knees to save her, but such weakness would likely piss Douglas off even more and hurt her chances of survival. Douglas knew him to be a cruel, no-nonsense type of asshole who never begged. Maybe he used to be like that, but now he knew he could find his next thrill in places other than busy prison rec rooms and dirty back alleys. Mia had shown him unconditional acceptance, and he owed her a debt he could never repay.

Mason swallowed hard, but the little saliva that traveled down his throat barely soothed his raw vocal cords. "Yeah, this nightmare can go in two directions. One—I'll do a lot of bad shit and eventually kill someone in cold blood. I'll live with the shame and guilt until I put a bullet in my head or drink myself to death, if Thorn doesn't put a hit out on me first. Two—I can fight back now, stop you, save her, and put an end to all this."

"You're screwed, Mase. You broke parole, and you'll break it ten times more before the day is over. Thorn will have to bribe a few people and take care of all the little details to make sure you stay far away from a jail cell. If you don't kiss his ass, kiss your freedom goodbye. Is a woman really worth time back in prison?"

"*This* woman is." He flicked his gaze to Jim. Her brother nodded, and Mason swore respect shone in his eyes. Ready to finish it, Mason swung his arrogant smirk back to Douglas. "I choose door number two."

And the metal door crashed open behind him.

Chapter Seventeen

Mia screamed a warning against the gag as Mason whipped around. Her brother's trusted friend charged inside the room, punched Mason in the gut, and knocked him over the dead guard. Mason slipped in the pool of blood and landed on his back. A hiss of pain escaped his lips. He rose to his knees a few feet from Jim, clutched his stomach as he doubled over, and his nostrils flared as he used the wall to hoist himself up.

"Giles?" Disbelief thickened Jim's voice. "You're involved in this?"

No shit, she wanted to shout.

The damn gag rubbed the corners of her mouth raw and doubled the saliva in her mouth. She drooled like an animal. Rope bound her hands behind the back of the uncomfortable wooden chair, and her shoulders ached from the strain. She'd jerked on the restraints for hours, scraped and broke her skin, and succeeded in loosening the knot. Rope also bound her ankles to the chair. Sweat clung to her body even though she shivered, and the barrel of the gun pressed to her temple burned a little too warm.

Dressed in civilian clothes, Narcotics Officer Giles Morrow brushed his fingers through his blond hair and glanced at her brother. He sighed as though in regret. "It's too bad you're messed up in this, Jim. I didn't want Mia involved either, but that's how things worked out."

"Why? How do you know this scum?" Jim nodded toward Douglas Udell.

Giles shrugged and glanced at the scum in question. "You care if I enlighten them?"

"Go ahead. We're all working together now, anyway." Douglas lowered the gun from her head, moved to stand beside her, and holstered the weapon in his slacks. Mia swallowed her sigh of relief as Douglas flicked his gaze toward Mason. "And we *are* working together. Even though you killed one of my guards, you're still exactly where I want you. You're a killer, now."

Mason clenched his fists.

"Self-defense is different from cold-blooded murder," Jim snapped. "I'll note that heavily in my report once we kick your asses and leave here."

Mason's brow lifted, and a tight smile curved his lips. "I didn't expect that."

"Shut up, Harding."

Mason's smile widened as he turned back to Giles. "Spill it. Tell us why you betrayed two friends and the damn law you promised to uphold. How crooked are you?"

Mia didn't care about his answer, but she assumed Mason tried to buy time as he fished for information. Anything they learned from their kidnappers could help turn the tide in their favor.

"My bitch ex-wife slapped me with a huge alimony obligation a few years back, and she won't even let me see my kids." Giles folded his arms across his broad chest. If Mia remembered right, Giles had cheated on his wife with a prostitute and faced only a minor reprimand for his illegal sexual activities. "Thorn provided me with the cash I needed to pay her off until a few weeks ago. My shit-for-brains police captain suspended me, and Thorn cut me from the payroll until the force reinstates me. Un—fucking—believable."

"You sent some petty hoodlum to the ER."

"So what, Jim? Dealers don't mean shit, especially dealers for rival gangs. I did my job and took a Capularia competitor off the street." Giles slapped his hands together. "Anyway, I couldn't believe my luck when I found out the man you paid me to track used to work for Onyx. Hot damn! Since Thorn wants Harding on the payroll and I want back in the big cheese's good graces, my pal Douglas and I cooked this up."

Giles then turned his cruel smile on her. He grabbed her chin and laughed as she tried to bite him despite the gag.

Mason and Jim shifted their feet as though they might launch into an attack, but Douglas grabbed his gun and they stayed back.

"Mia and I talked for a bit in her loft—she mostly berated me for tracking her boyfriend—and you wouldn't believe the shock on her face after I slapped her. We played a game of cat and mouse until I knocked her out cold and tossed her in the trunk of my car." Giles patted the bump on the side of her head, and she struggled not to flinch. He cast his gaze over his shoulder in her livid brother's direction. "I've always thought your little sister would be a firecracker in bed, Jim. If Harding doesn't follow orders, I'll find out soon enough how fiery she really is."

Mia closed her eyes as he trailed his fingers down her neck.

The long, bumpy ride in the trunk had jostled her awake, and Giles carried her inside a huge building as she kicked and screamed. He smacked her around and threatened to rape her as a shorter, smaller man watched from the corner. A demented grin stretched the stranger's face. Giles called him *Douglas*, and she suspected him to be Mason's old cellmate. Giles tied her up, and the men left her alone in the dank, dusty room for hours. Fear and paranoia had occupied her mind until she wanted to scream, and only the hazy sunlight streaming through the cracks in the boarded-up window kept her sane and level-headed.

Her eyes shot open as Jim's voice cut through her thoughts.

"She trusted you. We both did. We've known you for years." Jim cursed his college friend. "You're gonna pay for this, Giles. I swear it."

Fury burned in Mason's eyes. He seemed to watch the cop's every move before he turned toward her brother. "Remember when you said you don't keep company with lowlife scum? Bull."

Jim fisted his hands but kept quiet.

Giles withdrew from her side, slammed the door shut, and sneered at the unconscious guard. "Pathetic. Your bodyguards aren't worth a damn." He scowled at Douglas. "I parked the limo between the buildings, out of sight as requested, but this wouldn't have happened if I'd come in with you and not hid the vehicle. We should've used a SUV, not a limo like a bunch of fucking snobs desperate for attention. But you're a snob, aren't ya? You always gotta have the best." He rubbed his hand along his bristled jaw. "Not going according to plan, huh?"

"Fuck you, Morrow. It'll still work. Harding won't let his whore die." He cocked his eyebrow at Mason. "Right?"

Mason stepped forward, but Jim shot out his arm and kept him back.

"Don't play the hero." Douglas mocked. "It doesn't suit you. Besides, you're too smart. You know what we want, so you'd better do it. If not, she's dead. Her brother's dead. *You're dead* if you don't listen."

"I have one question." Mason sidestepped Jim and held out his arms as Giles flipped open one side of his jacket and showed off his holstered weapon. "How do you expect us to be friends after this? I will hate you until my dying breath. You must know that."

"You and civilian life don't mix, Mason. You're a badass Onyx bodyguard, much better than Stokes and Decker. You'll forgive me. You'll realize before long I did this with the best intentions, and you'll thank me, especially when the money and girls pour in like candy."

Mia rolled her eyes at the dribble Douglas sprouted.

Mason wore his anger like a cloak. Eyes narrowed and shoulders straight back, the stare he leveled on Douglas promised fire and retribution until something shifted on his face. He dropped his arms and shook his head, disappointment in his eyes.

She longed to hold him. He cared so much for Douglas, and this betrayal surely stabbed him like a knife in his heart.

Mason scrubbed his hands down his face. "All right, I guess I'm out of options."

Don't give in! Panic rose in her chest. Mia

chomped on the bandana and struggled for freedom, desperate to stop Mason from making the worst mistake of his life.

"Remove the gag. What's the point of it, Doug?"

"Your bed buddy bites." Giles answered for the smaller man and lifted the back of his hand to show off a bandage. She'd bitten him hard enough to draw blood, and he gagged her as a result. "The bitch also screams like a banshee."

She thrashed so hard the front legs of the chair popped off the floor.

"Don't hurt her, and I'll do what you guys want." Mason swiped his hand toward her. "Remove the damn gag. She can't breathe well."

Douglas huffed and pulled down the bandana.

Mia quieted and gulped air into her lungs. Her dry lips cracked. The smell of death wrecked havoc on her senses, and her stomach curdled into a nauseous pit. Blood and urine coated the stagnant air. Someone had lost control of his bladder, probably one or both of the guards. Decker's lifeless form lay in a pool of dark blood. If she survived today, she would have to re-examine her taste for bloody films, at least until she pushed this nightmare from her mind.

"Mia, look at me. Not at the blood. Stay calm."

Mason's deep voice drew her gaze. Little stress lines branched from the corners of his eyes and pursed lips. Perspiration plastered his hair to his chiseled face. His entire body shook, and his eyes, those hard, unforgiving green gemstones, strengthened her resolve.

She refused, downright refused, to let these nicely dressed gangbangers control her and the ones she loved.

As Douglas and Giles argued, they alternated their

attention between each other and their male captives, and seemed to ignore her entirely.

Fine by me.

Mia jerked on the rope again, gently so as to not draw attention, and bit her tongue to stop her smile as the rope slackened around her wrists. She maneuvered her hands free and rubbed at the rope burn. Mason shook his head, a bare shift of movement, as though he knew what she planned to do. Despite her pinned ankles, she leapt from the seat before she lost her nerve. The wooden chair legs screeched and the chair toppled over as she tackled Giles, the man closest to her, and she rammed her elbow in his groin. They crashed together on the floor.

His howl of pain rent the air. Giles fisted her hair in a meaty grip and slammed his knee into her stomach.

The force of his kick took her breath away and cut off her scream. Vomit burned up her throat, but she managed to swallow it. He thrust her aside and she cried out in pain. The concrete floor roughened her fall. Mia clutched her stomach, her legs twisted under the heavy chair, and she thrashed her legs to escape the binds. Every kick busted up her feet.

Mason grabbed her shoulders and dragged her back.

Giles staggered to his feet, his weapon in his hand, but Jim tackled him back down and punched the cop's jaw. The gun clanked and skidded across the floor. The men rolled in a tangle of flailing arms and legs, crashed into the guard's lifeless body, and blocked the door. Blood smeared their skin and clothes. The crush of their bodies blurred together as dusky light spilled throughout the room.

"Stay out of the way, darlin'. I mean it," Mason ordered, his tone rough, and he didn't bother to help her untie her ankles.

Douglas tried to leap over Jim and Giles for the door, but Mason rushed from her side and flung his old friend against the far wall. The gun fell from his hand as Douglas collapsed on his bottom. Mason straddled him and rained down his fists like mallets.

The coward shoved at Mason's chest, eyes wide with tears, and pled for mercy.

Bone crunched. Blood splattered from the little man's busted nose.

Mia pinched her eyes shut and clamped her hands over her ears, using all her strength to hold back her tears. *I have to help them. I'm not a damn damsel in distress.* She tightened her fingers in her hair. *Man up, Mia. Attack someone. You did it once before. Do it again.*

Her eyelids shot open. Mia loosened the knots and skimmed one foot at a time through the rope. Her skin burned. She rubbed her torn flesh and jerked her gaze between the two fights. Mason seemed to overpower Douglas with little effort, but Jim struggled to subdue the crooked cop.

Giles kicked her brother in the ribs, knocked him on his back, and stomped on his arm. A scream ripped from Jim's mouth as a bone snapped. Giles jumped on top of him just as Mia leapt on Giles's back like a wild spider monkey. He lurched sideways to shake her off, but she circled her arms around his neck and kneed him in the back. His throat bobbed as she tightened her hold against his windpipe.

Jim punched the cop's exposed chest and stomach

before shifting out from underneath him.

Giles elbowed her side and knocked Mia off.

She tumbled close to the fallen guard, Decker. His blood soaked her dirty clothes and coated her skin. Vomit rose again in her throat.

Giles dragged her toward him by her ankle, pinned her waist with the weight of his body, and wrapped his hands around her neck. His fingers dug against her skin, surely leaving bruises.

Her vision blurred and head pounded as he throttled her. She gripped his arms and scratched at his skin to draw his hands away from her, but he latched on and squeezed tighter.

The blast of a gun ricocheted off the walls. Gray dust billowed as the bullet hit the wall behind her.

Giles ceased choking her. His skin paled, shock filled his bloodshot eyes, and blood pooled in a circle on his chest. He fell on top of her like a load of bricks.

Mia screamed and shoved the corpse away from her.

Jim lay a few yards away on the floor, and he lowered the gun. Pain and relief creased his face in deep lines.

Mason scrambled on his knees to reach her.

She dropped her gaze to Douglas.

Splatters of blood circled the limp man's head and slicked his mangled face red. A few teeth lay scattered on the grimy floor.

Mason fisted a gun and had likely used it to bash Douglas's face in. "God, Mia. What happened?" Mason dropped the weapon and gripped her arms hard. "I told you to stay back. Why did the cop strangle you?"

"She attacked him." Jim swiped his arm over his

nose and scowled at her. "To help me."

Mason shook her. "Are you crazy? You attacked that bastard *twice*?"

The wicked heat of his gaze seared her, but he blinked several times and seemed to leash the molten firestorm in his deep-set eyes.

Sweat glistened on his skin, his dark hair stuck up in sharp points all over his head, and his warm breath hit her face. His gaze slid to Giles's lifeless body and then moved over Mia's face, neck, and chest as though he assessed her for damage.

"I'm so sorry." Mason cupped her face with his palms, gentler than before. "I love you so much. I'm sorry. I'm *so* fucking sorry. Are you okay? Tell me you're okay. *Please.*" He pulled her into his arms, buried one hand in her disheveled hair, and gripped her close with the other. He brushed soft kisses on her forehead and massaged her sore scalp.

His tender words pulled at her heartstrings. She held him tight, and her strong, moody man shuddered in her embrace. His lips trembled as she kissed him. He loved her, and she needed to tell him how much she loved him in return.

"Answer me. Are you okay?" He pulled back and feathered his fingers over the bump beneath her eye.

"I'm fine, really. Are you?" Mia hiccupped and grasped his hand.

He nodded, but several little cuts and bruises marred his arms, neck, and face. A hole ruined the front of his T-shirt. The metal in his jaw surely shot excruciating pain through his gums, but he managed it with a stoic face.

"I love you, too, baby. I knew it before you told me

you loved me at the park. I don't know what it is about you, Mason, but you've become everything to me. I would die for you. I'd do anything to protect you."

Tears spilled from his eyes. He wrapped his arms around her and kissed her as no one had done since she started to date at age fifteen. Heat flowed between them, and the intoxicating press of his lips on hers took her breath away.

A strange wheezing sound shattered the moment.

She glared at Douglas, the urge to spit strong.

Shallow puffs of air wheezed from his mouth with every rise and fall of his chest.

"He'll live, but he probably needs reconstructive surgery." Mason struggled to his feet and pulled Mia up with him. He held her close. "I never meant for this to happen. I don't know what to say to make it better."

"There's nothing you can say."

"If you two lovebirds are done with the mushy crap, get the hell over here." Jim's voice broke through the haze in her mind. "We're in a shitload of trouble."

Mia loosened her grip on Mason and tried to step back, but he pinned her to his chest. A deep growl resonated in his throat. She kissed the corner of his mouth to try to reassure him against whatever he feared, and he dropped his arms. They hurried to her brother's side together.

"What broke? Your arm? I heard a bone snap." She knelt beside Jim as he cradled his left arm to his chest. He struggled to sit up, but she pressed her palms on his shoulders and kept him down. "No, no. Relax."

"Like hell." Jim swatted her hands away.

Mason knelt behind him and slid his hands beneath her brother's arms to haul him into a sitting position.

Jim groaned and his face mottled red. He nodded at Mason. "Thanks, man."

Mason dropped his gaze and stalked back to Douglas's side. He withdrew a clean, unused 9mm handgun and a cell phone—*Jim's* gun and phone—from the inner pockets of Doug's blazer and then handed the items to her brother. Mason stroked his fingertips down her arm. His already dark scowl seemed to deepen as he noticed the cuts around her wrist.

Goose bumps prickled her skin. She held her lover's hand and offered him a small smile.

"Call for help," Mason demanded of Jim. "I'll cooperate with the police and—"

"No. This isn't right." She bit her nails into Mason's skin and shook her head.

"I killed someone, darlin'. So did Jim."

"The cops won't arrest you, either of you. You shot those guys in self-defense."

"You know better than that, Mia." Jim tossed the treacherous cop's standard-issue gun aside and winced as he shifted his broken arm to shove his weapon into the holster attached to his chest. "They *will* arrest us and we'll have to prove self-defense in court. I shot a cop."

"A *dirty* cop."

"That doesn't matter. A cop is a cop no matter how dirty in the eyes of the law. I'm screwed." He shifted his gaze toward Mason and back to her. "Mason violated parole out the wazoo, killed a man on top of that, and almost killed a second. Neither of us will make bail, but you'll be fine. You fought back but didn't cross the line." Jim scrubbed his hand down his drawn face. "Expect long, messy trials. Expect to testify."

Disbelief and shock coursed through her veins with the speed of a train. Her stomach rolled, threatened to upchuck last night's dinner, and she wanted to cry.

This can't be happening!

"We have to go. Stokes could wake up at any moment and try to fight us, but I don't think Doug could." Mason released her hand, retrieved the gun he'd used on Douglas, and shoved it in the waistband of his dirty jeans.

"Agreed." Jim slid his phone in his blazer pocket and scraped his feet on the floor in an effort to stand.

Mason wrapped his arm around her brother's shoulder and hefted him up.

Mia sidestepped a thick red puddle, careful not to disturb the bodies, and opened the heavy door. Mason and her brother followed her into the hall. Though they acted civil and kind to one another due to the crappy situation, she hoped they would put aside their differences for the long haul. Not that it would matter, anyway, if they went to prison.

Her boyfriend nuzzled the side of her head, and she drew back in pain. Giles had struck the hilt of his gun over her head to knock her unconscious in her home. Though the pain had dulled over the past few hours, fire shot through her scalp if anyone put pressure on the bump that resulted from the attack.

Mason stepped back, anger and shame in his expressive green eyes, and he turned from her to shut the storeroom door. The lever clanked as he swung it into place. They hurried down the hall, and Mia couldn't help but hug Mason close.

Stained, graffiti-covered walls surrounded them.

Stale, dry air filled her lungs. Not sure what they should do, Mia almost suggested they steal a car and head south for the Mexican border, but she didn't want to look over her shoulder for the rest of her life. She needed distance from the monsters who tried to kill them, so she could help the guys figure out their next move. Even with Douglas and Stokes locked in the cesspit of blood and death, Mia didn't feel safe, but she knew they shouldn't leave the scene of the crime unless they really did flee to Mexico.

They reached the midway point of the spacious factory floor just as the double doors creaked open across the room. Hope for survival plummeted in her chest.

Reinforcements? Oh, hell.

At least a dozen men entered. Dressed in black just like Decker and Stokes, the vultures spread out and their sure, steady steps echoed in the cavernous building. Their stern, callous faces and cold, cruel eyes chilled her to the bone.

Mason thrust her behind him.

She nearly bumped into Jim as he struggled to hold up his limp arm and to fist his gun at the same time.

The newcomers surrounded them on all sides but stayed several yards back. One man stalked closer until he stood a few yards away. Dressed in a navy-blue business suit, the tall, stocky criminal arched his eyebrow. His piercing brown-eyed gaze swept over them.

Mason and Jim aimed their weapons at the entourage. Even though their chances to win a gun battle weighed nil on her scale, the foolish males wanted to try. Neither the black-garbed men nor the one in the blue suit raised weapons in defense, and their lack of fear worried her.

She clutched her shaky hands behind her back. Mason needed to concentrate, not deal with her right now, and she bit her nails into her palms as he stepped forward. Mia trusted him, whether he planned to beg for their lives or shoot, but she doubted they would make it out of this in one piece.

Chapter Eighteen

Mason didn't recognize any of the men. Calm and collected, unlike Douglas's pawns, they likely belonged to Thorn and he couldn't fight them all and win.

Keep Mia safe.

A daunting task, but he didn't have a damn choice.

The scowling man in the blue suit leveled his gaze on Mason. An air of absolute power and authority radiated around him, but he appeared no older than his mid-thirties. He'd slicked his dark hair back over his head. A few wayward locks curled around his ears and added a false innocence to his hard, cruelly stamped face. Faint gray dusted his temples, and a diamond stud pierced each earlobe.

He's the leader, the master of this controlled pack of wolves.

Mason shifted his feet, on the ball and ready for action, and struggled to stay calm.

The leader flicked his gaze toward one of the other men. "Check for survivors."

The lackey headed across the room, presumably toward the hall, and then the screech of metal echoed off the walls.

Mason refused to look over his shoulder to check. The distraction could cost him more than he was willing to bear.

Silence spread until the sound of breathing and the

soft drip of water in a nearby puddle rang in Mason's ears. Rays of sunlight shimmered through slits in the boarded windows and broken glass panes. Footsteps echoed behind him.

The lackey returned, whispered in the leader's ear, and fell back into formation.

"I recognize you." Frustration laced Jim's tone, and a shiver of unease shot up Mason's spine. "You're Bristol Rieger, the eldest son of business mogul Axel Rieger. I've seen your picture on the cover of some magazines."

Shit. Douglas had hinted Thorn and a man named Rieger were the same person.

Thorn nodded, but his gaze never wavered from Mason. "All I've heard for the past few weeks is your name, Mr. Harding. It's time we met, but I would've preferred a meeting at my office, not at this cesspool. You're taller than I expected."

Mason tightened his grip on the gun. A sane man would never threaten someone of Thorn's caliber, but he couldn't chance a show of weakness. Wolves thrived on injured rabbits, but they respected gumption and he hoped the captain followed suit.

"Captain, I—" Mason snapped his mouth shut as Thorn held up his hand.

So much for gumption.

"I want answers, and I will not ask twice." Thorn folded his arms across his well-built chest. "Two men are dead. Who killed them?"

Mason coughed to steady his voice. "I killed the guard, Decker. Jim killed Officer Morrow. We acted in self-defense, but we had no intention of killing—"

"I never said you did, but I'm impressed. You and

Mr. Borden killed two armed assailants and incapacitated two others, unless I'm wrong in my assumption and Ms. Eddison also took up arms?"

"No, she didn't." Mason's quick answer stretched the captain's lips in a dubious smile. "I mean, she didn't seriously hurt anyone."

Thorn glanced toward Mia, an interested gleam in his dark eyes.

She stood a few feet behind Mason and breathed so loud he could hear the sound as though she stood right next to him. Whether the captain showed interest in Mia as a woman or in her courage to fight back, Mason didn't know, but waves of acid still churned in Mason's stomach.

"Anyway," Thorn drawled as he shifted his gaze back to Mason, "I received a message from my man, Stokes, a few hours ago. The GPS in his phone led to this shit-stained address. I came in from the mountains and would've been here sooner, if not for a traffic jam." He tapped his polished shoe on top of an old stain. "I told Douglas to leave you alone. He disobeyed my direct orders."

Mason frowned. "Douglas said you and the Scorpion orchestrated all this."

"Douglas lied, plain and simple." The other man's voice lowered an octave. "Your old cellmate petitioned the Scorpion and requested we bring you back in. The Scorpion refused, so the little shit asked his uncle and me to convince the general for him. We refused. I ordered Stokes, his regular bodyguard, to monitor his activities and to keep me updated from then on." He tsked. "Douglas thought Stokes, the man I'd hired, switched loyalties to him and *only* him. The fool lied to everyone who helped him, and he'll pay for his disobedience."

Mason's mouth dropped open. "You spoke to Oskar?"

"I did, and at great length. He spoke highly of you and believes his power-hungry nephew, my accountant, deserves whatever fate he receives. He never expected Douglas to screw up your life." The scowl on his face deepened. "You requested an out, Captain Udell vouched for you, and the Scorpion agreed out of respect for the captain. Oskar Udell later provided you with a service, but you owe him nothing because he wanted nothing from you. You have twice helped Capularia, and I'm in your debt." He tilted his head to one side. "Why did Douglas want you back in the ranks? For protection? I assign bodyguards to all my desk jockeys."

"Friendship." Mason coughed to soothe his sore throat. Pain shot through his bruised jawbone every time he opened his mouth to speak or breathe. "We were good friends, almost like brothers."

"I see. The fight is over. Lower your weapons. My men and I are not here to finish what Douglas Udell and Giles Morrow started." Thorn lifted his hands and slowly lowered them. His gaze shifted between Mason and Jim. "Keep them with you as a sign of good faith."

Mason licked his lips. Tension gnawed in his gut, and the hair on the back of his neck stood straight as Mia shifted behind him. He edged closer to the left to keep her back. Although a little insulted Thorn didn't seem afraid or even concerned as Mason pointed the gun at the captain's chest, Mason knew better than to let his idiot ego get in the way.

Of course you're not a threat to him. You're one man against a dozen trained assholes.

With no choice but to trust Thorn or die for insulting him, Mason secured the weapon in his jeans and held out his arms in surrender. "What does this mean? Jim and I killed two of your employees. In my experience, a captain would seek revenge and have no mercy."

"Revenge? Those jackasses deserved death in my book. I don't tolerate disobedience. No boss does." He tossed the non-too-subtle warning at the men in his entourage, but none of them flinched. "Captain Iversen killed the skinheads who slung drugs on my turf. Iversen thanks you for the information, as do I, and I decided to handle this current problem myself once Stokes informed me Officer Morrow abducted your girlfriend. I instructed Stokes to break his cover and step in to help her if anyone attempted to beat or sexually assault her, but he stayed back and followed Douglas's orders. Is that correct?"

"Yes, sir. Mia's fine, other than rope burn and a few slaps to her face. Morrow threatened to do much worse." He would do anything to hold her right now but couldn't risk it. "We had no idea Stokes wasn't our enemy. We didn't know *you* weren't our enemy."

"I believe you. Otherwise I would seek justice for Stokes's injuries and retribution for the deaths of my men. Morrow and Decker are my responsibility to do away with, not yours, and they'd fucked themselves long before you or your parole officer fired your weapons."

Jim scoffed, and Thorn's glare jumped over Mason's shoulder.

Mason rolled his hands into fists and turned to give Jim a shut-the-hell-up look. Jim stood a few feet back and off to the side as though he guarded Mia from the rear. Though they may not often get along, Mason trusted her brother to put Mia first. It felt right to him using Jim's given name as though they were friends, and since Mia didn't like it when he referred to her brother by the man's last name—her maiden name—he hoped this tentative truce would be permanent.

"What does that mean for us?" Jim lowered his weapon but kept it at his side. "Are we not as good as dead too? We know your identity."

"I understand your skepticism, Mr. Borden." Thorn rubbed his fingers along his thick, neatly trimmed goatee. "To the outside world, I'm a charming playboy with too many women and cars. I'm wealthy, somewhat respectable, but I do break the law on occasion. Usually just for speeding." A mischievous grin split his lips, but he quickly sobered back into the hard shell. "The man before you, a notorious criminal who dirties his hands and cleans up unexpected messes, is someone you don't want breathing down your neck. Denver and the surrounding areas are under my control. I take all threats seriously and handle them personally when trusted members of my set betray me. My mood is the deciding factor in a situation like this. All I have to do is snap my fingers and all of you are dead."

Mason coughed and drew the captain's attention. "You claimed to be in my debt, sir. I officially call in those debts. I want you to spare Mia's and Jim's lives. Two lives for two debts. I don't care about my own."

"Mason." Mia grabbed his arm, but he didn't turn around. "Are you crazy?"

He ignored her sharp, breathy words and focused on the crime boss. Though grateful Thorn decided to talk and to answer their questions, Mason knew their luck could change at any second.

"You would choose her brother over yourself?" Thorn asked, his eyebrows furrowed together. His lips firmed in a tight line.

As Mason hoped, the wolf seemed to respect his gumption.

"I would, no hesitation. You can read it in my records, so I don't mind telling you, but I have my own brother. The pain I put him through because I fucked up and landed in prison eats away at me. I know incarceration and death are two different things, but I don't want Mia to suffer the loss of her brother in any form." Though Alan would suffer *his* loss instead. "I don't want the survivor's guilt."

"That's commendable, but I must demand stipulations if I accept the deal." Thorn clasped his hands behind his back. "My men disobeyed and will face punishment. You and your friends are victims of their stupidity. If I can trust the three of you to keep silent, I see no reason why all of you shouldn't live."

"We can be trusted, sir."

"I believe *you* can, Mr. Harding, but I'm not so sure about the others." His gaze drifted toward Mia and Jim, and back to Mason. "Keep quiet about everything that happened here today. If you speak a word to anyone about my identity, I will slit your throats and drop your bodies in a ditch. I have more than enough connections to bury all rumors about my Onyx involvement. In return for your cooperation, I'll compensate each of you for your pain and distress. A physician on my payroll will tend to your injuries once you leave here." He leveled his stare at Jim. "No paperwork. No parole violations. Consider our peace treaty voided if I find any such documentation, and I *will* check."

"That's very generous, Thorn." Mason carefully worded his response. His blood pounded so hot and fast it might burst through his veins. "Are we your employees now? Do you want anything from us other than silence?"

"No, you are not, and silence is all. Those who work for the Scorpion or in Onyx do so willingly, not by blackmail or coercion, unless at a boss's discretion." Thorn stepped closer until he stood close enough to touch Mason, and he extended his hand. "I will hold you accountable if you or your friends speak of this incident to anyone, and you will not like my methods."

Mason shook the proffered hand. "I promise our silence. I cannot thank you enough."

"My associates will monitor the three of you now and then to ensure you keep to our deal. They will never inconvenience you. You will never know when they are around." Thorn crossed his arms. "The drug dealers who harassed your woman in her store, the parole officer who surrendered your classified files, and everyone else who assisted Douglas in this little event will face a stiff reprimand and never bother any of you again. Consider all the loose ends tied and the debts fulfilled."

"I understand, sir. That's a load off my mind." Mason reached behind his back but paused as the captain lifted an eyebrow. "I just intend to grab the gun. It belonged to Douglas. I shouldn't keep it." He slowly pulled the weapon from his jeans and offered it butt first to Thorn.

The criminal nodded at a nearby guard. The stranger approached, accepted the grimy gun, and retreated. Thorn's gaze traveled down Mason's tense body and back up. "It's too bad you don't want to join Capularia. There's always a spot open for a good man, especially one with bodyguard experience."

"It's appreciated, but no thank you."

Thorn smiled before he shifted his gaze toward three of his guards. "Escort the civilians across town to my on-call physician, wait with them, and take them home. Call me for further instructions when you're finished." He turned to a fourth man. "Take Stokes to my second on-call doctor and call me when you have a full report on his condition." His gaze swept over the rest of the men. "Dispose of the dead and keep watch as usual. Leave Douglas to me."

Mason pulled Mia close as several henchmen strode toward the storeroom while others spread further around the factory as though to keep watch.

Jim shoved his gun beneath his blazer and flushed red from anger or pain, probably both, as two of their escorts moved to stand behind him. Jim flicked his gaze toward the third escort who now stood at Mason's side.

The muscle-bound guard nodded at Mason, an impassive gleam in his eyes, and turned without a word.

Mason tightened his grip around Mia's waist as they followed the guard.

Sunlight spilled into the darkened cavity of the factory as another henchman opened the double doors. Five sleek cars and more guards waited in the parking lot.

Mason took the criminal at his word but couldn't let his guard down, not yet. He wanted to comfort Mia in the privacy of her home—a home ransacked by a treacherous friend—and to help her clean up. He would stay at her side for as long as she needed him. Jim probably wouldn't write him up for the missed curfew, even without Thorn's threat, but he would have to calm Alan down once he returned to his brother's apartment.

Whatever. Nothing mattered but Mia. She deserved so much better, and he would do everything in his power to make this up to her.

No matter what.

Epilogue

Two Weeks Later

"Why did you want to come here?" Mia asked after she sipped water from her glass.

Mason twisted a few fettuccini noodles and a portabello mushroom onto his fork but barely tasted the creamy Alfredo pasta as it slid down his throat. "No reason. I just wanted to take you someplace nice. You do like this place, right?"

"Yeah, very much, but you seem distracted."

Concern lit her eyes, and he dropped his gaze to his hands. Expensive automotive soap had removed every speck of oil from his stained skin, and his nails looked cleaner than they had in months. A few fight wounds still covered his knuckles. The scabs had torn off as he scrubbed his hands before he picked Mia up for their date, but the soreness barely fazed him.

The hostess in the Italian restaurant had seated them alongside a few other couples in a private room.

Low instrumental music drifted from discreet speakers, dim embossed lights glowed from the high ceiling, and candles burned in several nooks and crannies. A large potted fern partially concealed a vent in a nearby wall, and cool air blew in the direction of their table.

After hours of hard work in the July heat, he

welcomed any cold room he could find.

The upscale establishment surpassed his pay grade, but indulgence every now and then wouldn't break the bank. He carried a check for fifty grand in his wallet—courtesy of Bristol Rieger—but he refused to spend a cent until his parole ended. Mia and Jim wanted to throw their compensation checks away, but he convinced them that Thorn would take offense if they did, and that meant trouble. He planned to sign his check over to Mia at her bank tomorrow, since the State monitored his personal account, and she'd agreed to withdraw the deposited amount, so he could store it with the thirty grand he had already hidden behind the water heater.

He checked his watch and smiled at the late hour. After the incident at the factory, Jim had promised to accept Mason as a permanent fixture in Mia's life as long as Mason promised to never hurt her as Evan did. Mason swore to it, so Jim revoked every ridiculous parole restriction the previous week and transferred Mason's case to another State lapdog a few days later. Effective at midnight tonight, Jeremiah Borden would just be his girlfriend's brother, *not* his parole officer.

Mason missed the friend Douglas used to be—he couldn't imagine how the man screwed up his life so bad—and his stomach turned every time he thought about shooting Decker. He took a life. Though he would do it again in a heartbeat to protect Mia, the memory weighed on his conscience and would never leave him.

He'd spent the past few nights with Mia after Jim lifted the curfew. Unless his new PO added a bullshit restriction, his parole terms clearly stated he could spend three nights away from his legal residence within a seven-day period. After this night, he would have to wait four long days before he could stay with her again.

"Ask Jim to spend the night with you tomorrow. I don't want you left alone."

Mia glanced up in mid-bite. Shock widened her eyes. Her throat bobbed as she swallowed. "I'll be fine. The nightmares aren't so bad anymore."

"Not so bad? You don't sleep well. You've woken up in a cold sweat every night for the past two weeks." He jabbed his fork in the pasta. "I'm still mad you didn't tell me about this sooner. The first night I stayed over, I nearly had a heart attack when you cried out and thrashed in your sleep. I'll be with you tonight, but I can't be there tomorrow. Tell Jim about this, so he'll stay with you. Please, Mia. If you won't tell him, I will."

"Don't mention this to him." She tapped her fingers on the burgundy table cloth. "C'mon, Mason. It's not a big deal. I only relive what happened when I'm asleep. I'm not afraid. I know we're safe." Mia swiped her hair behind her ears and lowered her voice to a whisper. "Cut me some damn slack. It's not every day someone kidnaps me and threatens to blackmail me, to rape and kill me. It's not every day I see my brother and the man I love fight for their lives. I'm a big girl, and I'm handling the nightmares as best as I can."

His temper kicked into gear and the telltale tic throbbed in his cheek. He opened his mouth and stretched his jaw muscles to suppress it.

Mia's brow furrowed. "I don't want to argue, especially if it will hurt you. Just believe me, okay? I'm fine. I'll get through this."

"You shouldn't have to do it alone."

"I'm not alone. I have you for support." She broke a garlic breadstick in half and dipped it in the red sauce on her plate. "You're right, though. I should've told you about my bad dreams sooner, but I didn't want you to worry. You'll move in with me soon enough. If you can't, well, we still have three nights out of the week to be together. That's better than nothing."

Mason concurred, but he wanted more.

He also wanted her to see a psychiatrist to deal with her fucked-up subconscious, but he doubted a shrink could help if not up-to-date on what happened to her. He needed to ask Thorn for a favor, but he would have to call Oskar Udell first to find a way to contact him. If the Capularia captain kept psychiatrists on his payroll, Mia might find peace if she could speak openly with one.

That's a last case scenario. Just work this out on your own. Mason rubbed his tired eyes. Even though Thorn had presented himself as an ally a few weeks back, who knew what he would demand in return for his help. Mason cringed at the thought. *I'd owe him big.*

"What's on your mind?"

"Nothing." Mason sighed as a scowl crossed her face. He had to say something. "I'm thinking about tomorrow. I suck at making a good first impression, and I'll probably act like a dick if Cornell refuses to sign a change-of-home address form."

She blushed as a waiter walked by. "Well, first of all, I nearly broke your legs with my car the first time we met. So I have you trumped in the crappy-first-impressions department. Second, just act charming and

I'm sure Cornell will agree. I met him a few days ago at the parole office, and he seemed nice."

"You and I have different definitions of nice."

"I understand you're upset Jim wouldn't sign the form, but think about it. How could he? His supervisor already accused him of playing favorites when Jim withdrew those stupid restrictions, and Hamlin demanded to know why. If Jim agreed to let you live with me, a woman he once prohibited from entering your legal residence, Hamlin would probably override the decision."

"I know, but—"

"It sucks his boss found out we're a couple, but Jim had to tell him. Duane Hamlin claimed it would be a serious conflict of interest if Jim continued to act as your parole officer, so Jim transferred your case to avoid a career-hurting reprimand." Annoyance sharpened her tone. "Jim told your new PO about the request, and Cornell will make an impartial decision after he inspects the loft and interviews me. We'll likely have to follow a few rules, but it'll be worth it."

He held up his hand to silence her heated explanation. "I'm frustrated, but not mad. I don't want your brother in trouble, so I get why he wouldn't sign it."

A long sigh escaped her mouth. "I'm sorry, baby. I'm just a little overprotective. Jim's been so stressed lately. He tries to hide it, but I can see the strain in his eyes." Mia twirled her fork in the marinara-coated noodles on her plate. "Anyway, Cornell shouldn't find fault with me, the loft, or the neighborhood. LoDo is a clean, safe area for the most part. You're also closer to your job if you live there than in Westminster. That should be a plus for the PO."

"A definite plus, but don't forget about the bars and clubs a few streets down from the loft. It's a violation if I enter places that sell alcohol as their main item."

"You can't enter, yes, but your paperwork doesn't state you can't live near one. It's a gray issue." She shrugged and continued to eat. "Jim promised me Cornell is pretty lenient, so hopefully it won't be a problem."

Mason rolled his eyes. *He's probably a fucking hardass.* Determined to deal with Cornell the same way he dealt with Jim in the beginning, Mason would play nice, suck up now and then, and randomly spout off at the mouth to keep the man on his toes—after Cornell signed the form.

The air in his lungs stilled as Mia untwisted the scarf from around her neck. The V-neckline of her little black dress dipped low, and he almost pouted as she straightened out the silk fabric and let it shield her cleavage again. Mason yearned to reach over and push the scarf down her bare arms. He *would* if not for the other couples around them. Her small diamond hoop earrings sparkled in the candlelight, and a charm bracelet dangled from her wrist. Her lush, full lips teased him as she smiled. Thankfully, the cut on her cheek had healed quickly and without stitches. Makeup covered a few yellowish bruises on her face, but the marks no longer caused her pain.

He'd never seen a more beautiful woman.

Mason patted his hands down his sleek black jacket and wanted to thank Alan for forcing him to buy his one good suit. Without it, the maitre d' probably would've denied their entrance into the restaurant despite their reservations.

She shifted under his unblinking stare, but he didn't turn away.

He loved her protective nature. She defended him just as heatedly as she did Jim. No one but Mia ever made him feel so appreciated and cherished.

Mia frowned and dropped her fork. A nearby couple glanced over as it clanked on her plate. "What? Don't stare at me like a lovesick puppy, Mason."

Lovesick barely described his raw emotions. *Entranced* and *ravaged* summed it up better.

"Will you marry me?" The words slipped out and heat infused his cheeks. "I mean, I—um—oh, shit." He buried his fingers in his hair and pulled the strands, hard.

"Are you serious?" Surprise deepened her voice. "You want to get married?"

Mason swallowed the lump in his throat, determined to speak his mind and to get everything out in the open. "I'm very serious, Mia. I love you more than you know. You're everything to me. I want to spend the rest of my life with you. I want to argue, cry, and laugh with you. I want to make you happy and learn how to live with the gentler side to myself, the side you bring out. I need you. I nearly lost you, darlin'." He reached across the table and grasped her hand. Emotions he once thought himself incapable of feeling swelled in his heart, and he couldn't stop his confession. He didn't *want* to stop it. "You're the best thing that's happened to me in years, and I'm miserable without you. Marry me. Take me as yours. I swear you won't regret it."

A dusky hue flushed her face. "I don't know what to say. We already planned to move in together, but marriage, wow. That's sudden."

Rejection tightened his heart in a vise. He breathed deep and forced aside an onslaught of pain. "I just wanted a promise, a bigger commitment. I—"

"That's a *huge* commitment. I married Evan after just a year of dating, but I didn't really know him. We rushed into it, and I promised myself I would never do that again." She twisted her fingers with his and held up her free hand as he tried to speak. Her lips tilted on one side as she smiled. "You care more for me than any other man I've known. Evan wouldn't have risked his life to save mine as you did. I'd marry you tomorrow if you wanted me to, Mason. I love you. From the first moment I saw you, I knew you were special. You were the one."

Mason released a pent-up breath, unaware he'd trapped the air in his lungs. "I want kids, too, the whole nine-yards. I'll do my best to give you everything you ever dreamed of." He brought her hand to his mouth and kissed her knuckles. "If we got married, we could definitely live together then, but I don't want to jump the gun on this. Let's take our time and do it right. We still have so much to learn about each other."

Tears beaded under her lashes. Mia brushed her fingers along the straight line of his whiskered jaw, and Mason closed his eyes to savor her gentle touch.

He'd lied his ass off when his brother and coworkers hounded him about his bruises and his occasional grunts of pain. Everyone eventually dropped the subject, even Alan, but his brother's anger and worry shifted to disappointment. If Mason didn't know any better, he would swear Alan somehow knew what happened. His face took a beating but Thorn's doctor predicted no future problems. After the surgery on his jaw years ago, his gums had thickened around the metal plate and screws to help protect the bone from another break. He grew out a short beard to camouflage the marks, and he hoped like hell Cornell wouldn't notice.

"I'm so happy. I can't wait to tell Jim."

His eyelids snapped open. "No. It's not official yet." Mason traced his thumb over her bare ring finger. "Hamlin suspended him today. Jim's probably in a bad mood, and I don't know what he'd do or say if we tell him this."

"It's personal leave, not suspension. His supervisor told him to take some time off because his coworkers and parolees can't stand his crabby attitude anymore." Mia scowled at him. "And it *is* official. We don't need jewelry to prove it." She pressed his hand to her chest, right above her heart. "All that matters is what we feel in here."

"You're right, but I'll still get you a ring soon." He pulled back before he clasped her breast and humiliated both of them. "Let's just keep this bombshell quiet for a while. Okay?"

"All right, fine, but just wait until I'm pregnant. That'll be the *real* bombshell. Jim will either faint or have a stroke when he learns he'll be an uncle."

He chuckled. Mason scooted his chair closer to Mia, splayed his hand over her stomach, and wished life already grew inside her. A foolish wish since they still had so much to work on if they wanted their relationship to last for the long term, but it didn't hurt to dream.

"What's worse is we'll force your brother and mine to babysit the kids all the time." Mia laughed softly. "Oh, and tell Alan I want to babysit Danny. I need to get to know my future nephew better."

Mason couldn't stop the grin that spread across his face. She said yes. *Yes!* He wanted to jump up and shout. "I can't wait to spend the rest of my life with you, darlin'."

"We have all the time in the world. I'm yours, forever."

A word about the author...

Writing is the fruit of happiness. Amber Daulton lives her life by that one belief even though she normally isn't so zen.

As a fan of contemporary, paranormal, and historical romance novels alike, she can't get enough of feisty heroines and alpha heroes. Her mind is a wonderland of adventure, laughter, and awesome ways of kicking a guy when he's down. She probably wouldn't be too sane without her computer and notebooks. After all, what's a girl to do when people are jabbering away in her head and it's hard to shut them up? Write! Nothing else works.

http://www.amberdaultonauthor.blogspot.com

Thank you for purchasing
this publication of The Wild Rose Press, Inc.

If you enjoyed the story, we would appreciate your
letting others know by leaving a review.

For other wonderful stories,
please visit our on-line bookstore at
www.thewildrosepress.com.

For questions or more information
contact us at
info@thewildrosepress.com.

The Wild Rose Press, Inc.
www.thewildrosepress.com

Stay current with The Wild Rose Press, Inc.

Like us on Facebook

https://www.facebook.com/TheWildRosePress

And Follow us on Twitter
https://twitter.com/WildRosePress

www.ingramcontent.com/pod-product-compliance
Lightning Source LLC
Chambersburg PA
CBHW051522260626
47170CB00003B/743